I0673373

THE WEEK-END MYSTERY

The Author

THE WEEK-END MYSTERY

ROBERT A. SIMON

COACHWHIP PUBLICATIONS

Greenville, Ohio

The Week-End Mystery, by Robert A. Simon
© 2018 Coachwhip Publications
Introduction © Curtis Evans

First published 1926
Robert A. Simon (1897-1981)
No claims made on public domain material.

CoachwhipBooks.com

ISBN 1-61646-464-X
ISBN-13 978-1-61646-464-6

MURDER GONE META

'THE WEEK-END MYSTERY' (1926), BY ROBERT A. SIMON (1897-1981)

CURTIS EVANS

I. ROBERT A. SIMON

By 1926, when the 29-year-old American author and critic Robert A. Simon published his single detective novel, a charmingly whimsical murder story entitled *The Week-End Mystery*, the conventions of British and American detective fiction, then in its so-called Golden Age (conventionally dated as around 1920 to 1940), already were well-established, if not highly formalized. Long before Anglo-American hard-boiled crime writer Raymond Chandler in his essay "The Simple Art of Murder" (originally published in 1944 and revised for book publication in 1950) derided what he termed the "Cheesecake Manor" school of class-bound, hoity-toity mystery writing, the weekend country house party attended either by landed gentry (in the UK) or the merely wealthy (in the US) had become the classic, indeed clichéd, setting for fictional murder; and it is precisely this setting which Robert A. Simon employed and wryly lampooned in his clever detective novel.

Seemingly not quite getting the author's joke, the reviewer of the *The Week-End Mystery* in the *New York Times* lamented the novel's "hackneyed situations and conventional characters," while simultaneously allowing that these demerits did not much matter when "the story is so well told." "Mr. Simon has an ingratiating ability to take the reader into his confidence, to put him completely at his ease," pronounced the reviewer of the author's smooth narrative style, before concluding that "'The Week-End Mystery' must be classed among the superior detective stories." Yet despite receiving this and other accolades upon its publication in the US and

5

the UK (in the latter country by Collins, publisher that same year of Agatha Christie's *The Murder of Roger Ackroyd*), *The Week-End Mystery* was never reprinted and subsequently it nearly disappeared without a trace. Happily the novel is no longer a lost *Week-End*, having been recovered and reprinted by Coachwhip after its lamentable absence of ninety-two years.

The author of *The Week-End Mystery*, Robert Alfred Simon, was a member of the irrepressible American Jazz Age generation that during the Roaring Twenties took to detective fiction like it did to sitting on flagpoles—with, to be sure, less transitory results. Robert was born in Manhattan, New York, on February 18, 1897 (less than five months after Jazz Age bard F. Scott Fitzgerald), to Alfred Leopold Simon, a wealthy feather and silk manufacturer and milliner, and his wife Hedwig Meier, both of whom were of German Jewish heritage. In his early years he resided in Midtown at a four-story brownstone townhouse at 116 East 55th Street with his parents and younger sister, Helen, as well as an uncle and aunt, Leo and Anna (Meier) Simon, and their eldest son, Richard Leo Simon, a live-in maid and a German nanny. (German was Robert's first language.)[1] Two years younger than Robert, Richard would grow up to co-found the publishing firm of Simon and Schuster and father four children, including the famed singer-songwriter Carly Simon. Other cousins of Robert's included Richard's three brothers: George Thomas Simon, a jazz writer and early drummer in Glenn Miller's orchestra; Henry William Simon, an opera critic and professor of English at Teacher's College, Columbia University; and Alfred Edward Simon, a rehearsal pianist for George Gershwin and radio programmer of light opera and show music. In his own life and work Robert Alfred Simon evinced similar literary and musical interests to those of his multi-talented cousins.

Both Robert and Richard Simon attended Columbia University, where Robert received the degree of Bachelor of Literature in Journalism in 1921, after an interlude of a year's service during America's participation in the Great War as a Sergeant in Columbia University's School of Military Cinematography. During his college years Robert was a student in the renowned creative writing class of Dorothy Scarborough, who later became the author of the searing regional novel *The Wind* (1925) and the future teacher of acclaimed southern novelist Carson McCullers. After graduation Robert for a couple of years published articles on jazz and classical music in New York newspapers. Then in 1923 the prestigious firm of Boni and Liveright (among their authors in the Twenties were novelists Theodore Dreiser, Sherwood Anderson, Ernest Hemingway and William Faulkner, poets T. S. Eliot, E. E. Cummings and Hart Crane and playwright Eugene O'Neill) published Robert's first novel, *Our Little Girl*, an amusing satirical tale about "a young girl who was brought up to imagine herself a great singer and who came to believe it." At a party a year earlier Robert had wryly bet Boni and Liveright's owner, Horace Liveright, a single dollar that he could write a novel which Liveright's firm would accept. Having won the bet, Robert dedicated *Our Little Girl* to his cousin Richard, who was then Boni and Liveright's sales manager.

Over the next few years Robert continued to produce interesting literary work. In 1925 the newly launched *New Yorker* hired the young author as its first music critic (a position he would hold for the next 23 years) and Simon and Schuster, which Richard had co-founded the previous year, published his translation of *Fraulein Else*, Arthur Schnitzler's highly regarded tragic novella. The next year Robert produced his second and final novel, *The Week-End Mystery*. This book was published not by Simon and Schuster, which seems to have issued its first mystery title—Samuel Spewack's *Murder in the Gilded Cage*—three years later, in 1929, but rather by G. Howard Watt, publishers of Clinton Stagg, whose tales of the amazing sleuthing exploits of visually-impaired detective Thornley Colton, the so-called "blind problemist," were gently lampooned by Agatha Christie in her 1929 Tommy and Tuppence Beresford short story collection *Partners in Crime*. (The Thornley Colton cases have been reprinted by Coachwhip.)

Although *The Week-End Mystery* was the only detective novel Robert ever published, in 1927 he versatilely produced *Bronx Ballads*, a humorous collection of Jewish songs with illustrations by American humorist, cartoonist and radio personality Harry Hershfield, and served as general editor of Simon and Schuster's *The Pamphlet*

Poets series, designed "to promote poetry to the masses through paperback offerings sold for twenty-five cents."[2] Volumes in this laudable Simon and Schuster series included *Emily Dickinson, Edna St. Vincent Millay, Ralph Waldo Emerson, Witter Bytnner, Four National Negro Poets* (including Langston Hughes) and *The New York Wits,* the latter of which Robert personally edited.

Despite evident promise as a writer of both mainstream and mystery novels, Robert soon focused his creative writing energies exclusively in the field of music. In 1927 he produced a widely praised translation of Charles Gounod's *Faust* for Vladimir Rosing's American Opera Company; librettos for modern operas by Robert Russell Bennett, Albert Stoessel, and Vittorio Giannini followed in the Thirties. In 1928 he wed likeminded concert pianist and music teacher Madeleine Marshall, who the year before had co-authored a book of gaming scenarios, published by Simon and Schuster, for Guggenheim, a Twenties games craze similar to today's Scattergories. Madeleine was one of two talented daughters of Benjamin Marshall, a prosperous Syracuse, New York hide, fur, and leather manufacturer and a niece of Jewish community leader Louis Marshall, president of the American Jewish Committee and one of the most prominent constitutional attorneys in the United States (as a legal eminence he was considered an equal of the "other Louis," Louis Brandeis). Together Madeleine and Robert would have two children, John and Peggy, who as adults became, respectively, a Yale law professor and a theatrical producer, with her husband Max Traktman, of children's plays.[3]

Robert A. Simon died in 1981 at the age of 84, having lived a most interesting and rewarding life, though regrettably his sole detective novel—a comparative trifle, if rather a charming one—had been long forgotten at his death by the vintage mystery reading public. Happily modern-day murder fanciers at leisure can now take the opportunity to relax for a few happy hours with *The Week-End Mystery.*

II. *THE WEEK-END MYSTERY*

Robert A. Simon's *The Week-End Mystery* lies firmly within the tradition of the "Murder? What fun!" school of detective fiction associated with A. A. Milne's *The Red House Mystery* (1922) and several

Twenties works by Agatha Christie, including *The Secret Adversary* (1922) and *The Secret of Chimneys* (1925), all tales written with a light hand and the tongue in cheek. (Notorious sourpuss Raymond Chandler did not appreciate A. A. Milne's joke and spent a good chunk of his "Simple Art of Murder" essay dismantling *The Red House Mystery* for its lack of realism, in one of the great examples of utterly-beside-the-point literary criticism.) However, Simon's novel is even more "meta" than Milne's and Christie's books, in that it openly revels in mystery genre self-reference from nearly its first page.

The story opens in the "little office on 94th Street near Broadway" of Dr. Hugh Farrigan, orthopedic specialist. 28-year-old Jimmy Wrome, assistant to the head of the refined sugar department in the Universal Sugar Refining Company, has come to Dr. Farrigan's office seeking a cure for his aches and pains. The doctor quickly diagnoses Jimmy's malady as a broken heart and prescribes—but naturally—a steady diet of detective fiction, which Jimmy is to borrow from Curtin's, the drugstore around the corner.[4] Farrigan's playful prescription reads:

> Detective Stories.
> Read one daily until relieved. Dose may be increased if desired.
>
> Hugh Farrigan, M. D.

Dr. Farrigan starts Jimmy off with a mystery novel he happens to have on hand at the office: *The Shower Bath Enigma*, one of the many popular tales about series sleuth Bernard Gatlin, "the Man of a Million Masks." Responding well to his course of treatment, Jimmy next reads *The Porterhouse Murder*, another Bernard Gatlin exploit, and after that there is no return. From the Bernard Gatlin series Jimmy soon has devoured *What Happened in Rochester*, *The Pumblewaite Legacy* ("not so good, that one"), *Eighteen Minutes Past Five*, *The Face in the Dark*, *The Rosenbaum Case*, *The Cryptic Bride*, *The O'Reilly Affair* and the latest Gatlin opus, *The Statue of Liberty Tangle*, concerning the vexed question of just who "knifed the senator at midnight in the Statue of Liberty torch." Jimmy also reads tales about Great Detectives Hamilton Boone, Lord Hembury and Wilhelmine O'Connor, but the Man of the Million Masks

Original Cover (Curtis Evans Collection)

*For Mr. Howard M. Buffinton
with cordial greetings
Robert A. Simon
April 24
1 9 2 3*

Author Inscription (Curtis Evans Collection)

remains his mainstay. Soon he seemingly has gotten over his late love affair, but Dr. Farrigan starts to wonder whether the young man, who is now making Holmesian deductions about everyone he encounters, may be coming down with a severe attack of "detecti-vitis."

Jimmy feeds his raging fever for detection when Dr. Farrigan invites him to a weekend house party being held by his most prominent patient, wealthy bachelor banker Leed Payne, "the Mystery Man of Wall Street," at his country estate, Olean, in Bellechester. (Westchester?) Also among the weekend guests at Olean are New York assemblyman Francis Gulvin and his theater enthusiast wife; jive-spouting jazz saxophonist Eddie Endle, who plays nightly at the nearby Shuffle Inn; beautiful Claire Trevor, who just happens to be the woman who violently wrung Jimmy's withers; and Claire's mystifying new love interest, bland bond dealer Blake Hesbe. All these people, along with Olean's butler, Stelke (naturally there is a butler), become suspects when Leed Payne is discovered dead in his locked bedroom, having been mortally wounded from a single gunshot, seemingly self-inflicted.

Jimmy has other ideas about Payne's sudden death, however, and he promptly communicates them at length to a local reporter. Soon the case is being reluctantly investigated by Edgar Brinze, Captain of the Bellechester Police Reserve Force. Yet Jimmy has no confidence in the sleuthing capacities of Brinze, the son of a local cement manufacturer who had shown such "an alarming inaptitude for the niceties of the cement business" that he was foisted by his wealthy and politically influential father onto the police department, where he has proven every bit as inapt. Jimmy concludes that he will have to conduct his own investigation of the mystery, especially after Claire, whom it seems he has not quite gotten over after all, becomes Brinze's lead suspect! Can lessons from *The Shower Bath Enigma*, *The Porterhouse Murder* and *The Rosenbaum Case* help Jimmy mimic the crime-busting methods of the Man of a Million Masks and beat Bellechester's bullying and boorish Captain Brinze to the solution of the Leed Payne murder case?

Thus begins the competition for clues in one of the most meta mystery novels from the Golden Age of detective fiction. The reader will not fully appreciate just how much so until she has reached the last line of the last page. Please refrain from peeking, dear readers! Much enjoyment lies ahead of you in Robert A. Simon's winsome account of Jimmy Wrome's greatest case.

ENDNOTES

[1] The Simon's townhouse was later purchased by Robert B. Roosevelt, Jr., a cousin of President Theodore Roosevelt. It was torn down and replaced with an elegant neo-Georgian mansion at the behest of its new owner, millionaire William Ziegler, Jr., in 1927. Today the house is the site of the SUNY Global Center.

[2] Quoting Randy Mackin, *George Scarborough, Appalachian Poet: A Biographical and Literary Study with Unpublished Writings* (McFarland, 2011), 6. Dubbed the "Jewish Will Rogers" on account of his wryly humorous wit, Hershfield is best known today for his *Abie the Agent*, which featured the first Jewish protagonist in an American comic strip. He also created the comic strips *Desperate Desmond* and *Dauntless Durham of the U. S. A.*, in which he amusingly parodied cliffhanging crime melodrama. Simon and Schuster did not launch its celebrated "Inner Sanctum" mystery imprint, edited by Lee Thayer, until 1936. It would include such lauded mystery writers as Patrick Quentin, Anthony Boucher, Cornell Woolrich, and Craig Rice.

[3] On Madeleine Marshall Simon (1899-1993), see Sheri Cook-Cunningham, "The Many Facets of Madeleine Marshall," *International Journal of Research in Choral Singing* 4 (2): 52-76. Madeleine, who performed as a soloist with the New York Philharmonic under Arturo Toscanini, would later teach English diction at the Juilliard School for over a half-century (1935-86) and author the standard school text *The Singer's Manual of English Diction*. She was coach and accompanist for many artists, including Lily Pons,

Helen Traubel, Leontyne Pryce, Lawrence Tibbett, and Lauritz Melchior.

[4] Jimmy Wrome is of the same age as the author when he was writing *The Week-End Mystery*.

THE WEEK-END MYSTERY

I

A NEW CURE FOR AN ANCIENT EVIL

R. Hugh Farrigan hadn't enjoyed the sight of a broken leg for at least three weeks.

He was a frustrated orthopedist, although you might not have thought so, for he looked imposing in his little office on 94th Street near Broadway. Patients—when there were patients—were impressed with his authority. Sitting behind his glass-topped table, toying with a paper cutter in the form of a souvenir scalpel, he radiated power. His eyes invariably were described as "steely" by lady visitors who used words like "steely," and his hands were spoken of as "capable." Mrs. Bauerndorf, who lived in the apartment across the hall, thought that he was a fine, clean-cut young man; in fact, the sort of doctor you would let your daughter visit, unaccompanied. Mrs. Bauerndorf had no daughter.

Dr. Farrigan, staring abstractedly at the drizzle against his window pane, sighed. These warm May evenings were becoming monotonous. Somebody had suggested to him that it might be clever to have office hours between 7 and 9, and he was testing the idea. But apparently this two-hour period was not one of high-disease frequency. On many evenings he had sat at his table, waiting until inactivity had made him irritable. Then he would take up some volume of *Mysteria Medica* and become immersed in it, always hoping, however, that he would be dredged up by some sufferer from a really fine fracture, or a good healthy break. Now and then his reading was disturbed, either by someone who had a new work on abdominal neuroses to vend, or, more rarely, by some woman from a near-by flat, whose child was feeling something awful after eating frankfurters and marshmallow sundaes and who didn't like to bother her regular doctor with these little things. Dr. Farrigan had no objection to croup, colds and colic, but didn't anybody ever have an interesting ailment?

It was three years now that he had inhabited this office—three relentlessly uneventful years. He had intended to develop into an orthopedic specialist, but, as he explained in his lighter and confidential moments, "there was no practice in this line, to make no bones about the matter." It was the way of young specialists.

Mysteria Medica was absorbing enough, but it offered only vicarious experience. If only some strange disease, lodged in an alien body, would come marching into the consultation room! He wished that he could believe in the credo that one could have anything if only one desired it with sufficient fervor. It was a night for something to materialize, if things ever did materialize. The drizzle had trickled off into a thick mist which threw the lights in the windows across the court out of focus. Perhaps from this haze something would come to him, something tangible and exciting, yet something surrounded with the fanciful aura of the unknown.

He remembered the thrill that came when first he had treated Leed Payne. Payne was a banker, mentioned occasionally in the newspapers as "the mystery man of Wall Street." To his physicians, Payne was a powerful, short-tempered, middle-aged bachelor, whose quick whims made constant difficulties. He had severed relations with Dr. Unstrand, one of the three great orthopedists, because he didn't approve of Dr. Unstrand's eyes. The eminent specialist had been summoned to set a broken shoulder blade, incurred in a fall from a notoriously expensive horse. The operation was simple and successful, but Payne took a dislike to Dr. Unstrand, who sensed the banker's antipathy and intimated ironically but politely that a former student of his could handle the case from now on. Payne immediately demanded that Dr. Unstrand turn the case over to the student, and Dr. Farrigan became surgeon extraordinary to Leed Payne.

"There's nothing to do but look him over every week," Dr. Unstrand had told Hugh, "but hurt him a little when you do it or he'll think you don't know your business. And if you don't send in a good big bill, he'll be convinced that you don't. If he happens to like you at first sight, he'll be a life-time patient. If he doesn't, out you go. He's a man who works entirely on his prejudices."

Payne's prejudices seemed to be in Hugh's favor, and he sent for him frequently. Payne suffered little from his broken bones, but he felt that he had to be kept in condition.

"It's your business," he informed Hugh, in his brisk, rasping voice, "to keep me up to scratch. Most of the time I feel rotten. See that I don't. That's all."

Payne's "that's all" was one of the few familiar characteristics of the man. It was a masterpiece of literalism. It was a command which could not be questioned and which could not be disobeyed without a drastic penalty. Payne had concluded a famous interview with the greatest speculator of a decade with "that's all," and it was all. The speculator never recovered his fortunes or his standing.

So far, Hugh reflected, he had followed Payne's behest. Payne had immense vitality. He subjected his system to strains which might have injured any other man, and escaped with nothing worse than a bad frame of mind. Hugh's principal function was to cater to the banker's restlessness. The doctor gave no orders; it was the patient who prescribed.

"I feel rotten," he would say. "Get me a couple of good seats for a show tonight and come with me."

"Come with me on a party tonight," was another formula. "Be at my house at nine. That's all."

And these parties—!

Here the bell jangled. Hugh looked up from his reverie. Perhaps adventure had come out of the mists. He opened the door to admit a young man in evening clothes and a soft hat. The young man was slightly above medium height, with dark brown hair carefully plastered down, sharp but troubled brown eyes, a good jaw and a pleasant but unsteady smile.

"Doctor Farrigan?" he asked in a low voice, not altogether under control.

Hugh recognized it as the voice of a patient who had decided to consult a physician only after a hard internal conflict.

"I'm Doctor Farrigan," he said. "Won't you come in?"

The young man followed him into the consulting room and sat in the heavily upholstered chair near the desk.

Hugh drew from a drawer a large "History Card," prepared for and distributed to physicians by the manufacturers of Vitalol, "the peppy panacea."

"I'll take your history first, if you don't mind," he observed. "Name?"

"Wrome, W-R-O-M-E," said the young man. "James Wrome. I live across the street. I was going to a dinner party tonight but—"

"Just a minute," interrupted Hugh. "Let me take down the rest of the data. Business?"

"I'm with the Universal Sugar Refining Company. I'm assistant to the head of the refined sugar department."

"Your age?"

"Twenty-eight."

Hugh shoved the card to one side.

"It's this way, Doctor," said Wrome, rapidly and nervously. "I was going out to a dinner party tonight. That's why I got dressed up. Well, just as I was about to phone for a taxi, I felt weak and sick. Wrong all over. I never felt that way before. I couldn't understand it. So I thought it was something I'd eaten, and I took a pill and lay down. As soon as I lay down I began to tremble all over. I never had that before, either. In fact, I've always been in pretty good health.

"'Well,' I said to myself, 'this won't do.' So I went back to the phone, but as soon as I touched the receiver, I began to get nervous and sick again. I thought it was foolish of me. Here I had a little touch of indigestion and suddenly I was all unnerved. But my tongue went dry and I felt all in, and when I tried to lie down, I began to tremble again. I can't think of what I could have eaten—"

"Maybe it has nothing to do with what you've eaten," interrupted Hugh sharply.

Wrome seemed to be a little frightened by the suggestion.

"I can't think what else—"

"Let me ask you a few questions," said Hugh. "But first I think I'll look you over."

A rapid physical examination revealed no unusual conditions.

"I thought there wasn't much wrong," commented Hugh. "Have you been working hard lately?"

"No harder than ever. It isn't a very hard job. Raw sugar is, but not refined. Refined almost runs itself."

"Do you get enough exercise?"

"An hour or so of tennis a day. Sometimes a little golf. I keep in pretty good trim."

Hugh looked at him thoughtfully.

"Have you had anything disturbing happen to you lately?" he asked slowly.

Wrome fidgeted.

"Well—nothing that could have anything to do—"

"How do you know it couldn't have anything to do with your condition?" demanded Hugh.

"I don't," confessed Wrome.

He rubbed his hands against the glass-topped table.

"I might as well tell you, doctor," he said finally. "Maybe it'll do me good to get it out of my system. There isn't anybody I can talk to about it. Only, it'll sound terribly foolish to you, I'm afraid."

A deprecating smile helped to compose Wrome's somewhat overwrought features.

"Go ahead," Hugh suggested. "I'll light my pipe and listen."

Wrome changed his position in the chair several times before he began to speak.

"About three months ago," he began, "I met a girl—a young lady—"

"I thought so," Hugh emitted between puffs.

Wrome smiled, patently pleased by the physician's sympathetic understanding.

"I'll tell you the whole story," Wrome continued. "She was a lovely thing. We'll call her—well, I might as well use her name because it probably wouldn't mean much to you and it wouldn't matter if it did. Her name's Claire Barton. Claire isn't like any other girl I've ever known. That sounds like old stuff. I guess the real thing always sounds like old stuff. She's beautiful and clever and really unusual in every way. I mean she has brains and a heart—at least, I thought she had a heart.

"I met her at some little affair—and it happened. I never thought I'd fall for anybody. I have a little apartment across the street, and I thought I'd probably spend all my life there. I've known plenty of attractive girls, but none of them ever really got me. Claire did. I guess that's why I'm here now.

"She asked me to call on her. I didn't see much of her family, but she lives with them in an inexpensive apartment. Very simply, you know. She isn't at all spoiled. She's very natural and hasn't any affectations."

The thought of Claire seemed to impede Wrome's flow of speech. He looked at Hugh, who was nodding his head silently, and continued.

"She has a job downtown as secretary to a broker, and as she's working in my district, we used to go out to lunch together. In fact, it became a pretty common thing. That doesn't sound like much, I suppose, but it made a lot of difference to me. I've been sort of lonely ever since I came to New York to work, and Claire seemed to be a real friend. And I thought some day we'd be more than just friends. I suppose every man has an ideal girl somewhere in the back of his head, and Claire was the one that I must have had, there."

Wrome broke off again.

"I must sound silly," he remarked.

"Not at all," said Hugh. "Keep going."

"Claire and I used to see a good deal of each other. We went to shows together, and out dancing and all that sort of thing. We'd never discussed marriage or anything like that, but I felt that she understood. It's a hard thing to explain, but maybe you get the idea. As far as I knew, she wasn't interested in anybody else at the time, and she knew she was the only girl I'd ever cared for.

"So I began building air castles. I could see us married, with a home, and all that sentimental stuff. It sounds rather absurd, the way I tell it, but it was very real when I thought of it. I regarded her as my fiancée, although I don't suppose I had any right to without consulting her.

"Well, I'm not going to keep on with all that. You know what the feeling is, I imagine. Last week, I had a date with her for lunch and she didn't turn up—the first time that had happened. I rang up and she said she couldn't speak to me then. The next morning I had a note from her."

Wrome's voice became dry and he articulated the rest with difficulty.

"She said that we mustn't see each other anymore, that it was no fault of mine, but that it would be best if I forgot her."

Wrome paused and stared at the desk.

"That was a knock-out, all right," he went on, forcing a smile. "I couldn't think of anything but Claire for several days. Then I couldn't stand it any longer. I rang her up, and again she said that she couldn't talk to me. I wrote to her and had no answer. I realized that I was making a fool of myself, and yet I couldn't think of anything I'd done that could induce her to break off everything just like that.

"And that wasn't all. I felt that I had to see her, so I hung around the office building in which she works, waiting for her to come out and hoping that she might speak to me. I knew that something had happened to her—I didn't have any idea what, but I wanted to find out, and if it was something I'd said or done, to see if I couldn't right myself with her. It was a situation I couldn't get at all, because she'd been particularly lovely the last time I'd seen her.

"Somehow, I always missed her. Perhaps she wasn't working there any more. But this noon—"

Wrome's speech slowed up.

"This noon I saw her at last. She came out of the building. Of course there was a crowd coming out about that time so she didn't see me at once. I was about to speak to her, when a fellow I know slightly took her arm. He's a rather stupid young man. Works for some house in Wall Street. She smiled at Blake—his name's Blake Hesbe—and walked off with him, arm in arm, laughing and chatting with him as though—as though—"

Wrome again smiled his odd smile.

"This must sound almost hysterical to you, doctor," he concluded. "I suppose you thought I'd tell you something terribly shocking, and all you got was the story of a disappointed young man."

"It's more than that," asserted Hugh. "It explains what's wrong with you. The affair's hit your nerves and impaired your digestion.

You've been brooding over it and it's upset you. It's very common. I'm really an orthopedist, but such cases have interested me a good deal, and I've seen lots of them. You'll get over it."

"I hope so," said Wrome, "but I don't think so. Claire's before me all the time—Claire and that Hesbe, walking away arm in arm. Even now when I mention it—"

"Isn't there some other girl?" Hugh began.

"There can't be," Wrome declared. "I told you it was the only time I'd fallen. It's one of those things that happens only a few times in a century."

"It may happen oftener in the next quarter of a century," remarked Hugh. "You don't need medical attention. You need to know a few other girls—"

"I tell you, I know plenty of them but Claire's the only one—"

Wrome checked himself again.

"I certainly am letting the thing run away with me," he commented, with a certain detachment. "Now, doctor, I'm willing to do anything you say, but I know that it won't do me any good to try to fall in love with somebody else. As a matter of fact, I'd thought of that myself. Off with the old love doesn't mean on with the new. Everything reminds me of her. There's a song—'A Little Love, A Little Kiss'—she used to sing. Just to hum it would wreck me. I'm glad it's old. If I had to hear it often, I'd become a madman."

Hugh tapped the desk with his pipe.

"You'll have to get some sort of interest in life to keep your mind off the affair," he asserted. "Doesn't your business keep you occupied?"

"No," sighed Wrome. "I'm sorry, but when I lock my desk at five o'clock, every granule of sugar passes out of my system."

Hugh folded his hands and looked idly at *Mysteria Medica*. He gazed at the book cases in the room. Then he leaned across the desk and took a volume from a small collection held together by two skull-shaped book-ends.

"Let's try and experiment, Mr. Wrome," he said. "It can't do any harm, and it may be the very thing. Tell me, Mr. Wrome, do you read detective stories?"

Wrome was puzzled. Physicians had asked him about his habits, his diet, his family, his sleep, and all manner of personal matters but this was a new query.

"I've read them, of course," he admitted. "I'm not especially interested in them, and I haven't read any of them lately, but I know what they're like."

Hugh began to scribble on a pad.

"I'm giving you a strange prescription," he observed. "It's probably the first time in history that a physician has written it, but it may be just what you need."

He passed a slip to Wrome.

> "Detective Stories.
> "Read one daily until relieved. Dose may be increased
> if desired.
>
> > "Hugh Farrigan, M.D."

Wrome grinned.

"Is this serious?" he demanded.

"Absolutely. I've found that a detective story is the best mental eliminant when the mind is clogged with unwholesome material. It calls for an unusual train of thought, it takes you off the familiar mental track, and it brings you into new and absorbing surroundings. I might have added 'digest thoroughly' to that prescription. Put yourself in the detective's place and try to solve the puzzle before he does. It'll be a mental excursion from which you'll return refreshed, even if you can't get there ahead of the detective."

"And when am I to start on this journey?" inquired Wrome.

"Tonight. I recommend the mental drug store known as Curtin's, which you will find around the corner. The treatment won't be expensive, because you can rent the books at a quarter a week, and you won't keep them for more than a day or two. You'll find a very charming librarian in charge, and I think that she'll be able to keep you well supplied."

Hugh handed the book which he had taken from the rack to his patient.

"Here's your first dose," he explained. *"The Shower Bath Enigma.* I don't usually keep medicine in stock, but this happens to be here, and it ought to help you get a good night's sleep. Not over it, but because of it. By the time you figure out who killed the man in the gray sweater, you'll have forgotten all about your other troubles."

Wrome stood up and held the book in his hand doubtfully.

"Well, doctor," he said, "I'll try it. If it helps me get over this feeling, I'll certainly—"

"Be surprised?" cut in Hugh. "I'll be surprised if it doesn't help you. Now, I want you to come back in a few days and tell me how you feel. But be sure you do as I've told you. And stick to it."

Jimmy made his adieu and passed out of the door into the misty street. He entered his apartment and lit a lamp over his bed. He tossed his coat and vest on a chair and lay down. Come to think of it, he should have notified his host that he couldn't be at the dinner tonight. But it was too late now, anyhow, and he could explain in a note. He felt better. There was something soothing about the young physician, something that quieted his own thoughts and substituted Farrigan's. He must have been a curious figure when he entered there agitatedly in his evening clothes. He visualized himself, dressed for dinner, telling Farrigan the story of his infatuation and of its consequences. Nothing but a love-sick puppy! The boys at the office certainly would guffaw if they heard about this! He should have gone to the party in the first place. Then he looked at *The Shower Bath Enigma* and laughed. It all seemed like a dream now. And as he reviewed the evening, Claire again came into his mind. Claire's voice, asking him never to speak to her again. Claire, gladly greeting the sheepish, towheaded Blake Hesbe. Claire disappearing into the noonday crowd, arm in arm with Hesbe. He felt an unpleasant sensation in the knees and a faint shudder.

"What an ass you are, Jimmy!" he murmured. "Letting a girl get you this way!"

But self-condemnation didn't relieve him. He clenched his fists and shook himself. He'd have to fight this down. The dim face peering from the shower bath on the jacket of the book scowled at him.

"Here goes," he muttered with a perfunctory laugh.

He opened the book.

"*The Man in the Gray Sweater*," he read.

"*Sergeant Schuster sauntered casually up Pell Street,*" began the story. "*It was a blustery night, and the loungers who generally clustered about the entrances of dimly lighted doorways had taken themselves to other parts. From Wah Sing's Chop Suey House came—*"

At midnight, Jimmy was marching side by side with Bernard Gartlin, the Man of a Million Masks, into the secret passage behind one of Wah Sing's private parlors.

II
STARTING POINTS

Jimmy usually walked directly from the subway to his apartment, but this evening, he strolled along Broadway, looking for Curtin's. For once there had been a little excitement in the offices of the Universal Sugar Refining Co. A chemist, experimenting with non-spirituous but intoxicating syrup (add vichy and serve) had been overwhelmingly successful and had attempted to celebrate this new triumph of science by parading through the refined sugar department, volunteering to lick his weight in wild cats. No wild cats having offered their services, the chemist selected Gurney, a crabbed salesman, as his first opponent. Gurney, already exasperated by a trying day, warded off the chemist's attack with a telephone receiver, and it had been Jimmy's duty to restore tranquility before the matter reached the ears of the vice-president. As he looked about for the book shop, Jimmy was still enjoying his escapade, which consisted in smuggling the non-spirituously intoxicated chemist through the front door, at the very hour dedicated to the egress of the higher officials, and fitting the punisher of wild cats into the recesses of an unwilling chauffeur's taxicab. He felt better for his adventure. He felt a little like Bernard Gartlin, the Man of a Million Masks. He must become better acquainted with Gartlin, the suave old gentleman who always appeared on the scene after Scotland Yard and the United States Secret Service had relegated the case to the archives of the insoluble.

Curtin's, he discovered, was an attractive little store whose window sparkled with books bearing labels announcing "renting price" and "sales price." He felt a little self-conscious about going in and asking for detective stories, just as he had always fancied an ignominy

about going into a drug store and requesting liver pills. It would
be like wearing a broken heart on his sleeve. Still, there were many
detective story addicts. It was time that he got over this Claire nonsense, anyhow.

Seated behind a desk littered with index cards was a slender,
dark-haired young woman, with cryptic but delightful brown eyes and
a fascinating pout, put there by nature rather than by temperament.
Jimmy felt reassured in the presence of this attractive librarian. He
smiled at her and drew Farrigan's prescription from his pocket.

"Do you think that you could fill this prescription for me?" he
inquired.

She smiled back delightfully.

"I'd love to be a literary pharmacist," she said in a soft voice,
which, Jimmy thought, rippled. "Do you wish to become a subscriber?"

Jimmy filled out a blank and paid a deposit.

"Your physician doesn't specify the first treatment," she observed. "Have you any idea which book ought to be the first?"

"I'm sure you know more about them than I do," confessed Jimmy.

"Let's look at the chemicals," she suggested, "and I'll see if I can
find a suitable liniment."

Liniment? Jimmy looked at her sharply. Farrigan had said that
this was an uncommon treatment. The librarian spoke as though
most broken hearts were cured by reading. But there was nothing
knowing about her glances, and Jimmy charged his suspicions
against his sensitivity.

"Try this one," she said, handing him a green book which seemed
to have passed through many hands. "There's a great demand for it,
but it just happens to be on the shelves today."

He inspected *The Porterhouse Murder*.

"That's the latest Bernard Gartlin story," she explained. "Our
readers seem to like Bernard Gartlin better than any of the newer
detectives. He's the Man of a Million Masks. In this book he gets
into society, or what the author thinks is society. There's a character
named Viola Vandermere, but it's a good story, anyhow."

Her tone was a little too instructive for Jimmy's fancy. He didn't
like to be considered a novice at anything so ordinary as detective
stories.

"The usual thing, I suppose," he said casually.

"Certainly," she beamed. "If it weren't the usual thing it wouldn't pay Mr. Curtin to stock it. The usual detective story is the hardest to solve because the reader knows, that although the circumstances are stenciled, the criminal probably isn't the butler or the secretary or the quiet little man who hasn't any real function in the story. Life is like that. It's the everyday problems that give you the most worry. I rather suspect that you won't solve this one ahead of Gartlin."

"I'm not a detective," Jimmy retorted.

"Not yet," she added.

She returned to her desk and made notations on a card.

"One learns a good deal in a book store like this," she remarked. "I can tell quite a bit about our customers merely by looking over their cards."

She selected a card from one of the indices.

"Here's the card of a young woman, for instance," she went on. "She's been drawing books for about two years. At first she read only the very newest novels. Then the trend changed to love stories of a simple type. Suddenly she began to read Hardy and the Russians. Then there's a gap. Apparently she didn't read anything for several weeks. And then she began to draw two books at a time on home-making, cooking, household economics, and finally a work on the correct procedure at formal functions. That's all very obvious, of course. And the proof is in the fact that she had her membership transferred to one of our other branches under her married name. Society, love, disappointment, reconciliation, and marriage. The other branch could give you the sequel.

"This is a simple case. But here's the card of a well-to-do man of middle age. It shows nothing noteworthy until about a year ago. The titles of the novels which he drew wouldn't mean much to the casual observer, because they're mostly obscure or forgotten works. But I noticed that every book he drew after a certain date was about politics and that in almost every instance, the principal character went into politics with reform ideas. And the holder of this card was an unsuccessful candidate for the state senate on a reform platform last election. Perhaps he got the inspiration from his reading. I don't know, but it's not impossible."

She looked at Jimmy with an enigmatic smile, a smile that some-how seemed to match the mystery in her eyes.

"I don't know anything about you, of course, Mr. Wrome," she said, "and probably it's none of my business, but I shouldn't be sur-prised if your physician were trying to make a detective of you. If you were ten years younger, I'd be ready to predict that you were on the way to becoming a disciple of Bernard Gartlin."

"You're a little that way yourself, aren't you?" asked Jimmy.

"Most women are," she remarked. "That'll be twenty-five cents a week for that book, and two cents extra for every day it's overdue. But we've collected only six cents in fines on detective stories in the past year."

Jimmy and *The Porterhouse Murder* became inseparable within the next two hours. Again he was stalking along with Bernard Gart-lin, this time into Mrs. Vandermere's rose arbor, where certain vital footprints had been overlooked by the local police captain. He was puzzling over the strange agitation of Viola Vandermere when the telephone rang.

"How long do you expect us to wait dinner for you?" demanded an angry voice—

Jimmy recalled that a young man who had friends sufficiently hospitable to relieve him of the necessity of dining alone every eve-ning owed them a certain consideration. He left Bernard Gartlin in the rose arbor and Viola Vandermere in the den where the young Silesian's body had been found, and went lightheartedly in search of a taxicab.

An overcrowded morning at the clinic almost tempted Dr. Farri-gan to toss the penciled memorandum on his desk into a waste bas-ket already overflowing with complimentary blotters, but the word "Payne" on the sheet halted the despatch of the note.

"Mr. Payne called up, wants you to come to his ofice right away."

The maid had got the message. She always deprived "office" of an f.

Payne would say he felt rotten, what ought he to do about it, don't bother him, that's all. He liked to summon people to his of-fice. His mysterious transactions took place high up in a dingy, gray building on Wall Street, a building which looked as though it had been patched together from the left-over materials of its more impressive neighbors. A dull gold legend, "Leed Payne," on the lower left-hand corner of coarsely ground glass plate, set in a crudely painted door, served as a guide to the passer-by. Within was a weary, drab-voiced young woman who sat by a telephone. A large door led into the sanctum of Payne, a bare sanctum, concentrated entirely in a superannuated roll top desk, from which the shellac had been, rubbed many years ago. Payne had in his office no chair save that which he occupied. "People don't talk so long standing up," was his explanation.

"Mr. Payne was expecting you," drawled the secretary when Hugh arrived. "He wants you to wait a minute."

Hugh took an old cane chair facing the door, and looked about idly. A young woman in a neat blue serge suit entered on two of the loveliest ankles that Hugh ever had observed in a reasonably extensive and varied series of observations. From under an attractive little blue hat rolled a band of golden hair, and two blue eyes, bluer than the blue eyes usually associated with blondes, looked brightly but restlessly about. The coloring and the mouth completed the portrait appropriately. Hugh's gaze lost its idleness.

The door from Payne's office swung open creakily and the banker stepped to the threshold. His mezzo-forte gray checked suit, his pearl-gray spats, his brilliantly polished shoes, his blue and red striped necktie and the gargantuan carnation in his coat lapel seemed quaintly out of tone with the dull surroundings. He looked knowingly at his visitors, and revealed his large white teeth. When Payne was not looking knowingly, he was looking dully, and once in a while he looked fiercely. He was a man of three looks, light brown, dull brown and dark brown. Just now the prevailing tone color was light brown.

"Good afternoon, Dr. Farrigan," he remarked in a voice that always seemed a degree more raucous than necessary.

He stared curiously at the young woman.

"Ah," he said sweetly.

He always prefaced his remarks to pretty women with "Ah."

"Ah! Good afternoon, Miss Barton."

Hugh looked up sharply. Barton! Was Payne's visitor also Wrome's Claire Barton?

"You look as though you might know Miss Barton, doctor," commented Payne with a shrewd grimace. "If not, I'll introduce you. Miss Barton, may I present Dr. Hugh Farrigan? I hope that you'll excuse me for a few minutes longer. Then I'll see you for a moment, Miss Barton, and then I'll see you, Dr. Farrigan. I'm sorry that I haven't a more luxurious reception room for you."

He bowed himself back into his office jauntily. Evidently he was in one of his infrequent jocular moods today.

"You know me, Dr. Farrigan?" asked the young woman.

Hugh noted that the voice also fitted the picture. And that there was something vaguely anxious in its inflection.

"I don't know," he answered. "I think I've heard of you."

This response failed to put Miss Barton at ease. "Where?" she asked.

Hugh deliberated before answering. It wouldn't be professional ethics to discuss a patient, even so odd a patient as Jimmy Wrome, with a stranger. Yet Jimmy had mentioned Miss Barton socially rather than medically. Perhaps it would throw more light on Jimmy's trouble if Miss Barton could be led to speak of her relations with him.

"A friend of mine named Wrome knows a Miss Barton," he said. "Perhaps you're that Miss Barton."

Miss Barton acknowledged her identity by an uneasy movement of her captivating ankles.

"Yes," she admitted. "Are you a friend of his?"

"I know him slightly. And then, I believe, Mr. Hesbe knows you."

The reference to Hesbe manifestly annoyed Miss Barton.

"You seem to know quite a bit about me," she said lightly. "I wonder what you could have heard from Jimmy or Mr. Hesbe."

"Jimmy or Mr. Hesbe." Perhaps she cared more for Jimmy than Jimmy thought.

"Not a thing," answered Hugh.

"Now, that's hardly fair, Dr. Farrigan," she insisted, looking at him earnestly for all her playful speech. "You know that you've heard something, and it isn't right to arouse a woman's curiosity without satisfying it."

"Really, I haven't," said Hugh. "You won't take it amiss, however, if I add that I'd like to know more about you."

"There's not so very much to know," said Claire. "I have a job, and—and that's about all. Did you think that I had a highly colorful history?"

Distress had changed to charm.

"I didn't think at all."

Claire, in moments of badinage, was rather bewitching. It wasn't so easy to talk to her in those moments. Hugh reflected that this young woman might well upset the equilibrium of Jimmy Wrome— or of almost any man. Her beauty survived a first inspection and became more entrancing on closer acquaintance.

"Very few of us think when Miss Barton is around."

Payne had opened his door slightly.

"Won't you come in now, Miss Barton, and prevent me from thinking!"

Hugh didn't like Payne's attitude toward Claire. There was always a suppressed leer there. And what, he wondered, could Claire, apparently a simple, charming girl, have to do with Payne? Payne prided himself as a connoisseur of pretty women—the phrase was his own—and it wasn't unlikely that Claire attracted him. She might attract anybody. But why should she come to Payne's office? On business? Payne had told him of a man named Barton, with whom he had business relations—relations not altogether pleasant. Barton had had a daughter, "a young pip," Payne had said. But even if this were the young pip, what business could she have with a man who specialized only in large scale banking operations and who enjoyed nothing more than to reject business with a verdict concentrated in the caustic formula, "Chicken feed! I won't touch it! That's all!"?

But those who passed in and out of Payne's office always had puzzled Hugh. Payne often announced orotundly that "variety was the spice of life" and that he liked variety in the people he saw. Payne's famous week-end parties invariably brought together a curious assortment of guests. On one occasion, Payne had invited the illustrious

Vanity Lamar and her three divorced husbands, along with the other divorced wives of all of these worthies. Generally, however, there was not so much plan in Payne's selection of the company which was to inhabit Olean, his home in Bellechester, from Saturday to Monday. "Bring a friend with you—you know what I mean" was his favorite form of invitation, the "you know what I mean" being accompanied with a smirk which meant all things to all people. Perhaps Payne had nominated Claire as a possible week-end guest—but he wouldn't summon her to his office to issue an invitation.

And this was a bit of a coincidence—running into the cause of one patient's malady in the office of another. These little things were what made life interesting.

Claire's interview with Payne was brief. She walked rapidly out of the office within five minutes after she had entered, and it was evident that she was even more perturbed now than before. As she left, Payne came out of the inner office and looked after her grimly. Hugh rose as Claire passed him, but she was out of sight before he even could bow. Sometimes these short and stormy interviews in Payne's room were audible in the ante-chamber, but Hugh had heard nothing of what passed. Oh well! Payne's relations with people were beyond him.

A curt nod from the banker summoned Hugh into the sanctum. Payne slumped into his chair and looked up dully.

"I feel rotten," he announced.

That was like Payne. Periods of jocularity always were followed by this proclamation.

"Yes, rotten," he reiterated savagely.

"Shoulder?"

"That's for you to say," Payne snapped. "You're the doctor. If you think it's the shoulder, look at it."

Hugh examined it quickly.

"Mending nicely," he said. "Does it hurt much when I touch it."

"Yes—no—I don't know."

Payne tossed his head irritably as he spoke.

"Don't bother me about that damn shoulder," he commanded. "Wait till I ask you about it."

Payne's testiness didn't worry Hugh. He was acclimated to Payne.

"I didn't get you down here to talk about shoulders, anyhow," added Payne. "Have a cigar."

He thrust a box of sixty-cent Havanas at Hugh.

"Don't take one if you don't feel like it," he went on. "I didn't get you down here to hem and haw about cigars, either. Listen, now."

"Listen, now" was the signal for the passing of the depressed period and the beginning of an aggressive one.

"I'm going to have a party this week-end," said Payne, "and I want you to be there. All right?"

Hugh nodded and selected a cigar.

"Good. Now, I've got a pretty good collection of folks invited. Know Gulvin? No? No reason why you should. Then you don't know his wife, either."

Payne hauled a cigar out of the box and lighted it with an automatic lighter.

"He's one of those political fellows. He was the boy politician of the Bronx or one of those places. He's in the state assembly. I put him there. Otherwise, he's harmless. His wife's older than he is. She's a crank on little theaters and she likes to have me put up for them. The littler the theater, the better I like it."

Payne puffed at the window and stared at it as though waiting for the smoke to rebound before he continued.

"Then I'm giving Eddie Endle a repeat engagement. I told him I'd be glad to have him if he'd leave his saxophone at that Shuffle Inn dance hall of his. You'll like him anyhow. And then—"

Payne jabbed his cigar in Hugh's direction.

"You saw that sweet young woman?"

He laughed.

"You certainly saw her! Well, she's coming with a boyfriend. I always like to see those sweet things' boyfriends."

"Who's the boy friend?" asked Hugh.

"I thought you'd be curious," laughed Payne. "Well, curiosity once killed a cat."

Whenever Payne uttered something like this, he intoned it with the pride of origination.

"A young fellow," he added, "who likes to be seen with a pretty baby, just like you or me. Be that as it may, I want you to bring up a new face. Bring your whole practice, if you like. You try hard enough to turn the place into a sanitarium, as it is."

Payne smoked silently for a moment, and then his face furrowed over, indicating that a busy man mustn't waste time on social fripperies.

"Come out at the usual time," he concluded, "and bring somebody with you."

Hugh assented.

"That's all."

Payne puffed on his cigar as if to blow Hugh out of the office on a cloud of tobacco smoke.

"Good afternoon," remarked Hugh.

"Did you say something?" grunted Payne, sharply.

Jimmy, of course, would be the guest to invite for the week-end at Olean. He would come face to face with Claire—and with her companion, who, presumably, would be Hesbe. It might excite Jimmy, however, to meet the source of his sorrows. Hugh pondered on the ethical consequences of the proposed invitation. Did he have a right to bring anguish on a pleasant young man, whose only fault was that his affection had outrun his attraction? And yet, might it not be the very thing to bring Jimmy to his senses? It certainly would be an interesting contretemps and interesting contretemps were so scarce in this world of ours.

The matter didn't have to be settled at this moment, anyhow. Jimmy was to report back the day after tomorrow. If he seemed to be cured, the weekend experience would test the validity of the cure. Yes, Hugh reflected, Jimmy ought to be at Olean, if only to introduce a little drama in Payne's ordinarily talky parties.

Jimmy would meet Claire again—he would meet Hesbe (if Hesbe was the boyfriend)—he would meet Payne—

Now, come to think of it, how was it that Payne could unnerve Claire and still have her as a weekend guest? There was something in Payne's relations with Claire that could stand investigation. She was too nice a girl to—but anybody could see that. Still, women were deceptive. Why had she repelled Jimmy so suddenly? Could Payne—?

Hugh took down a volume of *Mysteria Medica*. It seemed a little less absorbing now. Had adventure come out of the mists? In the form of a case of nervous indigestion? Romance had started from less auspicious beginnings.

III
THE TRANSCENDED DETECTIVE

"Chinatown, my Chinatown,
Where the lights are low—"

A very old player-piano across the court was pumping a senescent refrain into Hugh's ears.

"I'll close the window if that disturbs you," he told his patient.

"No," she murmured. "No."

"Really?"

"No." Her English was limited. "How much?"

She paid Hugh's fee and walked briskly out of his office, muttering "Zanks, zanks," repeatedly.

A few minutes later, the bell rang. Hugh opened the door, and Jimmy, in a light gray summer suit and a straw hat with a bright band on it, entered breezily. Jimmy's appearance was sufficient to indicate that he was no longer the slightly neurotic young man in evening clothes who had shambled in a few nights ago.

"Hello, doctor," Jimmy called out. "How are you? Don't ask me how I am, because that's your business, but how are you? Ready to lick your weight in wildflowers?"

This was a transformation.

"Come in," suggested Hugh, "and tell me about it."

"I'll give you an ear full," assented Jimmy.

"That was a good job you made on that Italian woman's wrist," remarked Jimmy, as he sat down in the consultation room.

"What are you talking about?" demanded Hugh. "How did you know I attended to an Italian woman's wrist?"

"I know more than that."

Jimmy lit a cigarette, and flipped the match accurately into an ash-tray.

"She lives out of town—somewhere beyond New Rochelle—Port Chester, at a guess. She must have taken a mean fall when she hurt that wrist."

"Look here," interrupted Hugh. "I'll admit that my last patient was an Italian woman from Port Chester and that she fractured her wrist in a fall. She was sent up from the Clinic but how do you happen to know anything about it?"

"Elementary, my dear Dr. Watson, I mean Farrigan," rejoined Jimmy. "I'm surprised that you don't know how I happen to know. You're responsible not only for the case of the fractured wrist but for my knowledge of it."

"Had any more nervous trouble since I saw you last?" inquired Hugh.

"Not a bit. I'm cured. But about that wrist. To begin with, as I came out of the house, I saw this woman leaving your office. I take it that a woman leaving your office at this hour would be a patient. All right. I watched her as she walked down the street. She was murmuring some sort of benediction on you in Italian, and flexing her right wrist all the time. So you must have patched that wrist for her. Every time she moved the wrist, she stepped gingerly, from which I gather that she probably injured it when she slipped and fell, somewhere."

"I suppose that's all very good," conceded Hugh, "but where did you get the Port Chester idea? Did you stop her and ask?"

"I didn't have to. She had a time-table in her left hand, and she was trying to read it under a street lamp. I couldn't see it closely, but it was a small New York, New Haven and Hartford folder. The only folder of that size they issue includes the Port Chester schedules."

"It also includes Mount Vernon, Pelham, New Rochelle—" Hugh began caustically.

"So I've heard," agreed Jimmy. "But it wasn't raining in any of those places today. She obviously came from some place where it either was raining or threatening to rain this morning. Well, they had showers all the way down the line to New Rochelle this morning, as one of our best commuters insisted on telling me. I didn't think the information would have any value at the time. But your patient happened to be wearing rubbers, and my guess is Port Chester, because there's an Italian colony out that way. Now, that that's over, I feel fine and your prescription certainly worked."

"It seems to have made a detective of you," commented Hugh.

"If your friend Bernard Gartlin was a detective, I'm one too. It took him fourteen chapters to discover that Linderman was the man in the gray sweater. And eleven masks. Now, I can tell you without a mask that you've had a child with a sore throat in here some time within the past hour."

"Did you see the child coming out of the office with a tonsil from New Rochelle in its hand?" asked Hugh.

"Don't be facetious, doctor," countered Jimmy, smiling. "First of all, you've got that examining chair screwed up high. You've left a few tongue depressors, not yet wholly dry, on your desk. And there's a little stick, apparently soaked in argyrol, which was used in swabbing out the child's throat. But even Bernard Gartlin could have told you that."

"Is this the effect of my prescription?"

"Probably. It's one of the best prescriptions I ever got."

"And did you take it literally?"

"Sure. I read a book or two a day. After *The Shower Bath Enigma*, there was *The Porterhouse Murder*, *What Happened in Rochester*, *The Pumblewaite Legacy*—not so good, that one—*Eighteen Minutes Past Five*, *The Face in the Dark*, *The Rosenbaum Case*, *The Cryptic Bride*, and *The O'Reilly Affair*. I just drew another one for good measure—*The Statue of Liberty Tangle*."

"And you don't feel any more effects from your emotional disturbance?"

"Not an effect. By the way, how long have you had that patient with the skin disease?"

"Is this another demonstration of your skill?"

"Yes, and a simple one. You have a set of books on skin diseases in that book-case. It looks as though some agent had inflicted them on you, for they're dusty. One is missing, and on your desk. You wouldn't read them out of curiosity, for that's not your specialty.

"You haven't anything to do this week-end, have you?" asked Hugh.

"Is that deduction or a guess?"

"It's neither. I'm not trying to compete with you in the detective business. It's an invitation."

Jimmy nodded amiably.

There was no doubt about it, Hugh thought. Jimmy's sudden propensity for sleuthing would entertain Payne and probably would enliven the week-end. He would encounter Claire, but Claire seemed to be a disease of which he had been cured. And such a cure! The detective stories had acted as a too powerful counter-irritant, and Jimmy seemed to be obsessed with solving mysteries. Hugh wondered what Payne would say if Jimmy began making personal deductions from the book-cases at Olean. But there was no doubt about it. Jimmy ought to come to Bellechester.

"I want you to go to Bellechester with me," he explained. "I have a patient there named Payne, who likes to give week-end parties. That, by the way, isn't the trouble for which I'm treating him. He'll have various people there, politicians, saxophone players and other curios—and you'll probably enjoy it. You'll have a wonderful chance to practice your new art."

"Science," demurred Jimmy. "If you'd read as much about Bernard Gartlin, Hamilton Boone, Lord Hembury, Wilhelmine O'Connor and the rest of those detectives, as I have, you'd know that nothing is left to chance. It's only the local or police detective who bungles. The transcendent detective—isn't that a beautiful description? I found it in one of the books—may seem to be wrong, but that's only because he's sharper than the official sleuth and the reader. If you remember *The Pumblewaite Legacy*—"

"I don't," said Hugh. "But do you think you're a transcendental detective or whatever it is?"

Jimmy looked at him with an almost sardonic grin.

"I don't think I'm anything," he replied. "I believe you're beginning to doubt my sanity. I don't blame you. A little more than a week ago I came here because I felt shot to pieces and you were the nearest doctor. I must have been a pretty funny specimen, spilling a love story and trying to hitch it up with a case of indigestion."

"No, that was sound enough."

"Maybe it was. I know I don't want to go through it again. And now—here I am, cutting up like a storybook detective. But that was only kidding. And yet—"

Jimmy became serious.

"Somehow, I've got a hunch that there's something in it."

"In what?"

"In this story-book business."

Hugh began to consider referring Jimmy to a neurologist. It was evident that the young man was highly sensitized and that it didn't take long for his impressions to become beliefs. But there was nothing dangerous in his interest in the unraveling of things.

"I wouldn't take it too seriously," he advised him. "By the time you come back from that week-end, you'll have forgotten Bernard Gartlin and all the rest of the crew.

"All right. I'll drop in for you Saturday." Jimmy rose and lit another cigarette.

"I don't know why I should take up any more of your time, doctor," he said. "I might as well leave you to your troubles. You seem to have removed mine pretty well."

"Well," remarked Hugh a little dubiously, "you seem to be over your original disorder, but I hope you haven't picked up a strange new one in the form of detectivitis."

"Don't worry about that, doctor," laughed Jimmy, as he stood at the open door, looking sharply at the mirror in the hall.

"I wonder," he added, "if your maid is careless because she's left-handed."

"What made you think of her?" demanded Hugh.

"Well, she is careless, isn't she?" asked Jimmy. "And she is left-handed."

"Have you ever seen her?"

"Yes. Just now, in the mirror."

Hugh stared at Jimmy. Was the young man acquiring hallucinations of some sort?

"Come over here, doctor—where I'm standing—and look at the mirror."

Hugh obeyed.

"Now," Jimmy went on, "you don't see any physical presence in it. But this light makes it quite plain that somebody—presumably your maid—has been trying to wash the mirror lately. The drying wasn't a very thorough job, and the glass is streaked. Only a careless person would do that."

"Yes, she's careless," conceded Hugh.

"I've known that all evening," remarked Jimmy. "If she were at all thorough, she'd at least remove the newspapers of the day before yesterday from your wastebasket."

"Has that anything to do with her left-handedness," asked Hugh severely.

"Not a thing."

Jimmy smiled as he took his hat from the peg.

"But," he continued, "those streaks on the glass run from the upper left-hand corner down, diagonally, and the upper right-hand side hasn't been touched at all. Now, there may be back-handed window cleaners, but—"

Jimmy waved his hat genially.

"Good night, doctor. See you Saturday. I hope your watch is repaired by then."

"Huh?" asked Hugh, looking after Jimmy, who had descended the few steps to the street.

"You put your hand in your watch pocket and took it out again, looking foolish. And if that weren't enough you stared at my wristwatch. Didn't you read *The Shower Bath Enigma?*"

IV
THE NIGHT BEFORE

There was a guest book at Olean, in which all visitors were requested to inscribe some appropriate sentiment. This volume had come into being shortly after Payne had made several hundreds of thousands in the oil development from which his house had derived its name. The greatest oil operator of his time had been a week-end guest, and Payne had asked him to write something in the leather covered blank-book. Later on, it occurred to Payne that a guest-book containing a message from only one guest was a trifle ludicrous, no matter how distinguished that one guest might have been. And visitors certainly would be impressed by the autographs in the book. So it was thrown open to all comers.

John Gumbage, the only poet who ever had been honored with an invitation to stay at Olean, had commemorated the event with a few verses, composed, apparently on the spot, but later reprinted in his book, *A Sheaf for Melpomene.* Although the demands of rhyme—Gumbage was an old-fashioned versifier—had interfered slightly with topographical accuracy, the song gave a good notion of Olean:

"Olean"

(For L. P.)

"The roads that lead to Olean
  Go winding over hills;
The lawns that spread through Olean
  Are strewn with daffodils;
And through the night at Olean
  Are singing whip-poor-wills.

The great white house of Olean
 Lies smiling, gay and white;
The day is song at Olean,
 And music all the night.
The vagrant come to Olean
 Sees Heaven in the sight."

Jimmy, scanning the guest-book, thought that at least one vagrant come to Olean had not found the sight entirely a heaven. The broad, two-story structure, with its huge parlors on the first floor and its many sleeping rooms above, was too much like a summer hotel to be paradisiacal. It stood on a sunken terrace in a clearing near the edge of a heavily wooded estate. The interior reflected wealth and luxury, if not taste. Every painting had a little electric light hung over it, giving the effect of an art gallery in a smoking room. And he wondered why a replica of "Washington Crossing the Delaware" hung between two none too skillfully copied scenes from "The Rake's Progress."

Tea, the butler had announced, would be served in the sun parlor at four. Jimmy and Hugh strayed into this glass encased chamber a few minutes before the appointed hour. Payne, wearing golf knickerbockers which did not flatter his gnarled legs, entered a moment later.

"Early, I see, gentlemen," he called out. "Welcome to Olean!"

Hugh made the introductions.

"Make yourself at home, Mr. Wrome," remarked Payne, giving Jimmy a severe handshake. "That's a rhyme. Maybe I could be a poet, if I had the time—eh, doctor?"

He strutted about facetiously.

"Ah, here are others!" he announced.

Francis Gulvin and his wife entered. Gulvin was a young-looking young man, with rather intense blue eyes and thin brown hair. He always looked at people as though he were about to give them information which would do them a great deal of good. His wife was a heavy, pale blonde woman, whose baby-like features did not obscure the fact that she was older than her husband. Possibly because of her size she fancied the notion of petiteness and spoke in a sweet, light, almost infantile voice, illuminating her discourse with rapid gestures of her ornately ringed fingers.

Eddie Endle, the saxophone virtuoso, who looked the part of the leader of a smart dance orchestra, followed. He wore white flannels with broad blue stripes and he had tucked the ends of his washable bow tie under the folds of his removable silk collar.

After the usual desultory handshaking, the guests deposited themselves in various wicker chairs. Mrs. Gulvin insisted on sitting on the arm of Payne's rocker.

"There's nothing like making your husband jealous, is there, Mr. Payne?" she cooed. "It makes him appreciate you."

Gulvin merely glared at her and turned to Jimmy. "Is this your first visit here?" he inquired.

Jimmy admitted that it was.

"I like to come down here between sessions of the state legislature," continued Gulvin. "It's so restful. After the battles at Albany, I can always find peace here."

The manner was that of an unsuccessful orator, but Gulvin always was serious.

"I agree with you," said Jimmy. "Would you mind if I asked you a fairly personal question?"

"Not at all, not at all."

Gulvin executed this with a good flourish.

"If you like to go away for a rest," Jimmy went on, "why do you always take reports of one sort or another with you on your outings?"

Gulvin looked startled.

"Who's been saying that about me?" he demanded.

"Nobody," answered Jimmy. "But the way the pockets of your outing jacket bulge indicates very plainly that you must have pamphlets in them a good deal of the time."

Hugh interrupted at this point.

"Don't mind Mr. Wrome," he suggested. "He likes to deduct things about people. He's a transcendental detective."

"Are you connected with the service?" asked Gulvin, with sudden interest.

"No—and I'm not a detective either. Not even a transcendent one."

"Anybody mentioned detectives?"

Endle had sauntered over to the group.

"No."

Jimmy smiled at Eddie.

"By the way," he added, "how did you happen to forget your cuff-links?"

Endle looked at his sleeves.

"Me forget—?"

Jimmy picked a tiny tuft of cotton from one of the virtuoso's ornaments.

"These are new. You must have bought them at the station as you came out. I've never seen links like these on sale at any other place."

Endle grinned foolishly.

"I guess you're right about that," he confessed. "As I was comin' down in the taxi, I thought, 'Eddie, they's somethin' you've forgotten,' and I says 'What is it?' and then I remembered I'd left my cuff links in my room, and—"

"That's about the way I figured it out," Jimmy commented.

"Mr. Wrome can detect anything in everything," Hugh said.

"It's funny," agreed Jimmy, "but once you get interested in that sort of thing, it's surprising how much you can tell about people just by looking sharply. Life's a lot more like a detective story than you'd think."

He glanced about the room.

"This place," he observed, "would be a beautiful setting for a good mystery. A rich man's country home. Nothing for miles about. A group of guests not very well acquainted with one another."

"Don't," laughed Hugh. "It's creepy."

"Ladies and gentlemen!"

Payne's voice broke through the mild hubbub. "May I introduce Miss Claire Barton?"

Jimmy almost jumped. Why hadn't Hugh told him that Claire would be one of the guests? Of all people he didn't want to hear about, much less meet—but there she was, lovely as ever, and with her—Blake Hesbe. Payne evidently knew Hesbe, for he introduced him to the company. Jimmy took a strange delight in crushing the hand, a far from sturdy hand, of the tow-headed young man. Blake, with his watery gray eyes, his receding chin and his colorless yellow hair, seemed less than ever a suitable companion for the bewitching girl. Claire bowed to Jimmy gracefully but formally. He thought that she looked a little drawn, but he could deduce nothing. In Claire's presence it was not easy to rationalize matters.

The butler, a bald little man, served tea. Payne held a miniature court, surrounded by Mrs. Gulvin Claire and Hesbe. Jimmy and Hugh sat on a divan. Gulvin sipped his drink abstractedly, and Endle walked about the room, looking at the sky.

"Storm comin'," he announced.

Payne scowled at the clouds in the west.

"That's right."

The oncoming disturbance seemed to upset Payne's good humor. "Isn't this rotten?" he asked. "No golf—no tennis—no horseback."

He glowered moodily.

Eddie's meteorological prophecy was coming closer to fulfillment rapidly. A light breeze rattled the leaves. There was an ominous twittering of birds. The butler hurried to the veranda to furl the awnings against the rain. The sky looked as though a deep gray wind were blowing across it. Payne lit a shaded lamp near his chair. The butler crossed the room quietly, fastening the windows.

Mrs. Gulvin pushed aside her teacup.

"Let's tell ghost stories!" she cried enthusiastically.

Her husband shuddered.

"That's like her," he remarked to Jimmy. "She's crazy about theatricals and I suppose she finds this a good setting for a thriller."

"It is," said Jimmy.

"This reminds me so much of a play we produced last month," Mrs. Gulvin went on, despite the lack of encouragement. "It was a scene like this—a merry, merry party on a warm summer's afternoon. Only the scene was laid in Russia. It was a play by Tchekov, you know. Tchekov is so wonderful! Just the man for the Cosey Theatre which I hope someday to build!"

"I thought this was going to be a thriller," interrupted her husband.

She pouted.

"If you don't want to hear it, you don't have to!" she declared. "Does he, Mr. Payne?"

Payne looked up glumly.

"No," he growled.

She hesitated. Then she smiled at her audience and went on.

"It was a warm summer's afternoon, and a merry, merry party had just returned from a trip to Moscow. Minka, the charming daughter of—"

A sudden crash of thunder stopped short the recital. Mrs. Gulvin clapped her hands over her ears and rushed to her husband's side.

"Excuse me," she faltered. "It's silly, I know, but I'm so afraid of thunder!"

She showed her teeth apologetically.

"Now see what you brought on!" remonstrated Gulvin.

"You're a brute!" she cried. "Isn't he, Mr. Payne?"

Payne had no verdict to offer.

Hesbe, his pale face looking almost blue in the dim light, lit a cigarette and spoke. His voice had an edge in it and it quavered when he raised it.

"I heard a good story the other day," he volunteered. "It was a day like this, with a sudden storm. There was a man—down in Wall Street—who was sitting in his home, smoking. The storm made him feel bad. He hadn't been well, anyhow. And when he went to bed that night, he woke up in the middle of the night and it was still raining.

"All that got on his nerves and he took a gun from under his pillow and shot himself in the head. The next morning they found him dead, with a note saying he couldn't stand it anymore."

He subsided, as though the exertion of narration had been a strain.

So this, thought Jimmy, was the man who had supplanted him in Claire's affections. He had met Hesbe somewhere, but Hesbe had made little impression on him. Insignificant, he would have called him. He wondered what Claire thought of Hesbe's foolish tale. It had grown dark outside, and the rain was smashing at the windows. The electric lights flickered uncertainly for a moment and went out. Lights had a way of going out in Bellechester storms. A brilliant flash of lightning, which brought a vivid shriek from Mrs. Gulvin, illuminated the room. Jimmy caught a glimpse of Hesbe's narrow face, his pale eyes almost white in the glare, peering at Claire. There was something malignant in that look. He couldn't get Claire's reaction. A new idea came to Jimmy.

Was it affection or was it fear that brought Claire to Hesbe? The lightning had revealed something sinister in the man's make-up. Or was it Jimmy's imagination working overtime?

"I know a better one than that."

Eddie Endle had found voice in the gloom.

"Let's have candles until the light's going again." Payne's suggestion came out of the darkness.

"Oh, no, Mr. Payne!" Mrs. Gulvin, recovered from her fright, called out. "This is so delightfully spooky! Like the last act of—"

Eddie cleared his throat for attention.

"It seems," he began as though he were to tell an anecdote concerning two Irishmen, "there was a fellow who lived all alone on one of them old farms. He was blind or somethin' like that. Anyhow, he couldn't see nothin.' He was livin' on this old farm with his daughter and her husband, who wasn't no good for nothin' and he was waitin' for the old man to pass out so's he could get his money. The old man was a tough old bird so they was scared of him. He had a mean look, even if he couldn't see nothin.' Well, the daughter's husband got tired of waitin' for the end, but he was yellow and he was scared to do anything about it. So him and the girl got together to scare the old man to death somehow.

"They was always somethin' funny about the way the old lady—the old man's wife—had died, but nobody knew how it happened. They say the old man poisoned her slow with fish or somethin.' Anyhow he was leary o' fish and wouldn't eat none. So this couple got together and figured they'd scare the old man to death by handin' him fish at every meal. They put fish all around the place, so it smelt fierce, and when the old man said somethin' they acted innocent and said they couldn't smell nothin.' They made him eat fish, sayin' it was meat, and when he kicked they said he was sick and wouldn't he better see a doctor, but they knew he was scared of doctors and wouldn't do nothin' rather than have one around.

"One night there was a fierce storm like this one, and the husband brought in a lot o' fish. Just as he come in through the door they was a terrible flash o' lightnin', and there was the old man with a hatchet in his hand and his eyes starin' somethin' fierce. It seems the lightnin' had brought back his sight and he was wise to what was going on. The husband ast him what was he doing with that hatchet and the old man says what hatchet and the husband started to take it from him when he stumbled across somethin' and it was a body on the floor. He leans down to see who it is and—"

Here the lights went on again, suddenly.

"Sorry, the lights spoiled your story," observed Hugh.

He looked at Payne, who was in one of his dull spells.

"Maybe you'd better save the rest of it for another dark stretch," he added.

"They ain't much more," protested Endle, unwilling to discontinue his scene.

"Better not," whispered Hugh. "Mr. Payne isn't well, and it might affect his nerves."

"I got you," muttered Eddie intelligently.

Payne, indeed, looked anything but well. His eyes were lusterless, and his face was drawn and sallow.

"Maybe you'd better lie down a little while, Mr. Payne," suggested Hugh.

"I feel rotten," murmured Payne, oblivious of his company. "That damn shoulder—"

"It's the weather," explained Hugh.

Payne groaned.

"Get them away for a little while," Hugh whispered to Gulvin. "He'll feel better when he's alone."

Jimmy noticed Hesbe looking sharply at Claire as the guests left the room. Claire left rather rapidly and in marked agitation. He lingered for a moment. Hugh nodded for Jimmy to go.

"Here," thought Jimmy, "is the beginning—or is it the end?—of a mystery story."

"Get the butler," Hugh called out to Jimmy.

Jimmy rang various bells in the foyer. Several servants rushed out.

"Mr. Payne isn't well," he told the butler. "I think Dr. Farrigan would like you to help him." The man nodded and entered the sun parlor. Meanwhile, the guests had scattered about the house. Jimmy walked into the little den which served as a smoking room, and lit a cigarette. Endle came in.

"Honest," observed Eddie, "I hope my yarn didn't do him no harm."

Jimmy looked about.

"I wouldn't worry about that," he said, cheerfully. "He's been jumpy and nervous for a long time, they tell me."

"I'd feel like hell if I thought—"

Jimmy offered him a cigarette.

"I don't think there's any connection between your story and Mr. Payne's illness," he remarked. "I've been reading worse things than your little affair, and they haven't had any effect at all. Do you read detective stories?"

"Not since I was a kid," sniffed Eddie.

"This is all a little like one," continued Jimmy. "It begins with a party. Then a sudden storm. The lights go out, and when they come up again, the host—and he's just like the hosts in those stories—is all upset."

"Never read that kind," said Eddie. "Nick Carter was my speed."

"You'd like Bernard Gartlin," mused Jimmy. "The Man of a Million Masks."

Hugh led Payne past the den.

"Want any help?" asked Jimmy.

Payne looked about with a wan smile.

"Help?"

He laughed.

"I want you folks to have a good time."

His face became animated.

"You came out here for a good time and I'll see to it you'll get it!" he cried out. "Doctor, I want you to see they all have a good time."

"All right, Mr. Payne," Hugh said. "Now, suppose you rest for a while."

"Oh, I'll rest," snarled Payne. "You take charge of these people and amuse 'em."

He stopped at the stairs.

"Endle," he called out, "take everybody over to that dump of yours and give 'em a good dinner at my expense. Let 'em dance all night. That'll be the stuff."

Eddie stared at him dumbly.

"I mean it," insisted Payne. "Doctor, you gather 'em all together and Eddie'll take care of 'em over at Shuffle Inn or whatever you call the damn place."

"Better go up," urged Hugh.

Payne's face became fiercely set.

"I won't move a step—not a damn step—until you say you'll do as I tell you. That's all."

Hugh shrugged his shoulders. Payne's "that's all" was almost mesmeric. He bowed acquiescence and led Payne to his room.

"Good scene, don't you think?" remarked Jimmy.

"Huh?"

Endle didn't understand.

"Like one of those mystery stories I was telling you about," explained Jimmy. "The stern old bachelor goes up the stairs, his fiery spirit still glowing."

"Can't say I get you," apologized Eddie. "What do you mean— mystery stories?"

"Just a hobby of mine," laughed Jimmy. "I suppose I've got them on the brain. People are always having things on the brain nowadays. I suppose they always did, but they didn't make so much fuss about it before psycho-analysis became popular."

"What's that?"

"Psycho-analysis? It means you're hipped on something. Like these new novelists. You know—vermin in stones, crooks in the running brooks and sex in everything."

Eddie reached bewilderedly for a cigarette.

"Don't be alarmed," Jimmy continued.

He peered out of the window.

"Nice night for a ride over to your place," he commented.

"Storms is good for us," said Endle, glad to reach intelligible ground. "You mightn't think so now, but it's a fact they is. This time o' year lots o' them goes out ridin' and is caught unexpected sort

of and off they goes for the nearest roadhouse. Usually they's a little cold or somethin' when they arrives and we got to thaw 'em out
and then they stick around till it's clear and sometimes much later'n
that. I just have the boys play a little louder so's nobody hears the
thunder, that's the only difference to me. See, we work on a guaran-
tee and a percentage of the takin's, and they ain't many, specially if
they got a few girls with 'em, likes to be thought pikers. So the longer
they stay the more they order and I ain't got nothin' against storms.
It's the hot, quiet nights when nobody feels like eatin' or drinkin' or
anything that we lose out."

The Gulvins were coming down the stairs, carrying their coats.

"We'll have a full house tonight sure," added Eddie. "Guess I'd
better phone over and reserve a table. Let's see. There'll be them
two, and that blonde baby and her boy friend, and you, and maybe
the doc. That's six."

"Make it two tables," suggested Jimmy.

He didn't want to be at the table with Claire. It would be too
trying.

"What for?"

"It won't be so crowded."

Eddie sniffed.

"Say—we park away eight or ten at a table down there and nobody has no kicks. They's two kinds o' parties. Makin' parties—that's
a fella and a girl—which has to be alone in a corner, and we got a
lot o' corners for 'em—and these big blow-outs. Lucky' if we get one
good table this time o' day."

"You'd do me a great favor," said Jimmy, "if you could break up
the party into two tables."

Eddie grinned knowingly.

"Going to separate that blond goof and his girl?" he inquired.
"Say, I don't take to him, neither."

Did everybody know that he loved Claire?

"Nothing like that," Jimmy answered carelessly. "Just a fancy of
mine."

"Well, I'll try to frame it for you," agreed Eddie.

Jimmy looked into the rainy dusk as he dressed for the junket
to Shuffle Inn. It surely was a setting for a mystery. Stupid of him

always to be thinking of mysteries. Yet here was this sumptuous house—mysteries of a certain class always took place in sumptuous houses—with its queer assortment of guests and its somehow elusive host. Was Payne sending them all off to Shuffle Inn as a pretext for something? Claire was involved in this in some way. That was certain. Was Hesbe involved? What was the connection between Claire and Hesbe? Beyond doubt, Hesbe had some hold on her. Payne had some hold on her. Who else might have some hold on her?

"That's foolish," murmured Jimmy, as he battled with his dress tie. He often held forth to himself when he dressed.

"Foolish. You've been reading too much of this stuff and it's gone to your head. A man's sick. He doesn't want to spoil his guests' pleasure. So he makes a graceful compromise. And you turn it into blood and thunder stuff.

"Why are you such an ass about Claire? Maybe she likes Hesbe. You never can tell what a woman will like. She might like worse people than Hesbe. Maybe she likes Payne. That isn't impossible, either. Only, why can't she like you?"

Jimmy smiled bitterly into the mirror as this thought came to him.

"Well, that's life. You can't figure these things out. 'If she be not fair to me'—the only trouble is she is fair to me—much too fair for comfort. I'm not fair to her, so what difference does it make how much I care about her.

"Oh, bull!"

He broke off sharply. This was a singularly unprofitable trend of thought. He went down the stairs to the den. He seemed to be the first, except for the Gulvins, who had made terrific speed in dressing.

He sat down and looked at the Gulvins, who looked back. It was one of those dumb moments, when no one knows what to say or has much to say. Jimmy wondered whether he ought to read a newspaper. Then he thought of a better plan.

"I wish I were married, Mr. Gulvin," he began.

Mrs. Gulvin beamed on him. Her husband was puzzled.

"I do," continued Jimmy, "because then I wouldn't have to tie my own ties."

"See, Frank!" exclaimed Mrs. Gulvin delightedly. "Anybody can see you can't tie your own!"

"That isn't quite correct, Mrs. Gulvin," objected Jimmy. "I don't say that Mr. Gulvin can't tie his own. But I do say that you tie them for him. And I wonder why you still use the old-fashioned method of standing behind him when you do it."

"Now, you've been peeking through our key-hole," giggled Mrs. Gulvin.

"I didn't even know you had a key-hole," retorted Jimmy. "But the powder marks on your husband's shoulders, not to mention on his collar and shirt front, tell me pretty accurately which way the bow was bent."

"You're so clever!" cried Mrs. Gulvin. "Isn't he, Francis?"

"Very observant," was Mr. Gulvin's verdict, which might have been a confirmation or a correction.

"You'd be just the man for my little theater, Mr. Wrome," said Mrs. Gulvin. "I'm sure you'd make a splendid actor. Now, don't tell me you haven't acted!"

"I certainly will tell you," replied Jimmy, amiably. "I've never acted and I've never wanted to."

"But you will act at my Cosey Theater!"

Her tone was killing.

"Don't mind her, Mr. Wrome," interrupted Gulvin. "She's simply a crank on her Cosey Theater, as she calls it. She even tried to persuade me to introduce a bill in the legislature subsidizing this creature of her imagination."

He laughed lightly, as men who fancy themselves intellectually superior to their wives frequently do.

"Now, Francis—" protested Mrs. Gulvin.

The entrance of Hugh hushed the controversy.

"The cars are waiting outside," remarked Dr. Farrigan. "We'll be off in a few minutes."

"How is dear Mr. Payne?" gushed Mrs. Gulvin. "I do hope it's nothing serious."

"Nothing serious."

Hugh's tone was curt.

"He was so interested in the Cosey Theatre," she confided to Jimmy. "It would be terrible, if—"

She rolled her eyes sorrowfully.

Was this woman involved with Payne, too? Jimmy shook his head as if to brush off the reiterant notion that Payne was the center of a plot. He accompanied the Gulvins into one of Payne's limousines, while Claire and Hesbe went with Hugh in another. The rain had dwindled into a light drizzle, but it was warm again and humid. Jimmy felt uncomfortable in the closed car. He wanted air. He wanted to escape the too violent scent with which Mrs. Gulvin had adorned herself. He wanted to escape Gulvin's political cigar. He wanted a fresh breeze to clear his mind.

The brilliant lights of Shuffle Inn flickered in the mists. Endle had kept his promise. Jimmy found himself near the bandstand with the Gulvins. Far down the long, narrow room he saw Claire, resplendent in a striking evening gown, and Hesbe, looking out of place in evening clothes, with Hugh. Claire began dancing with Hesbe. Jimmy writhed at the sight. Hesbe was a cheek-by-jowl terpsichorean. It was evident that he had respect for Claire, for he didn't grip her as other young men on the floor clutched their partners. But he was an intimate, if not a gracile, dancer. Jimmy was tempted to cut in. The result of such a proceeding would be interesting. But there was already a barrier of distance between himself and Claire. She was a little like a stranger. If only she were more of a stranger or less of one!

The Gulvins were dancing. Gulvin was not the aggressor. He looked imploringly over his wife's shoulder, beseeching relief from Jimmy.

Eddie was wrapped up in and around his saxophone, blasting out his syncopations solemnly, almost spiritually. The light of art shone in his eyes. His shoulders twitched devotionally. His men swayed with him, through fox-trot after fox-trot. These serious musicians hardly ever paused in their labors. Did they desist for a moment, a stray handclap from a gay dancer would start them on their way once more. Jazz was no light-hearted assembly of noises. It was a ritual, a votive offering. They were like a choir, thought Jimmy, intoning an enlivening Laudamus.

The night was filled with music, and it was a long night. Jimmy forgot Claire, forgot the possible mystery surrounding Payne, forgot even the inconvenience of dancing with Mrs. Gulvin. Food came and went before him. Waiters glided by, whispering monosyllables which were answered by meaningless nods. Eddie's rhythmic incense had taken possession of the room.

It was a gorgeously liveried attendant who broke the spell. He muttered something to Endle, who answered with a nod of his saxophone in the direction of Claire's table. The attendant hurried to the table, where Hugh was sitting alone while Hesbe was swinging Claire giddily about the floor. Hugh jumped up, looked for Claire and Hesbe, made a little resigned motion with his hands, and followed the attendant. Jimmy hurried after him as he left the dining room. Something had happened! And yet—it might be only another Italian woman with a fractured wrist. He saw Hugh enter a telephone booth. Hugh spoke quickly and hung up the receiver decisively. He started as he saw Jimmy waiting for him.

"You've had unexpected news," began Jimmy pleasantly.

"There's no mystery about this!" snapped Hugh. "I'll have to go back to the house at once. Explain it to the rest."

"Anything serious?"

"Explain why I left. No—don't say it's anything serious. I don't know what it is."

He hurried to the cloak-room.

Jimmy entered the booth. The thing had happened. Something was in the air. His premonitions had not been products of a brain overfed with fiction. He would call Payne's house. A low voice answered his call.

"Who's this?"

It was the butler's voice, nearly inaudible, agonized.

"Mr. Wrome."

The voice lapsed.

"How's Mr. Payne?"

The repetition of Jimmy's question was ghastly. "He's—"

The voice became strident.

"Where's Dr. Farrigan? Isn't he coming? Tell him to hurry—hurry—"

"He's on his way," answered Jimmy. "Can I be of any use?"

"My God, sir, I don't know—no—don't—I can't say anything now, sir—you'd better not—not now—"

A click told Jimmy that the butler had no more to say.

He rushed to the door. He could hear the motor bearing Hugh down the road to Olean. Could he take the other car? And leave the rest here? He could send the chauffeur back.

He started for the dining-room again. How dull it seemed in there, with the music tick-tocking away and people shoving each other lazily about. He couldn't sit there again. He saw Mrs. Gulvin looking eagerly at him. No! He'd go back. What did he care!

He found the chauffeur in the courtyard. It was cooler now, and the stars blazed over the road to Olean.

"Mr. Payne's house," cried Jimmy, hoarse with excitement, "and drive like hell! "

The roads that lead to Olean"—where were they leading now?

V
THE MORNING AFTER

Jimmy's rappings on the windows of the limousine caused the driver to stop the car a few hundred yards from the house. Olean glittered in the moonlight, shining phosphorescently in the clearing. A dim arc at the entrance was a weak yellow guide post. But save for the reflection of the stars against the windows, there seemed to be no light about the house.

"Wait," Jimmy instructed the chauffeur.

He tiptoed up the damp road leading to the graveled ways about the house. He wondered whether he was tiptoeing to protect his patent leather shoes against the mud or to avoid detection. A slight breeze in the branches nearby sounded like the echo of footsteps.

"It's a promising beginning," Jimmy murmured as he crept carefully to the door.

There seemed to be no activity within. The screen door was insecurely fastened and the inner glass door was open. Anyone could have entered—or had Hugh failed to close up behind him? Jimmy dropped his hat on a chair and investigated the parlors and the den. No one was there.

He went warily up the stairs to the landing. If anything had happened, it must have been in Payne's room at the end of the corridor. The transom, covered with green cloth, showed a faint glow. Jimmy walked carefully on the thick rugs in the hall. He heard footsteps in Payne's room and stood in the darkness of the halls to see whether anyone would come out.

A flood of light was covering at him. And then there was a scream.

"My God!"

It was the butler, who had come out with a flash lamp.

Hugh strode savagely out of the room. Jimmy could see him snatch the lamp from the butler's twitching hand.

"What are you doing here?"

Hugh's voice was sharp.

Jimmy felt calm and amused. Whatever the mystery was, and the indications were that a mystery was to hand, he was coming to it early.

"I just thought I might be of assistance," he replied.

Hugh motioned for him to go to the other end of the corridor.

"Stay in Mr. Payne's room, Stelke," he snapped to the butler, apparently warding off a protest.

Hugh and Jimmy walked silently down the hall. Jimmy noticed that Hugh was in his shirt sleeves and that his eyes were unusually bright. He looked pale. No doubt about it. Something eventful had taken place. But what? This happening couldn't be deduced from shirt sleeves. Deduction seemed of little avail with so little to deduce from.

"Sit down on the stairs," commanded Hugh.

Jimmy made himself comfortable on the broad steps. Hugh sat beside him, switching the lamp on and off as he spoke.

"I don't know what your motive is in coming back here and sneaking about the hall," observed Hugh, "and, to be frank with you, I don't care. If you're not feeling well, go to bed. I'll give you something to put you to sleep, if that's what you want. I know you're fidgety, but I can't understand what possessed you to follow me and go stalking around like this."

"I could tell that something was seriously wrong with Mr. Payne," answered Jimmy, truthfully, "and I thought I could be of some use."

"Did anybody invite you?" demanded Hugh.

"No-o."

Jimmy didn't like to concede the point.

"Well, you can't be of the slightest use," continued Hugh. "In fact, you're more likely to be in the way. So you might just as well go back to the Inn and let out your spirit of adventure over there."

Jimmy wasn't going to be eliminated from a possible mystery as easily as that.

"But what's happened?" he asked.

Hugh turned the flash lamp on him and shook his head disgustedly.

"Merely as a matter of medical routine, if nothing more, I might say that it's none of your business," he said. "But if you've taken the trouble to go chasing all the way back, I'll satisfy your curiosity—partly. Mr. Payne has had—a seizure. Nothing can be done now, and its just as well that nobody knows until morning. Now, go back or go to bed, but for heaven's sake don't prowl around here. If it's anything for you to know, you'll know it soon enough."

Hugh rose from the step.

"I'm going back now," he said, brandishing the lamp, "and I advise you either to return to the Inn and help entertain or something or go to sleep. Nobody told you to go around chasing excitement."

"Is it serious?"

Hugh was becoming more irritated.

"Good night," he snapped.

Jimmy sat on the stairs, reflecting, as Hugh paced down the corridor. This was no ordinary seizure. Something had happened to Payne. Why the agitation of the butler? In detective stories, the butler always was agitated at the time of—the master's death! Was Payne dead? And how did he die? Did the butler kill him?

Jimmy paced down the stairs into the den and hunted a cigarette.

"You were looking for your situation," he told himself, "and you've found it—or you're inventing it. If Payne's dead, the butler's a likely suspect. It's always the butler. He always has some abstruse grievance which eventually leads him to finish up the boss.

"But who said the boss was finished up? And if he is, why the butler? The obvious suspect isn't the one you want. And would the butler telephone for the doctor if he were the guilty one? Yes, he certainly would. In a good many stories, anyhow. Of course, it might be one of the other servants, but it isn't—not usually. They always have alibis. The maid was sleeping with her sister, and the cook was a notoriously sound slumberer. They're always the first to be eliminated. For that matter, everybody else can be eliminated. All the guests were at the Inn when it happened."

Jimmy stopped chattering as he lit his cigarette.

"But who said it happened?"

He laughed. Of course, it hadn't happened. He had a faint suspicion that it might have—anything could happen—but he was manufacturing all of this. He went to the porch. Down the path he could see the searchlights of the automobile. Go back? Not while there was a life-and-death aroma about Olean. He'd send the chauffeur back.

The driver looked at Jimmy suspiciously. Jimmy reciprocated the look with the mental concept that the chauffeur might have—but that was improbable and a little more than that. Here he was, Jimmy thought, as the car sputtered back to the Inn, concocting fantastic theories about something that probably didn't exist. He trudged back to the house, and went to his room. There was a little balcony outside the window. Jimmy sat on the railing and looked out over the stretch of lawn ending in the woods. This solitary manor. This feeble light in the master's room. The butler's alarm. The doctor's irritation. The ironic contrast of the guests making merry at a distant Inn, while their host lay dead—if he lay dead.

Jimmy looked at the brilliant sky. On such a night as this—on such a night—what? He would like to have Claire at his side now, gazing at the heavens with him, silently, or perhaps whispering tender endearments. Claire, his lost love, Claire, the only one who ever had meant anything to him. Claire dancing in the clumsy arms of another only a few miles away.

"That's enough," he told himself. "You're getting maudlin, along with the rest of it. If you can't see a doctor working at midnight without fancying a murder and if you can't see the stars without thinking sentimentally of a particular girl—why, that's plenty."

He lit the lamp in his room. What would be the use of sitting here until dawn? Might as well sleep. He yawned at the thought. Read a little, and go to sleep. The others would be weary folk in the morning, while he would be fresh and ready for a day's amusement. It would be a wonderful day tomorrow. He tossed his cigarette stub out of the window and prepared for bed.

This was luxury. Lying in bed, with no real cares, reading a pleasant but not too stimulating book—*The St. Swithin's Robbery*, to be exact—and then a refreshing sleep. A deep dreamless slumber, they called it. Ah yes! Here was the same thing again. The senator had been found dead in the card room on the eve of a great debate on the limitation of immigration. His clothing showed that he had succumbed only after a fierce struggle with an unknown invader who had left no traces. But Genevieve, the senator's ward, found an ivory button under the carpet. The local detective was chagrined not to have discovered it himself. It was a curiously shaped button.

Ah, yes. The same old clew, inconspicuous in itself which eventually was to lead to the identification of the man who never could have been suspected of the crime had not—

It was a dazzling Sunday morning when Jimmy awoke. The lawn and the trees glittered, and the stretch of road visible from the window sparkled. There was a delicious breeze. Jimmy wriggled happily. He tossed aside the covers and consulted his watch. Eleven! It certainly had been the much-advertised sound, dreamless sleep. And what of Payne? Was there a mystery ahead, or had the events of the night before been the products of an overstimulated imagination? He hurried his dressing and went into the dining room.

Apparently, everyone had eaten except a new guest, a sallow, middle-aged man who was drinking coffee solemnly, stirring the beverage constantly and tapping the spoon thoughtfully against the side of the cup. Jimmy bowed to the newcomer, who returned the salutation disinterestedly. Who could this be?

Stelke entered, looking graver than ever. He moved about nervously as he saw Jimmy.

"Good morning," Jimmy called out almost boisterously.

Stelke returned the greeting in a dead tone.

"How's Mr. Payne this morning?" continued Jimmy cheerfully.

Stelke almost collapsed at the question and the stranger dropped his spoon with a clatter.

"What's your name?" demanded the sallow man.

Jimmy told him. So, he concluded, something had happened to his host.

"When did you get here?" the newcomer went on.

"About the same time as the others," Jimmy answered, "only they don't seem to sleep so well."

The sallow man stared at him penetratingly.

"Look here," he said brusquely. "Don't you know what's happened?"

Jimmy shook his head.

"Well, it's about time you knew."

The stranger pointed his remarks with the spoon. "Payne died last night. In fact, you might as well know now, he shot himself."

Jimmy gripped his knees. His premonitions had been true—too true. Payne had shot himself.

"I'm the coroner," added the stranger grimly.

Jimmy caught a smile before it broke out. Here was he, specialist in mysterious and violent deaths, practically sleeping through a dramatic suicide, and being informed of it condescendingly by a local official. Things were like that. He had been looking about for something like this, and when it happened almost under his nose, he was unaware of it.

"Dr. Farrigan called me this morning," explained the coroner. "I thought all the guests had gone on the ten o'clock train. Don't blame them, either. I don't see any holiday in staying in a house with a body."

"Everybody gone?"

Jimmy almost echoed the coroner's remarks.

"Dr. Farrigan is still here, sir," explained Stelke, "and Miss Barton and Mr. Hesbe."

Jimmy's waning interest in breakfast disappeared entirely. Why had Claire and Hesbe remained? Depend on it, this was no ordinary suicide. His intuition had told him that a catastrophe was impending at this party. It told him now that there might well be something more than suicide involved.

"Doctor—?"

"Miles. Miles is my name."

"Dr. Miles," Jimmy said, "I don't want to butt in where it's none of my business, but could I see the body?"

"You're certainly different from the rest," commented Miles. "They all wanted to get away as quick as they could."

"When did this happen?"

"About midnight. Stelke heard the shot and rushed to Payne's room. The door was locked. He phoned for Dr. Farrigan, and they broke in the door. It was all very obvious."

The coroner seemed to be almost bored with the case.

"Well, may I see the body?" persisted Jimmy.

"I was going now. I came early, without breakfast. Dr. Farrigan had me fixed up—but if you want to look, come along."

He led Jimmy to Payne's room. The door was partly open, and Hugh was sitting within.

"This young man wants to look at the body, Doctor," explained Miles.

Hugh stared at Jimmy in amusement and irritation. "Going to uncover a great mystery here?" he asked ironically.

Jimmy wouldn't answer. He waited for Miles to remove a sheet from the body on the bed. Payne had died in his night clothes. The shot had been fired through his right temple. The face was almost expressionless. The bedding evidently had been changed and the body had been composed.

Miles pointed to a revolver on the table near the bed.

"It was still in his hand when they found him," he observed.

"Mind if I look at it?"

Hugh and Miles exchanged glances denoting that Jimmy was a good-natured crank.

"Go as far as you like."

Jimmy balanced the weapon in his hand. It was an ordinary enough .32 calibre affair, apparently of recent purchase and it had Payne's initials on it.

"Is Payne's watch here?" asked Jimmy.

"Trying to hitch a robbery to this?" queried Hugh. "Everything's here. We examined the room while you were still asleep."

Miles laughed at the taunt.

"I didn't expect to find it missing," retorted Jimmy. "Please let me see it."

Hugh extracted it from Payne's bureau drawer and handed it to Jimmy, who glanced at it casually, and returned it.

"Thanks. Did Payne shave himself?"

"He used a gun—not a razor," said Hugh.

"I'd like to see his razor anyhow," insisted Jimmy.

Stelke brought it from the bathroom. Jimmy looked at it, nod-ded, and handed it back.

"The doors and windows were locked, I take it," he went on. "They always are. Nobody could have got in and out again without leaving traces."

"That's detective-story talk, Dr. Miles," laughed Hugh. "Mr. Wrome is a patient of mine. I recommended detective stories to him to take his mind off his troubles and this is the result."

"Everything was locked. And if you have any doubt about the suicide, Mr. Wrome, look at this."

Miles handed him a square sheet of paper. Jimmy read the message on it.

"There is no use going on. It is better to end it all."

"You've identified this as Payne's writing?"

"Certainly," said Miles, with a little asperity. "It's an unfortunate but ordinary case."

"Is your verdict that Payne met death by his own hand?" inquired Jimmy.

"Absolutely."

The coroner made it plain that he saw no point in wasting more of a beautiful Sunday over the matter.

"You're the boss," said Jimmy dubiously, "but I think we might—"

Here Stelke left the room, explaining that he had heard the front door-bell.

"Do you mean the butler shot him?" asked Miles.

"No."

The butler hadn't shot him. Of course, if Stelke should turn out to be a man whom Payne had swindled in business many years ago, it might be different. But the butler always was the first and obvious suspect—Jimmy refused to consider the contingency.

The coroner, however, didn't accept Jimmy's positive negative.

"You know, doctor," he said, turning to Hugh, "come to think of it, that man could have killed him, fixed it up to look like a suicide and then sent for you to throw off suspicion."

"Does he look or act like a murderer?" asked Hugh.

"No-o. I shouldn't say so. It doesn't look like a murder, anyhow."

He turned to Jimmy.

"You've been putting all this stuff into my head," he announced.

Jimmy grinned, as Stelke returned.

"There's a reporter here," he said.

"How do the papers happen to know anything about it?" wondered the coroner.

"At least three guests have left since the affair," said Jimmy, "and I dare say that the servants know what has happened."

"Hell!" complained Miles. "I'll never get away now. Well, I'll go down and see him."

Jimmy followed the coroner into the den, where Stelke had stored the reporter, a sturdy, sunburned young man, patently pleased with his assignment.

"My name's Heidelman," said the reporter. "I'm from the Bellechester *Chronicle*."

"My God," stormed Miles. "I thought you were from a regular paper."

"This is a beat," said Heidelman, who had read several works on practical journalism.

"Well, I know old man Cane and all the rest down at the *Chronicle*," continued the coroner, "but I never saw you before."

"I'm just working there for the summer—for experience," explained Heidelman. "I heard about Payne's death at the station and I thought I'd come right up."

"Nothing to say," snapped Miles. "Tell Cane to, ring me up tomorrow—not today—if he wants to talk to me."

"But the readers of—"

"That's all I've got to say now. I'll make my report tomorrow."

He brushed by Heidelman to the door.

"I've lost enough time as it is," he exclaimed, as he hurried to his automobile.

Heidelman turned to Jimmy, who was raiding the cigarette box.

"Maybe you could tell me something," he suggested.

"Have a smoke," said Jimmy, passing the reporter a cigarette.

"I never smoke when I'm on a story," demurred the virtuous Heidelman.

"Sit down, anyhow," urged Jimmy.

"This would be a scoop for me," said Heidelman. "I'm taking a correspondence course in journalism and people like to kid me about it. Well, I heard one of those hangers-on down at the station tell another that Payne had been found dead and all his guests had left suddenly. If I could rush that story to old Cane before the police or anybody gets it, it would certainly hit him between the eyes. So I'll be awfully obliged for anything you can tell me."

"Did anybody tell you it was a case for the police?" asked Jimmy.

"Why no. Isn't it?"

"The coroner doesn't think so. That isn't his official statement, but he took it for a plain case of suicide."

Jimmy outlined the events leading up to the arrival of Miles.

"—so when a man is found dead, with a revolver in his hands, a farewell note on the table, and all doors and windows locked, there's only one conclusion," he finished.

Something in Jimmy's voice prompted Heidelman to investigate further.

"And is that your conclusion, Mr. Wrome?" he asked.

"Who am I to have a conclusion?" retorted Jimmy. "I was a guest over the week-end. I was with the others at Shuffle Inn when it happened."

"But you have something more to say," persisted Heidelman.

"Why don't you interview Dr. Farrigan or Miss Barton or Mr. Hesbe?" countered Jimmy. "I believe they're still on the premises."

"Certainly," agreed Heidelman, with alacrity.

Jimmy rang for Stelke, who entered silently.

"Will you ask Dr. Farrigan whether he has anything to say to a *Chronicle* reporter?" he said. "And you might ask Miss Barton and Mr. Hesbe to step in here for a moment if you can find them."

"Could I ask him—?"

Jimmy shunted off Heidelman's attempt to interview Stelke.

"He's greatly distressed over Mr. Payne's death," he explained. "Don't harrow his feelings unnecessarily."

Jimmy toyed with the cigarettes in the box.

"I don't want to be quoted," he went on, "but there are a few things connected with this affair that could stand a little further inquiry. In the detective stories, it's often the reporter who solves the mystery."

"Is there a mystery?"

"I didn't say so."

Jimmy enjoyed Heidelman's perplexity. Perhaps for the first time in his life he was a fountainhead of knowledge for an anxious seeker after information, and the sensation was distinctly agreeable.

Stelke returned with the tidings that Hugh refused to be interviewed and that Miss Barton and Mr. Hesbe would be here directly.

"Do you think they'll be able to give me any more?" inquired the reporter.

"Maybe they won't want to," murmured Jimmy. It was a meaningless remark but it aroused Heidelman's curiosity visibly.

Jimmy smoked quietly until Claire and Hesbe came to the den. Claire was more ravishing than ever. Heidelman actually colored when he looked at her. She seemed depressed by the tragedy, but Claire depressed was more glorious than anyone else elated. Hesbe, as always, appeared insignificant.

"What'd you want us for?" demanded Hesbe.

"This charming young man," explained Jimmy, "is Mr. Heidelman, representing the Bellechester *Chronicle*, lack of acquaintance with which is, I am sure, your loss. He has heard of our late friend's mishap and is seeking data. Will you not set your views, which undoubtedly are of no small value, before Mr. Heidelman?"

Jimmy watched the effect of his airy speech on Claire. She seemed to pale, to become more disturbed. Claire was somehow connected with Payne's death. He wasn't so sure about Hesbe, but there was a link between Claire and Payne—a link which had disrupted his friendship with her—if links could be thought of as disruptive elements.

Hesbe's gaze shifted about the room.

"I don't see that there's anything for me to say," he answered. "No. I don't know any more about it than anybody else."

"And you, Miss Barton?"

Heidelman's suavity, which was intermittent, delighted Jimmy. However, it silenced Claire.

"No."

Even the one syllable, spoken almost unintelligibly, stirred Jimmy. If only he could summon together enough courage to face Claire frankly, to tell her what was in his heart, to put an end to a situation which left him at emotional odds and ends!

"I don't think there's much there," he remarked to Heidelman. "I've told you who was here, when it happened, and so on. Dr. Miles will have some sort of statement tomorrow. I don't know what else—"

He stopped and looked sharply at Claire and Hesbe, who were listening.

"This isn't anything authoritative, Mr. Heidelman," he went on deliberately, "and I'm offering it to you only as a suggestion which might occur to me if I were a reporter."

Claire and Hesbe, he noted, were all ears.

"If there were any more to the case—and it probably will develop that there isn't—than the suicide of a wealthy banker, recently not in the best of health, I should look into the gun which caused his death. It would be interesting, in any event, to know whether he had bought it in the last few days especially for this purpose or whether he was in the habit of sleeping with a gun under his pillow."

The effect on Claire and Hesbe exceeded Jimmy's expectations. Hesbe sneered. Claire's face became taut.

"Look here, Jimmy Wrome," she cried, "do you think you're a detective? Why—"

She calmed suddenly.

"We might as well go, Blake," she remarked coolly to her escort.

Jimmy followed her.

"Claire," he pleaded, "I only want to—"

She said. "Don't talk—I don't ever want to hear your voice again. Good morning."

Something was frozen inside Jimmy. He stood dumbly in the room. He put out his hands suppliantly.

"One more thing," Claire went on, "don't go out of your way to make a bigger fool of yourself than you have already."

Jimmy's hands were cold. He felt perspiration on his forehead. His tongue went dry, and there was a chilling sensation in his chest. And then he found his voice.

"Then here's one *more* thing," he called out. "And I'll bet anything I have or ever hope to have on it. Leed Payne was murdered, if ever a man was murdered. Not only that, but I know how it was done—and I know who did it!"

He dropped limply into a chair. He was exhausted. His eyes felt heavy and he hardly noticed Claire and Hesbe leaving. Heidelman came to him solicitously.

"Don't bother," murmured Jimmy, weakly. "I'll be all right in a few minutes. Just leave me alone. That's all—now."

VI
GETTING AWAY WITH MURDER

In every detective story, Jimmy had learned, the local sleuth eventually appears on the scene. Attached to the police department, he is a hardworking, arrogant, thick-headed constable, serviceable only as a foil for the quick-witted hero, and his conclusions point to the guilt of the very person whom the hero least wishes to implicate. But at the last moment, Bernard Gartlin, or your own favorite, turns the tables with the finesse of a spirit medium.

With the publication of Heidelman's efflorescent narrative in the palpitant columns of the *Chronicle*, the cue for the local detective had been given. The district attorney, whose life for the past two years had been clouded by unsolved shootings of well-known citizens, sighed wearily as Heidelman's story was called to his attention. It wasn't, strictly speaking, called to his attention; he read it himself, but he always liked to say that his attention had been called. Kenworthy knew that he was about to hear again that he was very harsh with minor law breakers but that he was powerless in really important criminal events. Why hadn't Miles told him about the Payne shooting? If Heidelman's story were correct, here was a *cause cèlébre*. If it were wrong, there would be a clamor for a trial of someone, anyhow.

"I don't know any more about it than you do," protested Miles, in answer to an irate call. "As far as I could see, the man had shot himself and that was all there was to it. I didn't know anything more about it until I saw that crazy yarn. Who's this Wrome anyhow? He hung around, hinting at things, but he looked like one of those cranks to me. I didn't know he gave out this crazy story."

"That's all very good, Miles," retorted Kenworthy, "but look at the evidence the paper scraped up. Wrome gives the impression that Payne didn't do it. You know people are always ready to believe it's a murder, even though the man may have shot himself in a public square."

"I don't see any evidence," said Miles. "He makes a few hints about the gun. They don't mean a thing."

"I'll grant you they don't," replied the exasperated district attorney, "but the yarn's gotten up so cleverly that the whole county'll be after me if I don't put up a stiff investigation. Why the hell did you let this Wrome hang around?"

"Hell, I didn't think he'd spill all this bunk to a reporter," shouted Miles. "He didn't tell me anything about it."

"Well, are you going to hand in a certificate of suicide?" demanded Kenworthy.

"How can I? It'll have to be death at the hands of persons unknown."

"Easy with that 'person unknown.' Those two words have had me jumping for years."

"Well, that's what it'll have to be now. I can't take any chances."

"Oh, go to hell."

The district attorney hung up angrily. He shoved papers about his desk aimlessly for a few minutes. Then he called up Edgar Brinze.

Brinze was the son of old man Brinze, of Hardell, Brinze and Coblin, cement manufacturers. Old man Brinze was reputed the richest man in the county and high in the councils of the governing party. Edgar had somehow made his way through Harvard, but had shown an alarming inaptitude for the niceties of the cement business, so old man Brinze decided to have him enter public life. Edgar thereupon was created a captain in the Bellechester Police Reserve Force. The police were not enthusiastic, for Edgar insisted on acting as unofficial head of the two-man detective department. Kenworthy, however, for obvious political reasons, found Edgar a useful ally, and employed him as a confidential investigator.

"Get this man Wrome out here," he instructed Brinze. "Go over the case with him. Make him dish up anything he's got. And put him out of the running. I don't want another one of these insoluble shootings on my hands."

And the local detective entered Jimmy's life. Jimmy discovered that this stout, amiably condescending, red-haired young man didn't match the picture of Bernard Gartlin's adversaries in the interests of Justice. Brinze had the confidence of a rich man's son. Otherwise, he wasn't exceptionally objectionable.

"Did the *Chronicle* quote you right?" asked Brinze, after introducing himself.

"I didn't intend to be quoted at all," said Jimmy. "The reporter is an amateur and doesn't know enough to conceal the source of his information. But his story was substantially correct. Why, by the way, should a little sheet like the *Chronicle* worry you?"

"It doesn't. But all the New York papers have reporters hanging around now. If the *Chronicle* hadn't printed all that stuff, they'd never have gotten the story. Now, what I want to get at is this: were you just talking in the air or did you really have something up your sleeve?"

"Neither. I merely made an observation to the effect that the origin of the gun would be worth investigating."

Brinze drew the revolver from his desk.

"Here's the gun," he said. "It looks like any ordinary .32 and it has Payne's initials on it. What more do you want?"

"What do you think of the engraving of the initials?"

"Are you trying to pull Sherlock Holmes stuff on me?"

"Not at all. I merely asked your opinion of the engraving. Does it look like a good job?"

Brinze examined the initials with a magnifying glass.

"It looks a little cheap," he said.

"Exactly. Now, Dr. Miles will tell you that I asked for Payne's watch and razor. Both of them were engraved. The style was entirely different. That's not so important. But the initials were J. L. P. Payne's whole name was John Leed Payne, and he seems to have liked the monogram, although he didn't retain his first name for any other purpose. I noticed that the silverware and the glasses at tea were monogrammed with three letters."

"What are you getting at?"

"That I don't believe this was Payne's pistol."

"But he had it in his hand when they found him."

"Suppose you ask that butler, Stelke, whether Payne owned a revolver. He would know."

Brinze sent a messenger for Stelke.

"If anybody had anything to do with this—in a criminal way—it would be Stelke," he observed. "There wasn't anybody else around who could have done it."

"I don't say that the criminal was in the room at the time of the shooting."

Brinze stared at Jimmy.

"That's nonsense. The doors and windows were closed. The powder marks and everything about the wound indicated that Payne could have been shot only when the muzzle was right up against his temple. He couldn't have been shot from the door, and the windows were locked. And he couldn't have been shot from the windows, even if they had been open."

"I don't say he was."

Brinze's expression showed that he doubted Jimmy's mental balance.

"Come down to cases," he urged. "If Stelke didn't do it, who did?"

"I'd have to prove any accusation I made, wouldn't I?"

"Of course."

"Such being the case, that's all I can say now. I haven't anything more than an opinion, and it might be wrong. I've given you my best lead—the revolver. It's up to you to track it down."

Jimmy lit a cigarette and smiled enigmatically. Brinze glared at him dully.

"You're just faking this thing," he declared. "I don't know why, and I don't care. But I'll tell you this much: You've started something you can't finish. I'll prove either that Payne killed himself or that Stelke did it."

"You'll have a hot time proving either. By the way, how long ago did you quit wearing your college frat pin, if that isn't too personal a question?"

"What's that got to do with it?"

"Not a thing. I was wondering whether I was right in supposing that you had worn it up to a short time ago."

"I haven't worn it since—"

Brinze flushed a little.

"I didn't mean to ask whether you'd given it to a young woman," laughed Jimmy, "but if you'll look at your shirt, you will see that there are two little holes which only some piece of jewelry like a frat pin could have put there. The shirt is a new design, so the holes must be fairly recent."

Brinze laughed sheepishly.

"That's rather clever," he conceded.

He inspected Jimmy as though to retaliate with a deduction of his own. But none was forthcoming.

Brinze's emissary brought in Stelke. Never before had Jimmy seen a butler in street clothes. Stelke, in mufti, seemed a stolid, indifferent middle-aged man, his civilian speech diverging sharply from his meticulous diction in the role of a gentleman's man.

"Don't be afraid of us, Stelke," remarked Brinze. "We're trying to clean up this thing as quickly as possible and you seem to be the only person who was at hand when it happened. Just tell us what took place, as you remember it."

Stelke repeated the familiar sequence of events. He had heard the shot. He had found the door locked. He thought of sending for Dr. Farrigan. Yes, the fear that he might be suspected of a crime prompted him to send for the doctor before opening the door.

"You had some questions, Mr. Wrome?"

Brinze turned the butler over to Jimmy with a grandiloquent air.

Jimmy felt like an attorney. A week ago he had been reading fictitious accounts of examinations of trusted servants. Here he was, conducting one himself.

"Stelke," he began impressively, "did Mr. Payne own a revolver?"

Stelke appeared perplexed.

"Not that I know of," he replied. "At least, he never had one in his rooms, and I used to fix things up there every day. If he kept one there, I never saw it."

"Did he have one anywhere in the house?"

"No. I'd have known of it if he had."

"Did you ever see this revolver before?" He pointed to the weapon on the desk.

"Only—only that night."

The hesitation in Stelke's answer was that of horror rather than of grief.

"You see," Jimmy remarked to Brinze, "I thought that this gun would bear a little investigating."

"But couldn't Payne have bought it specially for this purpose?"

Brinze smiled condescendingly.

"That's possible, but I doubt it. Stelke—did anyone enter the room after Mr. Payne went to bed?"

"Not that I know of. I'm pretty sure nobody did. Dr. Farrigan and I helped him to bed and then he ordered us to get out. I heard him turn the key in the door after us."

"My guess," observed Jimmy, "is that Payne didn't have that revolver on him when he went to bed. Of course, he might have concealed it somewhere and gone out to get it later. Perhaps, Stelke, you'll tell us whether Mr. Payne could have left his room unobserved after he retired."

"No, sir. I was worried about him, and I stayed down in the hall until about midnight. He said I was to wait up for the guests, anyhow. If he'd made any move I'd have heard him. About seven, I think it was, I went up, knocked at the door and asked him if he wanted anything. He told me to go to hell, so I figured he was feeling better."

Jimmy smiled at Brinze.

"Do you grant me the question of the revolver?" he asked.

"Well, there may be something in it."

"Another trifle. Have you the note which Payne left?"

Brinze extracted it from his desk.

"Look at this, Stelke," said Jimmy. "That's Payne's writing, isn't it?"

"Certainly."

"Now don't try to prove this a forgery," warned Brinze. "I'll let you have the gun—but that's too fantastic."

"Of course, it's too fantastic," agreed Jimmy. "It's so fantastic I'm surprised you thought of it. I wouldn't have."

"Then what are you getting at?"

"The background of this note, if I can. Stelke, is this some of Payne's regular notepaper?"

Stelke examined it cautiously as though he were touching a dead body.

"I never saw any like it before."

"As long as you have a magnifying glass, Mr. Brinze," suggested Jimmy, "would you mind looking at the top of this sheet."

Brinze felt that he ought to maintain his official dignity in the presence of a third person, even if that person were no more than a butler in civilian clothes.

"Is that intended to be funny?" he inquired.

Jimmy declined to be withered.

"Tragic," he said; "but if you don't care to take the trouble, I'll spare your exertion. This paper is a standard water-marked bond, and the top of it has been torn off. My conclusion is that Payne never bought, stole or otherwise annexed this particular sheet."

Brinze ran his fingers over the edge of the paper. "Certainly, certainly," he agreed irritably. "I didn't need you to tell me that."

"Tell you what?"

Brinze was becoming angry.

"Please get down to business, Mr. Wrome," he said sternly. "You talk about the engraving on the revolver and the tearing of this paper and heaven knows what's coming next. I didn't send for you to do tricks. I want to know what reason you had for calling Mr. Payne's death a murder."

"You've hit on two of my best reasons, Mr. Brinze," replied Jimmy sweetly.

He looked at Stelke as who should say "Do you expect me to tell you everything in front of this man?"

"Well, are you through with Stelke?"

Brinze brandished the magnifying glass menacingly. "Quite."

Brinze rapped against the desk indecisively.

"I haven't anything more to ask you now, Stelke," he announced. "You can go—but don't leave town until I tell you you can."

Stelke, who had regained his wavering self-possession, hesitated.

"Do you mind if I say something?" he demanded in anything but a servile tone.

"Go ahead," urged Jimmy. "Your ideas are as good as—mine, perhaps."

"It's this," explained Stelke. "You get me down here and you ask me what happened and I tell you and then you begin asking me a lot of fool questions about the gun and all that. Now, as sure as my name's Herman Stelke, Mr. Payne did away with himself. God only knows why, but he did, sure as you or me stands here. But if you still think somebody else did it, you're going about it wrong, all wrong. You'll pardon me for saying so, Mr. Brinze and Mr. Wrome, but you know what this reminds me of? The movies. It's like a detective story in the movies, with people looking for footprints and all that. If I was in your place and I thought anybody'd shot Mr. Payne, I wouldn't waste my time that way. No, sir! You know what I'd do? I'd look for the woman."

He paused, extremely satisfied with his address.

Brinze declined to degrade himself by commenting.

"Very interesting, Stelke," acquiesced Jimmy; "but which woman?"

"How should I know?" retorted Stelke. "I'm no detective. Mr. Payne knew lots of women, but I couldn't say any one of them had any reason for shooting him. All I say is, where there's so much smoke, there must be a woman."

Brinze glared at the butler.

"You have someone in mind, Stelke," he said. "I want to know her name."

Stelke smiled at Brinze's melodramatic assertion.

"I have not," he declared. "I didn't mean for you to think there was a woman in it. I only meant if there was anything to it, it was a woman. That's all."

Stelke's "that's all," a weak echo of Payne's famous ultimatum, amused Jimmy.

"That's all, Stelke," he said. "Mr. Brinze, I don't think Stelke has anything more to offer."

"I'm not so sure of that."

Brinze frowned at the butler, who was not at all nonplussed.

"But you can go, Stelke," he added, "and don't forget—you're not to leave town without reporting to me."

"Very good," replied Stelke. "I've got business here to finish up anyhow. Good night."

Brinze waited until Stelke had disappeared. He closed the door solemnly and stalked back to his desk.

"I'm getting tired of this," he remarked crisply. "I thought you were only talking for your own amusement or maybe for publicity when you gave that interview. Now, I'm just about convinced of it. I'll admit that the stuff about the gun is a little puzzling, but if there's no more to it than that, I don't see any sense in wasting time and getting the public excited over the case. It's no clew, anyhow. What else have you got up your sleeve?"

"I haven't anything up my sleeve," protested Jimmy. "It's merely my idea that Payne didn't meet a voluntary death. And it's not my business to follow up the case. I've given you what I have, and the rest, I should think, is up to you."

Jimmy lit a cigarette.

"Of course, you can drop the affair here, if you like," he went on. "But I imagine that you'd rather solve it, or at least investigate it yourself than have it done by the newspapers."

Brinze's hostility abated. The mask of the official dropped and he became a pleasant young man.

"You're right about the papers," he assented mournfully. "I don't know why the hell you had to get us into this. If there's one thing the New York papers like it's to kid Kenworthy and the police. We can't afford to have another mystery hanging over us. You're sure you haven't got something up your sleeve?"

"Sure. But—"

Jimmy stopped. He was going to make a facetious reference to Stelke's suggestion about the women when he recalled the enigma of Claire's relations with Payne. What if Claire were somehow implicated? He felt uncomfortable. His nervousness began to manifest itself. Brinze, he feared, was aware of it.

"But—?"

Brinze paced about the room.

"There is something else," he said. "And I have a pretty good idea what it is. It's a woman. Payne was pretty wild with them. I know."

He winked as rakishly as he could.

"I'm going to question every woman at that house party. That'll snap up things."

"Are you a disciple of Stelke?" inquired Jimmy, forcing a light manner.

"I'd thought of that myself," retorted Brinze, "long ago. I don't have to tell you everything. If there's anything in this, it'll come out when I get after those women."

The notion of getting after those women was undeniably palatable. Jimmy's fears for Claire increased.

"But they were all at the Inn when it happened," he objected.

"An accessory doesn't have to be on the scene," Brinze shot back. "I'll take your word for it that somebody, so far unknown, shot and killed Leed Payne with a revolver carefully engraved to give the impression of suicide. The murderer was instigated by a woman, who—well, I don't know what her motive was, but it's a sure thing it was the usual one. Yes, that's it, all right. I may have a little trouble spotting the woman—but hell, there were only two."

"Why," remonstrated Jimmy, "would it have to be one of the women at this particular party? You say Payne knew any number of them."

"It wouldn't have to be," replied Brinze scornfully, "but I'll look them over first anyhow."

He sat down for cerebration.

"Let's see," he mused. "There was Mrs. Gulvin and that blonde flicker."

Jimmy resented the description of Claire. He felt himself growing red in the face. If Brinze noticed his reaction he would be convinced that Claire ought to be examined and examined thoroughly. Jimmy bent his head, apparently to light another cigarette.

"Mrs. Gulvin," Brinze went on airily, "doesn't figure in this."

Jimmy became very preoccupied with his match.

"She's happily married—at least, I think so. She's a weak sort and anyhow Payne wasn't interested in her. I never could see why he had her around unless it was because he wanted something from Gulvin. We'll rule her out. Now the blonde—"

The blonde seemed to be a diverting fancy.

"Well, we don't know much about her. Miles saw her and he says she sure made him forget his wife. She looked kind of sad too, he said. That's interesting. Very interesting. Ve-ry, ve-ry interesting."

Jimmy looked at his watch.

"Well, I wish you luck," he said, dispiritedly. "I ought to be getting back to town. You know where to get me if you want me. But I'd look into that gun first."

"Chairchez la femm," laughed Brinze. "If there's anything in this, I've got it. It's the amateurs that look at guns and engraving. Motives are what we need—motives. Good night!"

Jimmy was miserable on the way back. The cool night breeze made him shudder. Or wasn't it the breeze? Why did he shudder? Why should he perspire so on a cool night? He clenched his hands in the vain hope of steadying himself. A horrible mess he had made of it! What a fool he had been to talk his head off to Heidelman! Brinze would persecute Claire and he might find—almost anything.

The more he muttered, the more he reflected, the worse he felt. He staggered through the lurching train for a drink of water. He staggered back to the smoking car, hoping to find solace in cigarettes. The aroma of cheap cigars sickened him. He went to the platform and breathed deeply. It was very quiet in these indistinguishable villages here. The little lights in distant cottages were so peaceful! The inhabitants weren't worried about futile love affairs and murder trials. He could be riding here tranquilly tonight, admiring the loveliness of the starlit fields and the little houses, if he weren't a plain damn fool. He lit a cigarette and watched the match die out as he tossed it from the train.

"That's how my happiness went," he chattered. "A little spark— and darkness. You're getting sentimental now. Don't. But what's the use? What does anything matter?"

His soliloquy went on as the train rattled into sight of the lights of New York. He returned to the car. Perhaps this mood would wear off. Perhaps it was all a bad dream. He walked unsteadily from the train to Forty-Second Street. Everyone seemed happy. Even the old woman selling newspapers was happy. He was alone in his misery. He took a taxi. The ride was cooling. Why did he have to be blocked in traffic? He watched the street numbers anxiously. He wanted to be home and asleep. He would feel better in the morning. But could he sleep? He handed two bills to the driver and entered his house without looking about. No. He couldn't go to sleep. He couldn't be with his thoughts.

Across the street he could see a lamp burning in Hugh's office. Hugh could give him something to relieve him. It was a terrible hour to see a doctor, but—

He rang Hugh's bell.

Hugh, in a deep blue dressing gown, answered the ring.

"Well, what's wrong with you now?" he demanded.

Jimmy blinked at him.

"Sorry to disturb you," he began, wearily.

"You're not disturbing me. I've been reading. I didn't expect company this time of night, though. Come in. Sit down."

Jimmy slumped into a chair.

"Same trouble," he grunted.

It was hard to speak.

"I thought I'd cured you of that," said Hugh, good naturedly.

He took his hand.

"You seem a little upset."

His voice was calming and the steady gaze of his eyes was reassuring.

"It's not love—this time," said Jimmy.

His voice wouldn't yield to him.

"Let's hear the story," suggested Hugh. "Get it off your chest."

"I was called to Bellechester. I told Brinze—that's the detective—about some crazy notions I had. And he—God, doctor, he suspects Claire of killing Payne!"

Hugh lit his pipe and stared at Jimmy deliberately. Jimmy felt exhausted. He had got something off his chest, but the delivery had not eased him. He was aware that his forehead was wet. He wiped it and twisted the handkerchief in his hands.

"Let me tell you something," said Hugh, at length. "I don't know any more about your early history than you've told me. But I take it that your life had been rather a simple one until the past few weeks."

Jimmy nodded impatiently. He didn't have to be told this. He wanted relief.

"You've had an even way," continued Hugh, "and a relatively slight disturbance has impressed you tremendously."

"Slight disturbance!"

Jimmy cried out bitterly.

"It's no slight disturbance to see the girl you love accused of murder!"

"Now, hold on," counseled Hugh, soothingly. "You don't get my point. And anyhow, she isn't accused of murder."

"Don't quibble," groaned Jimmy.

Hugh placed a pillow on the back of the easy-chair.

"Sit here," he said. "It'll help you relax. And listen to me before you work yourself up again."

Jimmy dropped wearily into the seat of comfort.

"This is what I'm driving at," Hugh went on. "You never had any serious emotional experiences. You became attached—more so than you suspected—to Miss Barton. The course of true love ran according to form. It ran off the track. And the effect was a jar to your nervous system. Not a very deep jar, although you won't agree with me now, but a comparatively heavy one for a man whose emotions weren't hardened to a blow."

Hugh smiled.

"This is really something for Dr. Villmers, the psycho-analyst. I'm only an orthopedist."

Jimmy resented the reference to the psycho-analyst. He wanted a remedy, not a talk about his hidden emotional mechanism.

"I've read up all this stuff about complexes and repressions and all the rest of it," he said querulously. "I haven't any suppressed desires or phobias or inhibitions or any of the rest of them. And if I have, it doesn't matter. This isn't a clinical case, doctor. I just want you to give me something to quiet me. I know what I've done, and tomorrow I'll just notify the office that I'm called away on urgent personal business and get at the bottom of it."

"Of what?"

"Of this murder."

"Why," demanded Hugh impatiently, "do you insist on making a murder of it?"

"I wish to God he *had* killed himself," said Jimmy, "but I saw a few suspicious things and I couldn't shut up about them. I never thought they'd lead to—where they have led."

"From what I've heard about your clews," Hugh remarked, "they're too vague to convict anybody of anything. You've started a little stir, but that won't last. The case'll drop out of sight before you know it. Don't worry about it. By the way, I'm a little surprised at your attitude towards Miss Barton."

"Surprised? What about?"

"I thought you'd recovered from your infatuation."

Jimmy sighed.

"I thought so, too—but I haven't. I wasn't really in love with her when I came here the first time. I didn't realize how much I loved her until Brinze began trying to hang the murder on her. I love her, and that's all there is to it! I'll always love her. And even if she killed Payne—but she didn't. Hesbe would be my choice. If only I could get evidence on him! But how can I? He was miles away when it happened. So was Claire, yet they think—"

He wanted to sob. It would have been a relief. But he felt that tears wouldn't be right.

"Stop!"

Hugh's voice trumpeted a command which startled Jimmy out of his mood.

"Sometimes," Hugh said crisply and cuttingly, "a little unvarnished talk is worth more than all the medicines and treatments anybody ever concocted. Your trouble isn't merely this imaginary murder mystery which you've practically created from a suddenly stimulated emotionalism and a too serious appreciation of wild detective stories. You're extremely suggestible, especially now, when you aren't altogether sure of yourself. Any suggestion takes hold of you and masters you. There are thousands, perhaps millions of people like that. They seize on a suggestion and it grows, often with amazing rapidity, into something approximating a hallucination. If I were to tell almost any of my patients that next week—about Thursday—he would have a sudden pain in the big toe of his right foot, the chances are twenty to one that he would develop that pain. When I was in medical school I went through the symptoms of each new disease as we studied it—and so did almost all of the others in the class. You brooded over your symptoms of love until they became a sort of disease. And now you've worried over this absurd murder business until it's become an affliction. There's nothing to it. Forget it. Go to work again tomorrow and help reduce the price of sugar. That's the best cure I can give you."

"But Brinze insists—"

"You insist, not Brinze. You have an idea that Brinze is determined to hurry Miss Barton to the electric chair. You're the only one who has it. You've taken up a chance remark and magnified it into an indictment. Suggestibility—that's all. That's what ails most of us."

Jimmy pulled himself up in his chair suddenly. He felt no less agitated, but something seemed to become clear in his mind. Hugh went to a cupboard and brought back a small bottle of white pills.

"Two or three of these in hot water will help you sleep," he said, "but an end of brooding will be more effective. Forget it. That doesn't sound professional, but it's an excellent prescription."

Jimmy stood up. He was breathing more freely. He was weak, but a mist seemed to have been dispelled.

"Thank you, doctor," he said, "I'll try to do what you say. I think you've shown me the way out."

"It's the only way out," remarked Hugh, escorting Jimmy to the door.

"Where did Payne come from?" asked Jimmy irrelevantly.

"Oh, forget Payne! As long as you continue to harp on the things connected with the week-end, you'll be miserable."

"But where did he come from?" Jimmy's eyes glistened eagerly.

"Charleston. Now that you know that, maybe you'll be able to sleep without the pills."

"Thank you, doctor. I'm going out of town tomorrow. I can get away, all right. Maybe the change of scene will do me good."

"Change of thought is enough. You can brood out of town just as well as in this office or in your apartment."

"No—I have to go. The answer may be down there."

"Where?"

"Charleston."

VII
THE MISTS OF MYSTERY

Not until the train had passed Trenton, the city of homes, did Jimmy begin to wonder why he had taken this quixotic journey to Charleston. There was something exhilarating about whirling through country on a Pullman. He was on the quest for the unknown. The stodgy old gentleman dozing in the seat ahead didn't realize that not six feet away sat a smartly dressed, keen-eyed young man who was about to dig into a pile of years and toss them aside carelessly until he struck ore which might assay gold or possibly brass or perhaps lead. The honeymoon couple across the aisle, caressing with ostentatious furtiveness, had no idea that the occupant of lower 5 was racing South on a mission that might result in town talk for weeks to come. The tremors and the weariness of last night were gone. Jimmy strolled into the smoking room and blew smoke contentedly out of the window.

His hypotheses were shelved temporarily. His deductions had been laid away. He would get the story of Payne's early life, select the passage most applicable to the present situation, and then construct the testimony which would release Claire. The thought of Claire this afternoon brought only a faint, almost a pleasant regret. The cover of the magazine which he had taken with him suggested the atmosphere in which Claire was enveloped now. Harlequin was weeping for his lost love. Harlequin's tears were wrung from his heart, yet it was the sorrow of Harlequin that made his life sweet. Claire was Columbine. Or wasn't it Columbine that broke Harlequin's heart? The further that Jimmy rode from New York, the more Claire became the bewitching heroine of a Harlequinade. He would come back from Charleston with a magic key, unlock the prison of the unhappy Columbine—

"Yes, it sure was hot in New York last night, brother—"

The pompous conversation of two heavy gentlemen smashed Jimmy's confused phantasmagoria.

"Not's 'ot 'stwas in Albany the night before."

"Guess you're right there. Hot's hell in Albany."

The clouds of distress would lift from Columbine's deep blue eyes and tears of anguish would be tears of gratitude.

"Don't see Jake much nowadays. He left town?"

"No. Still with Campbell."

"You don't say."

"Yeah. Jake's still with Campbell."

Harlequin would bend over the entrancing, yielding body of Columbine, stroke her soft golden hair gently from her white forehead, and—

"Last I seen of her was in Springfield."

"Ain't been to Springfield this trip. Nothin' doin' in Springfield this time o' year."

"Yeah, Springfield's sort o' dead now. Better in August."

"Good in August. That's right."

Under a sky of a million stars, a million moons, a million masks—

"That's what I told him, but you can't tell him nothin' when his mind's made up."

"That's right. Awful stubborn man once his mind's made up."

"You said it. Wont listen to nothin'."

Bernard Gartlin had donned the mask of a Hindoo and was wooing Columbine in the back alleys of New York's Syrian quarter. Gartlin could be undeniably seductive—

"Not tonight, I told her, not tonight."

"Thassa good one. Not tonight, I told her, not tonight."

Columbine threw a rose—

A stinging sensation between two fingers woke Jimmy. He has almost set himself on fire with his cigarette. He looked around dazedly. What was all this about Columbine, a million masks, not tonight, I told her, not tonight, a rose, awful stubborn man?

He lit another cigarette and looked over the landscapes. Curious how relaxed one became on a train. Perspective. That's what one got. Perspective. The mind wasn't cramped. He'd never have thought of Harlequin and Columbine and absorbed the drone about the heat in Albany anywhere else. It was warm here, but comfortable. Too warm to figure out why Claire had come to Payne's for the week-end. Too warm to ponder over the revolver. How had it come to Payne's room?

"'If you ever come near me again I'll throw you out of the office,' I said."

"It's the only way to treat those fellows. They don't know when they got it good."

"Yeah, they don't know when they got it good."

Jimmy didn't like the cigars which the rapid-fire conversationalists were smoking. He returned to his seat and went through a stack of Sunday papers. The President's latest speech, declaration of the dry chief, didn't shoot her husband, stock promoter says house is solvent—it was all boring. He picked up a sheet which had fluttered to the floor. He looked at a lettered diagram and drew out his pencil.

For the next three hours he was solving a cross word puzzle. The first call for dinner came just as he discovered that the three-letter word for "to soak" was "ret." Between other ingenuities (my first is in rock but not in stone, my second in rib but not in bone) and *The Death Sundae*, which he had rented from Mr. Curtin's emporium from force of habit, day and night passed. It was only when he had tipped the bellboy at his hotel in Charleston that Jimmy began to concentrate on the matter in hand.

His first subject was the desk clerk, who explained that he came from Goldsboro and had never heard of a man named Payne.

"But you might see Kirkman of the *Journal*," he suggested. "He's a newspaper man and newspaper men know everybody in Charleston."

The omniscient Kirkman proved to be a rotund, placid gentleman, whose snappy black mustache seemed incongruous with his lackadaisical manner.

"Payne? Leed Payne?"

Kirkman scratched his bald head reminiscently.

"Yes, there was a Leed Payne—why, I believe he died lately up North. Seems to me I wrote a piece about it at the time. Yes, certainly. He lived here twenty-five years ago, I think it was. Sam!"

Kirkman called the gray-haired city editor into consultation. The city editor, apparently relieved at being disturbed at his labors, held forth enthusiastically.

"Now, son," he told Jimmy, "there's just one man in this part of the world who can tell you anything about this man Payne. That's old man Ormer out in Boone Valley."

Jimmy inquired for a minute geographical prospectus of Boone Valley.

"That's a town out about ten miles—is that what you'd say, Kirkman?"

"I'd say twenty miles."

"Maybe so. You can't get there by train. It's a little place. A few farmers live there and maybe some people from the works. Ormer's a pretty old man. He lost all his money a long time ago and all he had left was this little shack out in Boone Valley. I guess you won't have much trouble finding him."

"What connection did he have with Payne?"

"I don't know. That was a little before my time. All I know is he comes in once in a while and asks us to print something about his flowers. He's a great horticulturist. And he certainly can tell stories about the old days when the town was gayer than it is now. I seem to recollect he mentioned Payne once. Payne shot a man or a man shot him. I don't remember."

Jimmy's brown eyes snapped as he hurried through the tranquil boulevards of Charleston to find a train to Boone Valley. Payne had shot a man, had he! Or a man had shot Payne? This might well be the turning point. His previous notions seemed strangely unreal with this exploration into an old vendetta before him. Who had shot Payne and why? Then he wished that he had asked for further information about Ormer. Ormer might be a crank, perhaps a little weak-minded. Ormer might not care to speak. If Ormer were at all peculiar—and the supposition was that Ormer was not entirely normal—he might regard the intrusion of a Northerner in Boone

Valley with suspicion. Yet Ormer came to Charleston now and then in search of a scrap of free publicity.

Something in *The Rosenbaum Case* flashed into Jimmy's mind. The detective had gone in the guise of a reporter to examine the suspect. Jimmy would go as horticultural editor of the *New York Times* and somehow veer the conversation over to Payne.

Trains to Boone Valley ran infrequently. But the hunt was up, and Jimmy couldn't idle in the warm sun of Charleston while the answer to his enigma reposed in Boone Valley. He walked until he found a garage where automobiles might be rented by the day. A listless young man volunteered to take him to Boone Valley and back for fifteen dollars and was surprised to find that his offer was accepted.

The dilapidated car worried its way over narrow dusty roads and through damp, shady stretches of clay into Boone Valley. Unshaven men in overalls loitered about the shed that served as a railroad depot, Jimmy instructed the driver to wait at the station until he returned and went to interview the ticket agent. This red-faced man informed Jimmy, between startlingly accurate expectorations of tobacco, that Ormer lived down the road—the white house about five minutes away. Jimmy strolled down the street. The weather-beaten cottages, with their ancient outhouses, seemed to him like a setting for a feature film. His quest led him into a new background, at any rate. Scrawny boys slouched about untidy gardens and fat, slovenly women waddled painfully but energetically up creaking steps. Jimmy, being a well-read Northerner, concluded that he had landed in the home of the hookworm.

Ormer's house, which was white in name only, was of a piece with its surroundings. Two shaggy trees, with dead branches dipping down, threw a shade over the front of it. A battered screen door was partly ajar. A sallow board had been nailed across a broken window-pane.

Jimmy walked through a decaying wooden gate which had long since ceased to function and traveled over the traces of what had once been a path to the house. He felt strangely cool in this sultry patch of land. Involuntarily he adjusted his bright cravat as he pushed the rusty doorbell. He could hear no sound within, nor was there any symptom of life in the house. He followed a line of scattered gravel—had this once been a walk?—to the rear of the house, where he saw an old man puttering about a tiny garden, in which a few feeble blooms sprouted anemically.

"Mr. Ormer?" inquired Jimmy.

Mr. Ormer looked up with a start. He was tall, flabby and stoop-shouldered, and his face was one which looked as though its owner always blinked. Ormer had long white hair and he was as clean shaven as a three days' growth of bristles would permit him to appear. His teeth were yellow from tobacco, and his small blue eyes were watery. He nodded uncertainly by way of identification.

"I'm from the *New York Times*," Jimmy began jauntily.

He was aware that Ormer was looking at his neatly pressed light-gray suit and his new cravat. Perhaps Jimmy had selected the wrong role. He might have done better as a rustic. But he might as well proceed along the lines of *The Rosenbaum Case*.

"I write about flowers and those things," explained Jimmy, not altogether convincingly.

He wished that he knew one flower from another.

"Flowahs."

Ormer repeated the word in a dull, cracked voice.

"They told me in Charleston that you had a wonderful collection," continued Jimmy, who wondered whether flowers could be spoken of as a collection. Stamps could—why not flowers?

"What about 'em?"

Ormer patted down a piece of earth about a sad little sprig and surveyed Jimmy more attentively.

"Why—I thought I'd like to write something about them. Could I interview you?"

The word "interview" brightened up the dull visage of Ormer.

"Certainly, sir. Won't you come into the house and sit down?"

A latent courtesy was breaking through the old man's apparent diffidence. Ormer seemed like a man unused to speaking.

Jimmy followed him to the cottage. It was even smaller inside than he had suspected. Ormer led him into a little parlor, decorated with dusty oil portraits of undistinguishable people and fading photographs. A table covered with a soiled green cloth and a few unstable chairs, covered with frayed blue plush, completed the inventory.

"Sit down, sir," requested Ormer, whose speech was growing easier. "What would you like to know?"

"About your flowers, now—"

What questions could one ask about flowers?

But the suggestions had touched the hidden springs and words gushed forth freely and eloquently. Jimmy wondered what all of this talk about peonies and roses and heliotrope and violets and syringas might mean. He nodded as intelligently as possible at every pause. Finally Ormer fished a crumpled clipping from his baggy gray trousers and thrust it at Jimmy. It was a short item from some local newspaper about Clayton Ormer's flowers. Jimmy stared at it with a show of intense interest and returned it.

"This is fine!" he exclaimed. "Just what I wanted. I'm more than obliged to you!"

"I can tell you much more, sir," said Ormer, whose voice had acquired a certain power. "The riches of nature are my hobby and flowers are my children."

"How long have you lived here?" asked Jimmy, trying to switch gradually to the subject of Payne.

"Upward of twenty years, sir."

"You come from Charleston?"

"Born and bred there, sir. Are you from New York, did I understand you to say?"

"Yes, I'm from New York."

How to bring up Payne?

"I knew a man who used to know you, I believe, Mr. Ormer."

Ormer's face clouded, but Jimmy was determined to drive for his point.

"He came from Charleston originally," he went on glibly. "His name was Payne. He—died a little while ago."

"Payne? Jack Payne?"

So Payne was "Jack" Payne in his day.

"That's the man."

"And he said he knew me, sir?"

Jimmy nodded.

"And he's dead?"

The news of Payne's death silenced Ormer for a moment. He opened the drawer of the table and drew out an old corncob pipe.

"You'll pardon me, sir?"

Jimmy produced a cigarette by way of answer.

"So Payne's dead," ruminated Ormer. "Died in his bed, I dare say."

"In his bed," said Jimmy truthfully. "Did you—did you think he might meet any other sort of end?"

He waited eagerly as Ormer scratched a match against his boot and lighted the pipe. As Ormer puffed away, Jimmy could almost hear his neglected mental machinery begin to operate again. Finally Ormer looked up.

"That's very interesting news, sir," he remarked. "Was he a friend of yours?"

"Just an acquaintance."

"Ah, yes. Very successful, I suppose."

"Very."

"I thought as much. He might have been a big man in Charleston, if—"

"Go on!"

Jimmy almost commanded the old man to tell his story.

"Well, sir," began Ormer, settling down comfortably to his pipe and his narrative, "in the old days, Jack Payne worked for me. That was before I—retired."

Ormer was covering up his failure loftily, Jimmy thought.

The old man bent over the table, apparently focusing his ideas on the green cloth before him. "Like to hear about Jack, sir?" he inquired.

"By all means, if it isn't troubling you."

"No trouble at all, sir," smiled Ormer. "It does me good to talk over some things."

He shoved his pipe into his mouth as though to secure it and settled back for his story.

"My memory isn't what it used to be," he began. "I can recall faces and events but details slip. However, Jack Payne came to work for me when he was a young fellow. He was a right smart, handsome boy and I thought some day he might succeed me.

Ormer became melancholy.

"That was when I was making money, sir," he explained in a peculiarly humble way. "Later on, my ventures didn't turn out as well as I might have expected, and—

"But that has nothing to do with Jack Payne. You'll pardon me, sir, if I wander. Payne made good progress with me. I started him as a clerk in my office—I was a broker, sir—and soon he became my right-hand man. I don't say he wasn't always honest, but he gambled—gambled more than a young man in his position had a right to. He played the races heavily and he speculated. I forbade him to speculate, but I knew he did it behind my back. Speculation isn't good for any man, sir. It brings financial ruin to some and misfortune to all.

"But Jack was known as a lucky gambler. He never lost on the races and his speculations were uncanny. He seemed to have no system, like other speculators. He operated entirely on his intuition. He used to say that he could feel the movement of a security and he never was very far wrong. Some little thing would give him the idea that a stock would rise and his money would be in it. Impulse governed his life. It almost amounted to superstition, sir. A chance remark by a negro boy would somehow be his cue to buy a certain stock.

"You know, sir, that a successful gambler makes enemies. Payne was a sharp trader and many men hated him. They envied his luck and his successful intuition."

"You mean that he worked on hunches?" asked Jimmy.

"Hunches, I believe, they call them now, sir. Yes, you might say that he worked on hunches. As I was saying, Payne played a lone hand. He had no close friends. I trusted him in a business way, but I never had his confidence. What he did outside of office hours was not my business. I should have liked to have been a friend to him, but he was cold and independent.

"Now and then they tried to break him in the market, but they never got him. And if he suspected that any man was trying to thwart him, Payne would go to any length to defeat that man. He never failed. Sometimes it took him several years to even a score, but he always evened it—and more."

Ormer paused to relight his pipe.

"As it was in money matters, so it was with women. Jack was a hot-blooded boy, no more so perhaps than many others, but he couldn't stay away from women. He was involved in several ugly affairs and once I cautioned him as gently as I could. I told him that many a good man had come to grief through women. He laughed at me and walked out of the office with his head high. He was a very proud young man. But in the end I was right. It was because of a woman that he left Charleston."

Ormer's dull face had become animated by memories, and he went on fluently.

"There were still duels in those days. We didn't say much about them, and they were fought across the river. Many a good man died at dawn, with the river mists rising like a soul on its way to heaven. That was my fancy then. Even now, when I see the mist on the river—

"You'll pardon me, sir. I'm getting away from Jack again.

"Jack fell in love with a woman named—I can't recall her name. It was twenty-five years ago if it was a day. It was something like Nagle, and she came from a small town near Lexington."

"Nagle?" interrupted Jimmy. "Are you sure it was Nagle?"

"I'm sorry, sir," apologized Ormer. "Nagle is the name as I remember it, and yet it wasn't Nagle. Her name doesn't matter."

Jimmy wanted to insist that the name mattered enormously, but he saw that it was futile to press the matter.

"I never saw her. I heard about her. She was a simple girl, they said, beautiful and innocent. She had come to Charleston to spend the summer with kin. Jack fell in love with her, and when I heard of it I was happy, for I thought he might turn over a new leaf if he married her.

"But there was another man—a man from up North. And one week-end, when Jack had gone away with a few companions who were merrier than they were wise, the man from the North and the woman Jack loved went across the river, where so many young couples went to be married, and were united.

"When Jack returned from his debauch—it's the only word, sir—he was like a wild man. He drank incessantly for a day, and went through the city with a gun in his pocket, looking for the man who had taken away the woman he loved. He swore that he would meet him in a duel to death and kill him.

"He found the man late at night. He made him go with him to a saloon, saying that he wanted to celebrate with him his great fortune in winning so wonderful a woman. Jack was so insistent that the man came along to humor him.

"In the saloon, Jack called all the men—and it was a meeting place for the gay bloods of the city—together. He mounted a table and made a speech. He pointed out the young husband as the man who had been tricked into marriage. And he sneered at the man, saying that he had known this woman intimately long before her husband had held her in his arms. It was a vile accusation and the husband leaped to the defense of his wife's good name.

"There was a disgraceful brawl, in which Jack lost all control of himself and fired several shots at his successful rival. The police came in, but Jack disappeared through a side door. His friends would not reveal what had taken place. But Jack Payne was never again seen in Charleston.

"That was the last I knew of him until you told me of his death."

Ormer shook his head regretfully. He had an affection for Payne or for Payne's memory.

"You never heard of him again?"

Jimmy prompted the old man in the hope of learning something of Payne's subsequent movements. "Never—except once."

Ormer smiled humbly as he ran his hand through his white hair.

"I forget so much, sir. I've had reasons for trying not to remember things. But I did hear of Jack once after he left. He wrote me a short note from New York. It was written on the train, I think, and it wasn't signed, but I should have known his hand anywhere. He said he had to leave, that he was sorry he couldn't say good-bye, and he ended up by saying that he would even up matters with the man who had ruined his life."

"What was his name?"

"I don't know that, sir."

Ormer's manner was again defensive. He seemed to be sensitive about his failure to recollect details.

"But it isn't my memory that's at fault this time," he went on, with a touch of pride. "I never knew the man's name. He was a stranger in town. Payne didn't use the name in his letter. He referred to him with a vile expression. He said he'd even matters with him if it took twenty years. I wonder if he did."

Jimmy would have given anything to know the answer to the implied question.

He lit another cigarette and rose to go.

"But about my flowers," began Ormer. "I was going to tell you more, sir."

"You've told me just what I wanted to know," said Jimmy. "I don't want to take up any more of your time."

"Not at all, sir."

Ormer had risen with his guest.

"I could talk all day about my flowers. They are all I have left."

"I don't doubt it."

Jimmy checked the too ready reply.

"And you'll send me a copy of your article, sir?" Ormer's eyes were wistful.

Jimmy felt guilty. But perhaps he could get some newspaper man—possibly Heidelman—to print a few lines about the old man of Boone Valley.

"I'll be delighted to."

"Please do."

Ormer was quaintly beseeching.

"You don't know what it means to me."

Jimmy gripped Ormer's dry hand and went on his way, murmuring meaningless thanks. As he walked down the hot road to his rented vehicle he was trying to fit Ormer's story into the evidence already at hand. Find the woman! It wasn't Claire. That, at least, was certain now. Who was this Nagle woman? What really was her name? Nagle, Nagley, what other variants were likely? And what was her husband's name? Perhaps there might be only a man in the case. She came from a small town near Lexington. That couldn't be followed up. Jimmy absent-mindedly beckoned to his driver and slouched back in the car, as the motor worried its way back to Charleston.

Here was a motive. If Payne had evened matters with the man, had not the man revenged himself? But, if so, when could he have entered the house? Could any of the guests—?

Claire and Hesbe were too young. Endle was too young. Gulvin—no, he was too young, and Mrs. Gulvin spoke with a fine New York accent. She couldn't have been the mysterious Nagle woman in any event. Stelke? Stelke was unmarried and it was absurd to think that he would have gone to such melodramatic extremes to kill Payne. He would have had to have a disguise to avoid recognition. Bosh!

A few more days in Charleston, a search of old newspaper files, a few interviews with old inhabitants. Gartlin used to do things like that and step in just as the innocent suspect was about to be indicted or arraigned with complete proof and the criminal within convenient reach. In this case, the innocent suspect was Claire.

The thought of Claire again obsessed Jimmy. Brinze might already have put her through a third degree and held her on suspicion. He might even have scraped together sufficient circumstantial evidence to present a case. The information which Jimmy had gathered from Ormer would at least be adequate to cast doubt on anything that Brinze might have in mind. Old files and old inhabitants disappeared from Jimmy's thoughts. The next train back!

Jimmy arrived in New York in a state of mental breathlessness. He had to tell someone his discoveries. It was hard for him not to confide in the conductor and his fellow-passengers. He almost told the taxi driver who drove him to his apartment. He almost told the doorman.

This thing had to be talked over. Hugh would be the man to hear about it. Hugh had been skeptical of the value of the Charleston trip, and he certainly would be surprised to hear what it had yielded.

"Been in Charleston?" asked Hugh, almost jeeringly.

"I have," asserted Jimmy.

"Bring back the murderer with you?"

"No—but—"

He couldn't resist the impulse.

"When did you break that razor blade?"

"The boy detective at it again! This morning."

"I thought so. That cut near your ear looks like the work of a safety razor blade chipped at the corners. You want to be more careful with your self-stropper."

"I'll admit all that," laughed Hugh. "Tell me what you found."

Jimmy retailed Ormer's short history of Payne's career.

Hugh regarded him quietly as he finished.

"My boy," he admonished, "go back to work. I don't pretend to be a sleuth. I don't know anything about the fine art of crime detection. But all that I can see in this lurid tale of yours is an episode in the life of a man who probably went through more than one such experience. Still, I don't say it was a fool's errand. The change of air seems to have done you good."

"Oh, you don't understand and don't want to understand," retorted Jimmy.

"Probably I don't. As I say, it's out of my field. And let me give you a little sound medical advice. Now that you've worked off all this emotional energy, resume your regular way of living and forget the rest. You're a little late, anyhow."

Late! Jimmy felt himself tingling.

"Well—how am I late?"

"There's been a coroner's inquest, finding death at the hands of persons unknown. Payne's will has been offered for probate. He left almost everything to institutions. And there's been an arrest in the case. You may credit yourself with it indirectly, for if you hadn't got this man Brinze excited, the whole affair would have passed over by now."

"Yes—but who—who is it?"

Hugh smiled tantalizingly.

"Gulvin," he said. "They found him searching Payne's room two nights ago."

Jimmy stamped his foot in confusion.

"You see," added Hugh, "while you were hunting ghosts in the sunny South, the practical detective managed to get down to cases."

VIII
SHADOWS

Jimmy surprised Hugh by his high spirits on hearing of the arrest of Gulvin.

"Couldn't be better," Jimmy laughed. "Of course, he would land on Gulvin."

"Why 'of course'?" demanded Hugh. "There's no 'of course' about it. Gulvin, as I told you, was found rummaging around Payne's rooms."

"What was he looking for?"

"I don't know anything about that. Brinze declined to tell the papers anything more, and I don't think he would have told them about Gulvin's arrest if Gulvin hadn't beaten him to it."

"Where is Gulvin? In the county jail?"

"If that's where they keep them, that's where Gulvin is."

"He won't be there long."

Jimmy gazed thoughtfully out of the window.

"There's one point you might help me to clear up, doctor," he remarked. "I've been persecuting Brinze with Payne's revolver. To your knowledge, did he ever own one?"

"How should I know that?" demanded Hugh. "He must have owned, begged, borrowed or stolen one to shoot himself with it!"

"Oh-h!"

Jimmy resumed his research through the window.

"You still believe it was suicide?"

"Yes, I do," responded the physician, "and anybody not obsessed with crime hunting or persecuted by crime hunters would have the same opinion."

He smiled benignly.

"It's none of my business," he went on, "to tell you what you ought to be doing except in a medical way, but, as man to man, don't you think you're wasting a lot of time?"

"No, I don't!"

Jimmy jumped up from his chair.

"And I'll prove it to you yet," he added, as he went rather abruptly out of the office.

The next move wasn't altogether apparent. The arrest of Gulvin was characteristic of the local detective who had his own methods, although Brinze wasn't like the local detective who had cooperated grudgingly with Bernard Gartlin. Gulvin had an alibi. He was several miles away at the time that the shooting took place, and there were plenty of witnesses. Why he had searched Payne's room wasn't explicable at this moment, but Jimmy had a notion. "Chairchez la femm," as Brinze put it. It would be a simple matter to exonerate Gulvin if Gulvin couldn't extricate himself from the enforced hospitality of the country jail. He put Gulvin out of his mind.

Tonight he would interview a more important witness. Meanwhile, he would relax by reading the diary of Samuel Pepys, as agreeable a sedative as ever was at the disposal of man.

But Pepys received little attention. Jimmy skimmed through the small accumulation of mail on his desk and tossed away, unopened, the efforts of mail order men to attract his attention. He was a poor name for a mailing list. Only a plain envelope with a badly typewritten address interested him. A small folded sheet, also typewritten, fluttered from the envelope.

EVERYBODY IS LAUGHING AT YOUR SILLY DE-
TECTIVE STUNTS. YOU'D BETTER DROP THEM?
OR IT WILL BE THE WORSE FOR YOU. ONE WHO
KNOWS.

Jimmy gaped at the note. For a moment it seemed as though his senses had been paralyzed. Then he found himself in a state of amazing calm, studying the note with a smile. This might easily be a practical joke. The use of capital letters was artificial. It was obviously the trick of someone who wanted the letter to look like a bona-fide threat. The question mark was perplexing. Probably it was part of the scheme to make this a Black Hand counterfeit.

He locked up the note and its envelope in his little strong box.

Nothing could be done about the note now, at any rate.

He smoothed out his evening clothes and prepared to go to Shuffle Inn. Eddie Endle, at least, didn't know that he was following the Payne affair, and he might know something about Payne's entanglements. It would be necessary to examine more thoroughly all of the guests at the party. Brinze was saving him the trouble of questioning Gulvin, but Gulvin was of no significance in the matter.

He went into the street in search of a taxi. As usual, there was none in sight. He started for Broadway. It occurred to him that he had dressed too rapidly and he stopped to adjust his tie, using a window as a mirror. He noticed a man across the street stopping to stare at him. It was a tall, thin, shabby figure with a dirty panama hat pulled far over the face. Jimmy turned around sharply to inspect the man, who averted his head as Jimmy faced in his direction and slumped nonchalantly down the street.

Turning the corner, Jimmy looked back and perceived that the man was following him.

"Shadowed?"

The melodramatic thought came to him and wouldn't down. He walked a few blocks, passing several inviting taxis. Then he wheeled about. His shadow was still with him. First the note, and now a shadow. The pursuer was becoming the pursued.

The persistence of the seedy figure increased Jimmy's interest in his quest. It was only meet that the detective should be stalked by an unknown adversary. He was tempted to whirl about, grasp the shadow, rip off the panama and demand to know his business.

"Now, in the stories," he reflected, "they don't do that. It would end the story prematurely. But I'll take a whack at this mannikin and see what he means—if anything."

He performed a correct military about-face and marched briskly and directly to the shadow. The shadow, at Jimmy's approach, faltered and suddenly ran for a Broadway car. He boarded the red vehicle as Jimmy tried to follow him and the car went uptown.

"My clew would be to hail, as they say, a taxi," Jimmy muttered, "follow the car, and grab him when he gets off.

"But," he added out loud, "to hell with him."

He lifted his straw hat in gay apology to two middle-aged matrons who positively bounced as they heard his cheerful damnation of the shadow.

And now the long, long trail went winding into Bellechester again and from Bellechester across the glazed roads that led not to Olean but Shuffle Inn. It was early for the restaurant, and only a few respectable patrons hauled one another across the floor as Eddie's orchestra tootled plaintively boisterous melodies into the empty cuddle corners of the institution.

Jimmy took a table near the band and perfunctorily ordered an orangeade. Two dollars, he thought, was enough to spend in this hostel. He sat facing Eddie and looking fascinatedly at the curious gyrations which accompanied Eddie's performance. The rhythm apparently seized Eddie and tormented him, forcing him to sway back and forth as it impinged on various parts of his body. Eddie's shining saxophone indicated the tempo for his assistants and sparkled like a gargantuan firefly through the artificial dusk of Shuffle Inn. Jimmy's eyes followed the magnetic horn. Suddenly his gaze became intense and he concentrated on the lower side of the instrument. He almost stood on his head in his efforts to examine one certain spot. The waiters were a little uneasy about his contortions, for few patrons of Shuffle Inn stood on their heads before midnight.

The scattered handclaps didn't encourage Eddie's entourage to respond with an encore, and Eddie left the platform. Jimmy greeted him cordially.

"Why—hello."

Eddie seemed a trifle startled to see Jimmy.

"Haven't seen you since he died," he remarked lamely.

The "he" was almost superstitious in its inflection.

"Too bad, wasn't it?" commented Jimmy.

"A shame."

Eddie's superlatives were not the strongest.

"You know," he went on, "I was sort o' shocked when I saw you just then. Last time you was here was the time he died and seein' you there sort o' brought it all back, if you know what I mean."

Jimmy was disappointed. He had hoped that Eddie's momentary tremor was in some way connected with the mystery, and it was nothing more than the shudder which a certain type of person manifests on meeting anything or anybody associated even remotely with a sudden death.

Eddie and Jimmy sat at a little table back of the palms about the podium.

"I see some of 'em says he didn't do it himself," observed Eddie, by way of making pleasant conversation.

"What do you think?"

Jimmy's eyes were unnecessarily severe and his jaw was needlessly squared as he fired this question.

"How'm I to know anything about it?" asked Eddie, naïvely. "I don't see why a man who's got everything he wants and then some wants to go off and end it all, and then again maybe there was something none of us knows nothin' about. It's too deep for me. I don't make it."

"Did you ever hear him speak of—suicide?"

Eddie wrinkled his brow.

"Can't say I did. No, he was cheerful enough, I guess. Of course, his bum shoulder sort o' made him cranky sometimes, but I never heard him say nothin' about wantin' to end it."

"Suppose—now I'm just asking this as a hypothetical question—"

"A what?"

Eddie hated highbrows.

"Let's just pretend," Jimmy said in mincing irony, "that Payne was afraid of someone."

"Aw, he wasn't afraid of nobody," scoffed Eddie. "He had guts!"

"I made no aspersions on his entrails," Jimmy demurred. "No, I'm just saying—mightn't he have had some enemy who wanted to see him out of the way?"

"We all got guys who don't like us," philosophized Eddie. "That guy Herschman over at Fig Leaf Terrace is sore as hell because I got this job when he was biddin' for it, but that wouldn't make me lose no sleep."

"Herschman wouldn't want to put you out of the way," suggested Jimmy.

"If he ever tried anything dirty," announced Eddie, with a near snarl, "I'd hand him a young rap in the puss."

Jimmy wondered whether this formula might not well be applied to Blake Hesbe. Even a middle-aged rap would incapacitate that unprepossessing Romeo. But Hesbe was a problem to be considered later.

"But if it were a row over a woman," Jimmy continued.

"If you're talkin' about me," said Eddie, "I don't get in no rows over women; I get in rows *with* 'em. If you're talkin' about Payne, he didn't have to have no rows. When he wanted 'em he got 'em. He had technique."

Eddie was proud of his imported two-syllable word.

"By the way," Jimmy remarked, glancing at the platform, "what kind of saxophone are you using tonight?"

"That's an E flat," explained Eddie. "I like it for straight stuff. Later on you'll hear a baby sax that'll make you feel lovin' as hell, but this old bird's a good reliable old horse."

Jimmy craved an inspection of Pegasus, the bird-horse. Eddie put the instrument in his hands.

"Now, if you're anything like the rest o' the customers," he said, "you'll ask me if it's hard to play and I'll tell you it is. Funny thing—every man you meet wants to play a sax. If that's on your mind, lay off it. It's an overcrowded profession. Lot's more money for beginners in tubas; especially if you double on the bull fiddle."

"I wasn't looking for a new vocation," explained Jimmy.

He ran his fingers over a monogram on the lower side of the horn.

"I see you have it initialed."

"I'll say I have! People are so crazy about saxes they steal so many you can't hardly get insurance on 'em."

"Where did you have this monogram put on?"

"I've got that on all my saxes—all nine of 'em. You ought to see a little melody sax I bought off a guy in the Philharmonic—I guess you know what that is—the other day. It's a pip. I didn't like the mouthpiece, but when I get a new one, it'll make Herschman's sax sound like an old woman hollerin' for a hot-water bottle."

Jimmy had no interest in Fig Leaf Terrace's Mr. Herschman.

"Where did you say you had them monogrammed?" he ventured.

"Down at Wicker's. That's in Maiden Lane. I get a lot of jewelry off him and he done this as a favor. If you want to get some good lookin' rocks, that's a fine place to get 'em."

"Wicker's, did you say?"

"Yes, Wicker's. Ask for a lanky guy named Keats. Tell him you're a friend o' mine and he'll sure treat you right."

"I'll do that."

Jimmy fretted. At least a part of his solution lay at Wicker's—possibly in the hands of the attenuated Keats—and he would have to wait until morning to pursue his inquiries.

"Give 'em a fox," remarked Eddie, rising. "Dead crowd this time o' night. Waitin' for somebody?"

"No—I'm alone."

"Pickin's ain't so good this early. Wait till 'round eleven and I'll tip you off to somethin' hot."

Jimmy smiled at Eddie's imputations.

"No—I'll be taking an early train back," he answered. "I was feeling a little blue tonight, and I like to hear you play."

While Eddie's cohorts were declaiming lyrically the virtues of somebody's eyes, Jimmy slipped out of Shuffle Inn and went over the roads that led to New York. He thought that he might doze on the train but Eddie's identification of Wicker's as the jewelry shop in which his instrument had been embellished had induced an excitement which precluded slumber.

"Brinze is out of luck," he ruminated, as the train clattered along. "What hunch was it that led me to Shuffle Inn tonight? Endle's monogram and Payne's were the work of the same hand. Now, if Wicker's can tell me who had that revolver initialed—"

Why not Eddie?

He had never thought of the saxophone king as a murderer. Eddie had even betrayed a mild shock at seeing Jimmy tonight.

"Now that," he went on, "is the sort of thing that Bernard Gartlin always threw out. In the stories, you can ask a man whether he thinks it's going to rain and his face blanches. Every time somebody turns pale, or speaks in a broken voice, that's a clew. Only, it's never a clew that works.

"No, Jimmy—Endle had no more to do with this than Gulvin. You've run across a piece of circumstantial evidence. The saxophone and the gun were monogrammed in the same store. Which doesn't mean that every customer of Wicker's is a murderer."

Nothing could be done about it until morning—and yet the initials on the revolver wouldn't go from his mind. He brooded over the possibilities of the monogram until the train reached the Grand Central Station. Still mulling over the problem, he stepped into a taxi and went riding up Fifth Avenue.

A jarring stop interrupted his meditations. He saw the driver step from his seat and raise the hood of the machine. The delay made Jimmy fretful. He hated to be held up en route anywhere. Impatiently he lit a cigarette and resumed his contemplation of events past and revelations to come.

Finally the taxi jerked on its way through Central Park, and deposited Jimmy at his door.

He tried to read the meter, but the light was poor. "How much?" he asked the driver.

The man lit a match and held it before the clock. And then Jimmy lost all interest in the fare. The man driving the taxi was his shadow!

IX
BRASS TACKS

"I have a little shadow who goes in and out with me, but what can be the use of him is more than I can see?"

Jimmy changed the rhyme thoughtfully. The shadow, whoever he might be, was an expert in the art of concealing his features, and his appearance on the driver's seat of the taxi was a triumph of ubiquity. Shadows usually turned out to be villains in disguise. (See *The Pumblewaite Legacy*.) Sometimes they were helpful detectives ready to intercept the powerful malefactor. (See *The Rosenbaum Case*.) That this long slender figure was a detective was improbable, and that it was a really well-equipped villain was unlikely.

"You were searching Payne's rooms," he continued.

"But *what* can be the use of him is more" than Jimmy could decide at the moment. He was impressed with his own stolidity in the face—or possibly in the lack of a face—of a phenomenon which sometimes made even the imperturbable Gartlin show "fine lines of care." The story books were coming to life, were bringing life to him—*were* life!

The doorman told Jimmy that he was to call Mr. Brinze at Bellechester as soon as he came in.

"Well, I'm glad I can lay my hands on you," exclaimed the voice of Brinze, "even at this hour. We're getting down to brass tacks now, and as you started this business, you might as well be in on the finish."

Jimmy noted the exultant tone of the local detective. It convinced him that the finish was not so near as Brinze imagined.

"Going to hang Danny Deever or Gulvin or somebody?" he inquired.

"Don't be a fool!"

Brinze's voice cracked angrily.

"All I've got to say to you now," the detective continued, "is that I know all I want to know, and I'm going to have an informal examination tomorrow morning at ten. I want everybody who was a guest at the party in my office at that hour, and that means you, too."

"Very good of you to invite me."

"Don't try to be so damn funny!"

Brinze was in the worst of humor.

"I might as well tell you now that we'll have the newspapermen in on this," he went on, "and I'll show them what's what."

"*What's* what?"

"You'll know all about that in the morning!"

Jimmy could picture Brinze slamming the receiver on the hook viciously. He smiled as he went to bed and woke up the next morning with a keen appetite for the proceedings. He looked out of the window for his shadow. The shadow was eating a late breakfast, apparently. He wasn't there.

As Jimmy scrutinized the menu at the dairy restaurant around the corner, one of the shadow's stratagets became clear. The shadow hadn't been the driver who had started from Grand Central. When the alleged break-down occurred, the shadow had replaced the chauffeur.

"I wonder," Jimmy confided to his eggs, "whether he thought of that himself or whether he read it somewhere and tried it out."

Brinze's inquisition was a grim echo of the animated party which Payne had arranged. Gulvin had the conventional pallor which results from incarceration, even in the county jail. Mrs. Gulvin wept gushily. Claire looked solemn, beautiful and unhappy. Hesbe still appeared to be the recipient of the double blank when the dominoes of life were distributed. Eddie was Eddie. And Hugh sat about calmly but obviously anxious to get back to more interesting duties.

Brinze, in full glory resplendent, seated himself behind his desk, and rapped for attention, as though he was convocating the House of Lords. Heidelman and three blasé reportorial associates sat at a table which Brinze had designated as reserved for the press.

"First of all," began Brinze, "I want to say that this is unofficial. I admit that the proceeding is unusual, but we're not going to get anywhere with cut-and-dried methods."

He waited for this manifesto to impress the reporters.

"The only thing that interests me," he proceeded, "is to get at the bottom of this business. I want the facts. And I intend to get them."

Another flourish to the press.

"I don't expect anybody to say anything which might tend to incriminate or degrade them. I'm not going to put anybody under oath. But I'm after the facts, and I'm going to get them or know the reason why!"

What meat, Jimmy asked, had this Cæsar fed on?

"All that passes here, gentlemen of the press, must be regarded as confidential. I'm willing to take the newspapers into my confidence, but I don't want a word of this printed until I say so. Is that clear?"

He glowered at the four reporters.

"It's clear," growled a stout reporter, "but what the hell use is all this?"

Brinze was palpably shocked, but expressed his contempt only by a withering shake of his head.

"Mr. Gulvin!"

Gulvin rose in his place. He was white and he rubbed his fingers nervously.

"Now, Mr. Gulvin," Brinze began, "do you admit that you visited Mr. Payne's rooms since his death?"

Gulvin gulped and nodded.

"Very good."

"What's very good about that?" interrupted Jimmy.

"I'll show you in a minute!"

Brinze brought his fist down on the desk, injured it against the edge and sucked his hand unmagisterially.

"I'm conducting this examination," he snapped. "Anyone who has questions to ask may do so at the proper time."

"You were searching Payne's rooms," he continued. "Now, Mr. Gulvin, just what did you expect to find there?"

"I refuse to answer that," declared Gulvin. "I object to these proceedings."

"Maybe you'd prefer to answer to the examining magistrate," sneered Brinze.

"I certainly would!"

"Sit down!"

Brinze shut off Gulvin's examination with as much drama as he could command.

"Mrs. Gulvin!" he bellowed.

His manner now became oleaginous.

"Mrs. Gulvin," he smirked, "you don't want to see you husband prosecuted, do you?"

"Of course she doesn't!" interpolated Jimmy. "Why not ask her whether she'd like to have him electrocuted?"

"Now you shut up!"

Brinze apologized to the press for his lapse from dignity.

"We must have order," he explained.

"Now, Mrs. Gulvin"—several more gallons of oil entered the stream of talk—"will you tell us what you know about your husband's relations with Payne?"

"Don't you answer!" cried Gulvin.

"I won't!" confirmed his wife lachrymosely.

Jimmy rose.

"Mr. Brinze," he said, "I'm confident that I can clear up this angle of the case if you'll let me ask Mrs. Gulvin a few questions."

"I'm conducting this—"

"Let him ask them!" growled the fat reporter. The press backed him up with assenting grunts. Brinze spread his hands on the desk helplessly.

"Go ahead," he said grudgingly. "If it brings us any nearer the truth—"

His resignation was magnificent.

"Mrs. Gulvin," Jimmy began, "you were interested in the Posey Theatre or the Cosey Theatre or some such enterprise?"

"Indeed, yes," she acknowledged in relief. "The little theater is something for which I am fighting."

"Now *that*," Jimmy declared, "is *very* good. Oh, you'll agree with me, Mr. Brinze. Furthermore, Mrs. Gulvin, you had hoped to interest our late friend in the worthy project of endowing one of these artistic institutions?"

"Ah, but it's too late now!" she sobbed. "And he was *so* interested!"

"And you wrote him letters on the subject?" continued Jimmy, sympathetically. "Nice, long, enthusiastic letters?"

"He asked me to put it in writing."

"Thank you. Mr. Gulvin, will you answer me two innocent questions?"

"If they seem proper—and only if they seem proper."

"They'll be most proper. These proceedings being strictly unconventional, I'll ask you to recall that you told me that your wife was given to extravagances of expression in promoting her dramatic projects."

"Yes, but is this relevant?"

"Nothing could be more so. And you knew that she was in communication with Mr. Payne on the matter?"

"Of course."

"Then," concluded Jimmy, "you feared that her letters to Mr. Payne might contain language which might be misconstrued in print. And you thought you'd rescue those letters before they became public property. Am I right?"

Gulvin blushed and nodded.

"Mr. Brinze," Jimmy remarked, "I have established the motive for Mr. Gulvin's researches among the effects of the deceased. His extra-legal methods, I admit, were not what we might have expected from so distinguished a legislator, but if you are holding him on no other grounds—"

He sat down.

"That's what I call sense!" declared the stout reporter.

Brinze was plainly beaten in the Gulvin matter. "I don't see what business it is of yours," he grunted. "Nobody asked you to defend him."

"I thought," suggested Jimmy pleasantly, "that you were anxious to get at the facts or know the reason why, and I've tried to bring out the facts and the reason why."

"That's enough of that, Mr. Wrome," announced Brinze. "There are other witnesses. Mr. Hesbe."

Blake shambled to his feet, stroking his smooth blond hair.

"What, Mr. Hesbe," said Brinze, "can you tell us that might help us to find a solution for the so-called mystery surrounding the death of Mr. Payne."

Hesbe twisted his hair.

"Why—I don't know anything. All I know is I was at the party and went out dancing with the rest of them later and next morning I heard he was dead."

"Have you any theories?"

"No—I don't know as I have."

"Maybe," Brinze commented sarcastically, "our friend Mr. Wrome would like to question Mr. Hesbe."

"There's nothing that I want to ask Mr. Hesbe now," said Jimmy coldly. "He's told his story very illuminatingly, I think."

"That's all, Mr. Hesbe."

Brinze eliminated Hesbe.

"Miss Barton."

Claire steadied herself against a chair, and Brinze repeated his formula for information.

"I don't know anything about it," she said softly.

Jimmy felt an uncomfortable thrill at hearing her voice again.

"Would this witness suit you, Mr. Wrome?" inquired Brinze.

"I once asked Miss Barton some questions," murmured Jimmy. "That was long ago. At least a month ago. I don't believe that Miss Barton cares to have traffic with me."

Claire didn't look at him.

"That surely is unfortunate," grinned Brinze. "That will be all, Miss Barton."

Eddie proved to be a slightly more loquacious but equally uninformative witness, and Hugh merely confirmed the medical verdict of suicide. The reporters were restless.

"It's getting late," asserted the stout one. "Where's the story?"

"What about that gun?" asked Heidelman.

"Mr. Wrome is the authority on the gun," replied Brinze. "What about the gun, Mr. Wrome?"

Jimmy smiled cryptically.

"This is your show, Mr. Brinze," he said. "I've nothing to add to what I told Mr. Heidelman."

The impasse annoyed Brinze. He rose and announced that he was through for the morning, that there would be another session later on, that the reporters were pledged to print nothing that had taken place, and that he wished them a good morning.

"Just a minute," interrupted Jimmy. "Is Mr. Gulvin still a prisoner?"

"He can go to hell for all I care." shouted Brinze, "and you, too."

It was a gloomy party that took the 2.17 back to New York. Only Mrs. Gulvin was animated, and she seemed to be on the verge of publishing her husband's recent activities to the souls condemned to ride on this train. Her husband restrained her almost by violence and lectured sullenly on the maladministration of law in Bellechester. At the next session in Albany, he would have something to say!

Jimmy deliberately chose the car ahead of Claire and Hesbe. His constant activity had diffused the impression which Claire had made on his mind, and he could think of her almost calmly, yet he preferred not to sit too near his whilom love. He didn't yet trust his nerves. He was amused at Brinze's blundering examination. At least Brinze had fitted his role of local detective. His posturings, his thunderings, his smirkings and his fine gestures to the newspapermen had been a diverting spectacle.

As the train plodded along, Jimmy strolled to the smoking car. He passed Claire, purposely looking aside, but a soft "Jimmy" called him back. Hesbe was not in the car, and Claire's blue eyes were pained and imploring. Jimmy stood irresolutely for a moment, and then sat beside her.

"Jimmy," she whispered hurriedly, "I haven't been fair to you."

He shrugged his shoulders. Claire, as ever, was unanswerable. Of course she hadn't been fair to him! What had he done to deserve his sudden *coup de grace?* But what could he say to her?

"Jimmy," she went on, more calmly, "I know you think I'm heartless. But there are things one can't explain. When I asked you not to see me, I didn't mean to be cruel, Jimmy. I've felt terrible about it, and it's been on my mind. I didn't want you to think—"

This incoherent apology had a strange sound to it. There was something else on her mind.

A latent pugnacity suddenly overwhelmed Jimmy. "Look here!"

He was amazed at the asperity in his voice, and not at all displeased with it.

"You know as well as I do that you're not much worried about my feelings. If you had been, you wouldn't have acted the way you did. So, young lady, let's set aside apologetics and get down, as our friend Brinze so crisply says, to brass tacks."

"I don't know what you mean!"

"They always say 'I don't know what you mean' at this stage."

"Where do they always say it?"

Claire's voice had wonder in it and alarm.

"In detective stories."

"*What* are you talking about?"

"You'll find out!"

"Jimmy," she said, "I really don't know what all of this means. But I want you to be my friend. I'm frightened, Jimmy."

"Of what?"

"Oh, please don't ask me!"

He nodded as though he understood.

"Only—whatever happens—please—be my friend!"

She was sobbing now.

"Of course I'll be your friend," said Jimmy, reassuringly. "But I thought you'd adopted another—and better—friend."

Claire began to weep. Jimmy sat with her for a moment and discovered that he was no longer militant. He couldn't press his questions now. He had gone too far with his assault on her emotions. He left her silently and continued his broken journey to the smoking car.

As he passed into the next car, he encountered Hesbe, apparently returning from the smoker. He couldn't resist the temptation to speak to his detested rival.

"Miss Barton needs you, I think," he remarked caustically.

Hesbe stopped and regarded him sourly.

"What have you been saying to her?" he demanded.

"Nothing of consequence," Jimmy answered lightly.

"Now look here," said Hesbe, his thin voice displaying a tremolo as he tried to sound important, "you think everybody's a fool except yourself. But I've been watching you up there with her, and I want to tell you to keep away."

"Are you going to tell me that I ain't done right by your Nell?" inquired Jimmy.

"I'm just telling you to keep away," reiterated Hesbe, shaking a wavering finger at Jimmy. "I'm not going to have anybody hanging around the woman who's going to be my wife."

The piping announcement crashed into Jimmy's consciousness with terrific force. He stood in front of Hesbe like a pugilist waiting for the blow that is to bring senselessness. Jimmy was aware that the tow-headed figure shambled away from him with a final gesture, but something seemed to be wrong with his eyes. Finally he clenched his fists and worked his way into the smoking car, walking unsteadily, as though the ground beneath him were trembling. He discerned Hugh, smoking his familiar pipe, and dropped into the seat beside him.

"You look like a ghost," said Hugh. "What's wrong?"

"Claire's—Claire's engaged to Hesbe," Jimmy gasped.

Hugh put his firm hand on Jimmy's shoulder.

"Don't take it so hard," he counseled. "I know it's a mean thing to hear, but it happens to almost everybody, and it's all a part of life. A year from now you'll wonder what you saw in her."

Jimmy slumped miserably.

"A year from now!" he cried. "A year from now! I wish to God it was a year from now!"

"Buck up," Hugh went on. "She's gone and you can dismiss her from your mind. It's all for the best. She started you on your wild adventures. She got you into this mystery mess. Forget it all."

"Forget it all!" Jimmy echoed bitterly. "It's not so easy to forget! Hesbe, of all people!"

He brooded and puffed morosely on his cigarette as the train neared the station. Hugh insisted on taking him home in a taxi. Jimmy left him without a word. He entered his apartment and lay on the bed. The bright sunshine disturbed him. He went to lower the shade. A thin figure outside the house made him release the cord, and the shade fluttered up with a smash.

"So he's with us again!" muttered Jimmy.

He watched the seedy man whose face still was hidden by the battered panama hat. The shadow paced up and down the street always looking front.

"I wonder whether he's trying to get on my nerves—as though there were room for anything more," Jimmy mumbled. "I wonder—"

There was a note on his desk-pad—"Wicker's." Jimmy crossed it through as he sat at the telephone and ordered a taxi. Then he pulled an old gray overcoat and a worn felt hat from a closet. He put them on and grinned. Then he stuffed an outing cap in his pocket, and answered the ring of the house telephone by hurrying downstairs and into the taxi.

X
ONE OF THOSE CLEWS

"Drive uptown fast," Jimmy instructed the driver, "and I'll tell you where to on the way."

The mystified chauffeur saluted and sped along Broadway. Jimmy removed his overcoat and felt hat and put on his cap.

"We're going to be followed," he told the driver, "but we've got a good start."

He glanced back. The shadow would have to pick up a taxi in the street, and the delay would give Jimmy time to execute his scheme.

"Drop me at the Ninety-Sixth Street Subway," he went on, handing the man a bill, "and drive right on for a mile or so."

He propped up the coat and hat against the back window of the cab.

"It worked in *The Rosenbaum Case*," he ruminated. "Why not now?"

He jumped from the door at the subway station and hurried down the stairs into a downtown express. Whether the shadow followed the taxi or whether he had seen him leave it made little difference now. At least he could go to Wicker's without being followed.

Keats was on duty, and mention of Endle made him communicative.

"Yes, Mr. Endle is one of our best customers," said Keats. "I sold him some mighty fine stickpins last week. He certainly must be making money."

"He's a very fine saxophone player," remarked Jimmy.

"Very fine," agreed Keats.

"You don't happen to sell saxophones?" inquired Jimmy.

"Well, that's hardly in our line."

"I only asked because Mr. Endle told me you monogrammed his for him."

"Oh, yes—we monogram anything."

Jimmy drew out his watch.

"I was wondering whether you could put my initials on this."

"Surest thing you know."

"What styles of monograms have you?"

Keats produced a card. Jimmy pointed to 7-A, which corresponded with the design on Eddie's instrument and Payne's revolver.

"Is that a popular style?"

"Yes, but not for watches. It's a little big for watches."

"Better for saxophones?"

Keats laughed.

"Good for saxophones, loving cups, roast beef platters, and almost anything big enough to carry it."

"I wonder whether it would go well on an old revolver I have home."

Jimmy fumbled with his cap, in apparent shyness.

"Do people have revolvers engraved?" he asked cautiously.

"Well, not so much. People don't carry guns as much as they used to. But, come to think of it, I had a customer a few weeks ago who had a revolver monogrammed with this very design."

"Really!"

Jimmy was working hard to restrain his curiosity.

"And the funny thing about it was, it was a woman. Some looker, too!"

Keats seemed to enjoy looking back on his pulchritudinous client.

"Do women carry revolvers?" Jimmy asked innocently.

"She was so good looking, I wouldn't blame her. She might have been a Follies girl or something."

"Well, that's one Follies girl I'd better look out for," Jimmy commented. "A jealous blonde, I suppose."

"Blonde is right," assented Keats.

The jaunty look faded from Jimmy's face. The thought which had come to him was anything but pleasant. He shifted his position so that he was in the shadow. He was afraid that he was betraying his thoughts, and he didn't want Keats to ask counter-questions.

"It must have been Lillian—Peabody," he volunteered, as airily as he could.

Keats looked surprised.

"I don't know Lillian Peabody," he said, "but if that's the name of a swell blonde, that's the girl. Those were the initials."

"L. P.?"

"Yes, L. P. I guess you know 'em all, brother."

Jimmy forced himself to ask another question.

"Did her hair come out under her hat in a sort of band?"

"It certainly did! Look out for Lillian!"

Jimmy's ghastly guess had been correct. Claire had had this revolver monogrammed with Payne's initials. He was aware of Keats' curious gaze.

"Well, well," he said. "Well, well."

"Hope you're insured," remarked Keats.

"Quite so."

Jimmy laid the watch on the counter.

"You can put my monogram on this," he said. "J. W. I'll call back when it's ready."

Keats made out a slip.

"By the way," asked Jimmy, "*was* her name Lillian—er, Peabody?"

"Darned if I know," answered Keats, handing him the paper. "I just gave her a ticket like this with a number on it."

Jimmy stumbled into the street. Beyond doubt, Claire was involved in the murder of Leed Payne. The identification wasn't complete, but it was staggeringly clear. He was about to go home, but he couldn't. He would have to find why Claire had the revolver monogrammed. And if she really did have a hand in Payne's death—the thoughts bounded maddeningly—what could have been her motive? He could have sworn that she had had no relations with the dead banker. If she did it, it was for another person. But for whom?

"They always do it to save the fine old father's honor."

The postulate, gathered from the adventures of Bernard Gartlin, irritated him. And yet, consider old man Barton. He had lost money in recent years. Jimmy had met him only once, but he recalled him as a prematurely bowed gentleman, who always looked sad. He had, like the heroine in the song, seen better days. Perhaps he had lost his fortune in Payne's offices. The idea was almost too pat, and yet the obvious often was true. Had Payne ruined Barton and had Claire taken it on herself to avenge him? Too melodramatic. Yet, melodramatic or not, the notion persisted. And if Claire, upset by her venture into murder, had decided that she must break with all her friends, would that not explain her quixotic attitude? It must have been just after the revolver had been monogrammed that she had ordered Jimmy never to try to see her again. But there was Hesbe.

In his bewilderment, Jimmy sought Hesbe's office. Hesbe did a small brokerage business from a little two-room suite in John Street. Jimmy would draw from Hesbe further information about Claire's family. If Hesbe was going to marry her, Jimmy thought, he ought to know something of the family history.

Hesbe glared at Jimmy as he entered the office.

"I came to apologize," explained Jimmy, humbly. "I've been a little excited lately and maybe I said some things I shouldn't have."

Hesbe's pale eyes looked up vacantly.

Jimmy extended his hand.

"I want to apologize," he said, "and I want to congratulate you. Miss Barton's a wonderful girl."

He marveled at the return of his poise.

"Thanks."

Hesbe seemed to have nothing more to say.

"I'm sure her parents are very happy," Jimmy went on smoothly.

He assumed a fine air of heartiness.

"I suppose you'll be going into business with Mr. Barton now," he remarked.

"He isn't in business," said Hesbe, glad to show superior knowledge.

"Isn't he? I thought he was."

"Not for a long time. Things went wrong and he quit."

"Wasn't Mrs. Barton's family wealthy?"

It was an outrageous bluff, and Jimmy knew it.

"No."

"I thought they came from Boston and owned some big—"

What big thing could they own?

"Some big furniture stores up there," Jimmy finished.

"That's wrong."

Hesbe spoke authoritatively.

"Mrs. Barton came from Charleston," he explained.

Again the thoughts popped in Jimmy's brain.

"Ah, yes," he remarked, putting his hands in his pockets to create a nonchalant effect. "The name was something like Nagle, wasn't it?"

He could have brained Hesbe for his deliberation in answering.

"No. It was Nagleby."

"That's right!"

Jimmy almost shouted at Hesbe.

"And they left Charleston about twenty-five years ago?"

He was balancing himself alternately on one foot and the other.

"Yes."

Hesbe was indifferent to Jimmy's increasing excitement.

"Well—good luck, old man!"

Jimmy thrust a perfunctory handshake on Hesbe and scurried to the street.

"Good luck, old man!"

He laughed.

He became sober, and started slowly for the subway.

"This next interview," he told himself, "isn't going to be quite so easy."

XI
CÆSAR'S FIANCÉE

Memories of brief refusals over the telephone and of letters unanswered determined Jimmy's course. He would have to see Claire. No matter what the interview might bring forth, it was imperative that he question her. The elusive lady would decline to see him if he requested permission. He had not the skill to compose a note which might compel an entrance to her presence There was only one way and that way led directly to Claire's apartment.

The gaudy but neglected lobby of the house didn't deter Jimmy from stepping into the frayed elevator and demanding of the perspiring attendant that he be carried to Barton's corner of the building. "Guests Must Be Announced," proclaimed a dingy card in the elevator, but guests had plied their ways about Cerulean Court for many years with no questions asked. Jimmy rang the bell of 10 E and waited. How many times had he rung this same bell! But the pleasing palpitation which used to prelude his entry into the company of his beloved was gone. There was still a palpitation, but it was scarcely pleasing, and Jimmy couldn't define what it meant.

A rustle from behind the door indicated an answer to his summons. Unwittingly he adjusted his cravat as he used to straighten it in the ages long past—a month ago. And then Claire opened the door.

Jimmy stepped within silently. More than once had a door been shut decisively on the determined mask of Bernard Gartlin. Justice before courtesy was Jimmy's motto. Claire's hand lingered on the door-knob, but Jimmy pushed the door shut with his elbow. In the weak, yellow light of the narrow corridor, Claire stared at him.

Jimmy regarded her sadly. She was as beautiful as ever, but she looked tired tonight and worn out. Her adventure had marked her. The last time that he had been here she had rushed to him with an ineffable smile and welcomed him in rich, laughing tones. And he had responded delightedly, thanking the fates for bringing into his life so wonderful a girl.

Tonight, Claire merely stared and Jimmy returned the stare.

"I'm not here socially," he said, finally. "I have to talk to you. Heaven knows, I don't want to—not about what I have to talk to you about."

It was all snarled, but he didn't care. She leaned against the wall, tapping the shredded carpet with her foot.

"I can't imagine what you want, Jimmy," she remarked finally. "I thought you understood—"

"Oh, that!"

Jimmy laughed impatiently.

"I haven't come to make love to you," he explained, a little surprised by the coldness of his voice. "You asked me not to, and I'm obeying you. This is something much worse."

Claire rubbed her fingers together.

"I really can't see you, Jimmy," she murmured. "Really, I can't. I'm too—too upset."

"I'm upset, too," said Jimmy. "That makes us even. I wish I didn't have to be here tonight. But there's something I must say, and I won't leave before I've said it."

He stopped.

"Anybody home?" he inquired.

"Father and mother are at the movies. I can't see what difference that makes."

"I didn't want anybody to hear what I'm going to ask you."

"Ask me?"

Claire looked pale and horrified.

"Yes. Can't we sit down somewhere?"

She sighed despairingly and led Jimmy into the old-fashioned sitting room. The cheap prints in their haphazard frames seemed to mock him. The last time he was here—but he resolved to put away memories of the last time. He sank into an armchair with broken springs.

"Claire," he began, "I want to ask you a few questions, not as your friend—at least, I'm not asking you to look on me as a friend if you don't care to—"

"I want to be your friend, Jimmy," she said. "I told you on the train—"

"There are things you didn't tell me on the train!" The recollection of Hesbe's threats enraged him. "You didn't tell me you were engaged!"

"To whom?"

She asked the question wonderingly.

"Please don't try to act at me."

He regretted the bark in his voice, but he couldn't control it.

"Hesbe told me."

"What?"

Jimmy began to walk about the room. He couldn't sit still.

"He told me plainly enough that he was going to marry you."

"He had no right—!"

She checked herself suddenly.

"Well, it makes no difference now, I suppose," said Jimmy wearily. "That isn't what I wanted to ask you."

He resumed his none too comfortable seat.

"I want to ask you a few simple questions, not about yourself, but about somebody else.

"Let me smoke, please," he added; "it's sort of calming."

She handed him an ash tray. It was almost like the last time—

"I can't tell you now why I'm asking these questions," he continued. "But you'll lose nothing by answering them. First, what was your mother's maiden name?"

"Nagleby."

Claire's face showed surprise.

"And she came from a little town near Lexington?"

"Yes. Why do you ask?"

"Let's say for information. Some day you may cross-examine me as much as you like on this, and I'll answer every question in as

much detail as you require, but please don't try to go behind the
returns tonight.

"I don't like to do this, Claire," he went on, almost pleadingly. "I
have to. That's all. And you'll understand why before long, I hope.

"Your father came from the same part of the country?"

"No," Claire replied, her fear apparently subsiding. "He came
from Allentown, Pennsylvania, but he met mother while he was
visiting in Charleston."

"And they were married in Charleston?"

"Somewhere near there."

"And they lived in Charleston a long time?"

"No. Oh, why did you ask me that?"

"Please trust me."

"I trust you, but—it's so strange that you should come up here
suddenly tonight and ask me such peculiar questions."

"They're not peculiar. They're very much to the point."

Jimmy reflected. So Claire's mother had been the woman for
love of whom Payne had gone rioting through Charleston on that
eventful night twenty-five years ago. And Barton had been the successful rival who had accompanied Payne into the saloon. And it was
Barton whom Payne had sworn to break, though it took him the rest
of his life. It all dove-tailed only too well.

"Is your father in business now?"

"Yes, in a way. He has desk room downtown and he does a little
commission business in various lines, but he's practically retired.
Father isn't very well."

Jimmy visualized Barton, that unhappy-looking, bent man,
whose fringe of black hair encircled a large bald spot as though it
were the halo of a vanished splendor. Barton said little, and he shuffled about the house quietly, always as if looking forward to a sleep
and a forgetting.

"I'm not asking this next question from curiosity," he continued,
"and it's not polite. But please answer it. Wasn't your father rather
well to do at one time."

Claire bowed her head.

"He lost most of his money downtown," she said softly.

"In Wall Street?"

"He said it went in a venture that didn't turn out well."

"How long ago?"

"I don't know. About five years ago mother and I noticed that he was acting worried about something. He wouldn't tell us what it was. But one day he said that he'd lost a great deal of money—"

She was on the point of tears. Jimmy's admiration for her was great at this moment. What she had revealed had been no disgrace, but it always was humiliating to admit financial reverses, especially reverses incurred in speculation.

"You don't know how I hate to go on," he confessed. "I feel rotten about probing away like this. But try not to worry too much about this question. It's about the last, anyhow. Has your father any friends? I mean—does he see many people?"

"No."

"He's something of a recluse?"

"He—he isn't very well."

"I know that. Claire, please forgive me, but I have to know this. This will be the last and most painful one. Do you know of any reason in your father's past why he should have become so quiet and almost frightened in his manner?"

Claire began to sob. Then she rose angrily.

"I don't know what you mean or what you're driving at!" she cried. "My father's done nothing to be ashamed of. I won't answer another question. I don't know why I've permitted you to go as far as you have! Please go!"

She stamped into the corridor.

Jimmy followed her.

"I didn't intend to insult you," he said, "and I haven't been asking questions to uncover old wounds. I don't suppose I have any right to expect you to understand that, but you will."

"I don't know what's happened to you," she retorted, tearfully, "but I'm sure I don't understand. You've been talking like an amateur detective ever since—"

She stopped suddenly, and stood very straight, waiting for Jimmy to go.

"Why don't you say 'Ever since Payne was murdered'?" he flung at her.

Claire's eyes lost their luster, and she steadied herself against the door.

"Please go," she begged. "I'll break down in a minute if—"

"If I go on?"

His brown eyes were glittering and his jaw had assumed an unwontedly pugnacious angle. "Please—please go!"

She was weeping now. There was no anger in her face, only misery. Jimmy felt that he had behaved too severely.

"I don't want to go and have you think I'm a brute," he said. "I don't want you to think I've come here to persecute you. If I'd known you'd feel this way about it, I'd never have said anything."

"It's too late now," she sobbed bitterly.

"Too late for what?"

"Oh, go! Go!"

She reiterated her command like a chant.

"But I don't want to go and have you think that I'm your enemy."

"I can't think anything now. Only go, please, and don't—"

"'Don't ever come again!'"

Jimmy finished her sentence mockingly.

She nodded wretchedly.

"I'll go," he said finally, "but I don't intend to take your instructions as final. You'll feel differently about things soon. Good night, Claire. Won't you shake hands?"

She disregarded the extended hand.

"Good night," she muttered.

Jimmy sighed as he closed the door behind him. This interview had been a mistake. To be sure, he had learned the identity of Barton, but was it worth while? It established a motive for Claire's connection with the revolver that had ended Payne's life. Perhaps she had shot Payne to protect her father?

The hypothesis didn't fit in with Jimmy's previous ideas, but it seemed painfully logical. There was something in Barton's life which had to be kept hidden. Jimmy had deduced as much from the man's hunted look, and Claire's evasions on the subject were equivalent to confirmation. Payne doubtless knew of this dark spot and was about to bring it to light. The banker had been in a position to know of Barton's ventures in Wall Street. But were they really ventures in Wall

Street? Subtract the "s" from "speculation" and the answer was un-pleasant but apparently accurate. So many men had described their financial vagaries as unsuccessful investments!

Worse than any possible revelation concerning Barton was the loss of Claire. Detective stories had diverted his mind, had brought him into a new and perplexing set of problems, but neither they nor anything that had followed his study of them had eradicated the thought of Claire. Even in her confused, tearful, angry mood she was more attractive than any girl that had come into his life. Love, after all, was a personal equation. One could argue Claire out of one's mind; but when the argument was over, Claire would return insidi-ously. Why couldn't it have been some other girl?

Jimmy pondered the ways of the cosmic disease as he walked the few blocks from Cerulean Court to his apartment. He should have been figuring out the connection of Claire's confessions with the cir-cumstances surrounding the death of Leed Payne. Gartlin had had a way of shutting himself up with this ratiocination on such occasions and emerging with a neatly worked out set of conclusions. But Gar-tlin's author hadn't supplied him with emotions which centered on Claire Barton. Jimmy's author had.

As he approached the entrance to the house, Jimmy saw his shadow again.

"This part of it is going to end now!" he announced to himself.

As he started in the direction of the shadow, the shadow walked easily but rapidly up the street.

Jimmy followed quickly and suddenly broke into a sprint. The shadow also hurried, but Jimmy's speed was too much for the man. Jimmy came up to him and grasped him by the arm. The shadow had a thin arm, the proper arm for a shadow.

"If you try to get away, I'll turn you over to the police," said Jimmy sharply. "Or I'll beat you up and explain why to the nearest magistrate."

The shadow cringed and tried to hide his face. It was a long thin face, with a foolish little mustache on it.

"If you don't think I'm on to you," continued Jimmy, "you lose. You can have your choice. Either you can tell me who's engaged you for this little job or you can break the news to one of our sympathetic judges."

The shadow refused to make any observations. He was edging and sidling and otherwise trying to elude Jimmy's grip. A passerby on the dark street stopped, looked, listened, concluded that an amiable citizen was bearing the burden of an inebriated kinsprit and passed by. Jimmy applied a hammerlock on the shadow and wondered what to do with him.

Gartlin had always had a humorous assistant whose custom it was to bob up when the detective had seized a suspect, bringing an automobile and many waggish profundities. There was no one to aid Jimmy, nor did he know what to do with his captive. He could have found a policeman, but he didn't want the man arrested. He wanted information.

"Come with me," he commanded, "and if you try anything funny, I'll do something even funnier to you. I've been watching your little tours of inspection since they started, and this, I think, is your last one, young man—or old man, or whatever you are."

He applied more pressure and the shadow winced.

"Wait till I really use a little science on you," Jimmy remarked. "Then you'll raise your noble voice in something more than a grunt."

He dragged the man to the apartment house.

"Now, if you'd like to come in quietly and talk this over peacefully, all will be merry," he said. "If not, I'll recruit a few fine, upstanding black hallboys and we'll simply kidnap you."

He punched the man lightly in the ribs.

"Will you come in?"

The shadow grunted assent.

Jimmy relaxed his grip, forgetting Gartlin's maxim that grips should never be relaxed. The shadow deftly wriggled free, and swung an inexpert uppercut at Jimmy's jaw. Jimmy's knowledge of boxing didn't equal his wrestling technique. He swung wildly at the shadow, who whirled about and started to run at amazing speed. Jimmy dived at his head, hoping to hurl him to the ground. The shadow ducked, and Jimmy fell to the ground, clutching something soft and stringy in his hand. The shadow, meanwhile, had turned the corner and was out of sight.

A little dazed by his sudden descent to the pavement, Jimmy scrambled to his feet, and realized that pursuit would be useless.

Angrily he threw the object in his hand to the ground. Then he picked it up again. It was a clew, of course.

The clew proved to be a disheveled false mustache of inferior quality.

"He's certainly a musical comedy shadow," mused Jimmy, as he went slowly to his apartment. "Whoever's putting him up to this must be a librettist."

He sat down to a serious contemplation of his booty. It was an every-day bit of theatrical property, totally undistinguished.

"It ought to have the maker's name, address and telephone number on it," Jimmy thought.

But it had nothing on it except traces of spirit gum and dust.

Jimmy placed the trophy in his strong box to join the threatening letter which had warned him against participating in his search for the murderer. What a legacy for his grandchildren!

The adversary who had engaged the shadow had brought Jimmy into a curious harlequinade. It was almost too fantastic to think of a man with a false mustache carrying on espionage in West 94th Street, New York City. Yet the mysterious figure, alert and elusive, certainly existed in the flesh, if not in very much flesh. Jimmy decided that at the next encounter he would first knock the shadow cold and then investigate.

There was a letter from Brinze.

"We have been following out certain suggestions which you made to this office," ran this official document, "and we have made some important discoveries by following up your leads. We should like to have a conference with you at your early convenience."

Was this a vindication of Jimmy's theories? He had told Brinze little except that the revolver ought to be looked into. That, undoubtedly, was what Brinze had done. And, therefore, Brinze was on the trail of Claire.

"Chairchez la Femm."

The false mustache no longer interested jimmy. Claire was in danger, if Brinze had unearthed the facts about the revolver. Jimmy swore at himself uproariously. If he had had any sense, if he had recalled even the elementary rules of the Man of a Million Masks, he would never have handed over an unexplored clew to a rival. He didn't care about the credit which Brinze would be certain to pre-empt. Brinze was welcome to all of the glory which accrued to the solver of the mystery. But Brinze's next move would be to arrest Claire. He had captured Gulvin with less provocation.

Jimmy knew that he was tangling up the affair at every move. He had led to the trail to Claire. It would be simple enough to make out a circumstantial case against her. Of course, she had been at Shuffle Inn at the hour when the shot was heard in Payne's room. She could establish an alibi—

Jimmy glanced at his watch. It was almost eleven o'clock. It would hardly do to telephone Brinze at this hour and acknowledge his note. Yet—

He found Brinze's number in the suburban directory and asked for it. There was a long pause. Finally a sleepy voice answered. Jimmy asked for Edgar Brinze. He insisted that it was important. It was Mr. Wrome.

"What do you want?" snarled Brinze.

"I just got your letter," Jimmy bungled.

"All I can say to that," barked Brinze, "is that they must have a hell of a peculiar system of mail deliveries in New York."

"I've been out—working on the case," explained Jimmy.

"Do you have to ring me up now to tell me that?"

"I didn't ring you up to tell you that."

"Then what the hell did you ring up for? My sleep is valuable, even if your time isn't."

"I've got something that seems to fit into what you wrote. I want to clean it up tonight."

"Well, you have all day tomorrow to clean it up."

"No, I haven't!"

Jimmy almost bit off the transmitter in his anxiety.

"Well, what do you want?"

"What did you mean by saying that you were working along my lines?"

"Oh—that?"

Brinze's annoying laugh came over the wire. "You remember your talk about the gun?" he continued. "Well, you were right. We traced that gun."

Brinze's laugh brought no joy to Jimmy this time.

"I suppose you had that all doped out, too," concluded Brinze ironically.

"No—I can't say—but are you sure?"

"Sure's anything."

"Will you make an arrest?"

"Not so fast, old sleuth. We know who bought the gun. But that doesn't prove that she fired it."

"No, it certainly doesn't."

Jimmy's tone had a wealth of relief in it.

"Well, that's easy enough for you to say. How do you know she didn't?"

"For one thing, she was at Shuffle Inn—"

"Oh, the perfect alibi! Well, I don't blame you for trying to defend so charming a creature, but that sort of thing has ruined plenty of perfectly good professional detectives, not to mention amateurs. Don't be fooled by the beautiful and innocent looking lady!"

Brinze mustn't suspect Jimmy of any interest in Claire.

"I don't say she didn't," Jimmy added.

"Oh, you don't!" jeered Brinze. "You don't say she did and you don't say she didn't! Maybe you can tell us who did! Are you still so quick at those things?"

"I'm not ready to say anything now. Anyhow, I can't discuss it over the 'phone."

It was an easy way out.

"Or over anything else," Brinze finished. "I want to see you in a day or two. I want to ask you a few questions about the behavior of certain people at a certain time. Maybe you'll solve everything by then and show us all up for a lot of boobs. Good night!"

The instrument clicked. It almost chuckled at Jimmy as Brinze rang off.

"Monica Wells!"

Jimmy repeated the name slowly. He sat for a moment at the telephone, drawing his hand across his chin. Then he made a note on his little used date pad.

"Oh, Claire," he murmured sentimentally, "what a botch you made of that! 'Monica Wells'!"

"How?"

"How could anybody trace a gun? You can't buy a gun in New Yo
without a permit. We checked up on the permits and we checked ι
on the sales of guns in New York. It was a sweet job."

"Who bought it?"

"That's really for you to find out at this stage of the game, old man

"I haven't access to pistol permits."

"No, I guess not. They don't let amateurs examine all the re
cords, do they?"

Jimmy saw that nothing was to be wrung from Brinze by direc
questioning. He took a bold chance.

"Where did the man buy the gun?" he asked.

He held his breath as the answer came.

"It wasn't a man, you young sleuth!"

Again the laugh, but this time it pleased Jimmy. He had taken
Brinze off his guard.

"Then it was a woman!"

"No, it was a kangaroo!"

Brinze enjoyed his sarcasm immensely.

"And I suppose the kangaroo was Mrs. Gulvin," Jimmy remarked
as carelessly as possible.

"That shows how much you know about it!"

Brinze was gloating in high good humor.

"You never even heard of the person who got the permit," he
went on. "Just for fun, I'll tell you the name. It was Monica Wells."

Jimmy excitedly knocked a full ash tray from the telephone table.

"What!" he shouted.

"What are you hollering for? I bet you never heard the name
before."

Jimmy checked a reply. "I—don't—think—I—have," he confessec

"Certainly you haven't! There ain't any sich girl! But we kno
who she was, and I guess you do, too!"

"How should I?"

"How should you? Well, the lady giving her name as Mor
Wells is a great beauty, young and slender, with wonderful gol
hair, which she wears in a band across her forehead. Now, if
don't know—"

He looked at his watch impatiently.

"Nothing to do till tomorrow," he remarked to the telephone.

As he lay in bed, his deductive processes seemed to be paralyzed. There was a greater problem ahead of him now. He would have to save Claire. She evidently cared little for him now. If Brinze could prove her even an accessory to the crime, she would pass out of his life. And with the passing of Claire, there would be peace.

But he didn't want peace. He didn't want anything now except Claire. Perhaps it was the warm summer night that made him emotional. He tried to drive out the thoughts, but they wouldn't go. He emulated William James' professor who clenched his jaws and repeated "I must relax, I *must* relax" until it struck him as a silly thing to do.

He reverted to Hugh's formula. His mind went back over the series of books which he had rented from Curtin's. Suddenly all of them were swept from his thoughts.

"Monica Wells," he murmured. "That's very funny."

And after many hours (actually, fifteen minutes) he went to sleep.

XII
THE NATURAL PHILOSOPHY OF LOVE

Curtin's hardly had got under way for the day's business when Jimmy entered. It was a bright, warm morning, and the librarian wondered why her customer had found it necessary to come in on the run at this hour.

"I've saved a new detective story for you, Mr. Wrome," she remarked.

She drew a volume from a little shelf under her desk.

"No, thanks."

Jimmy was a trifle abrupt.

"I wanted to *buy* a book this morning."

The lady of the brown eyes and the amusing bobbed hair smiled tolerantly.

"Some definite book?" she asked.

"A very definite book. A most definite book. The definite book. *THE* book."

Jimmy rattled off his crescendo.

"And what," inquired the mild-voiced librarian, "is this most tangible, concrete and otherwise unmistakable work?"

If this was banter, Jimmy decided, it was charming banter. A delightful girl, in her fresh, white, clinging dress. But there was no time for that, now.

"*The Porterhouse Murder*," he said.

"Why you've read that, Mr. Wrome," she protested uncommercially.

"I've read it, and I want to keep it. Not only that, but I want to buy the copy that I read. Or do you keep more than one copy in circulation? If so I want to buy all of them."

The pouting mouth displayed as much of a grin as a pouting mouth can.

"Only one copy, Mr. Wrome. But that's been pretty well circulated. I can give you a fresh copy."

"No, no. Not a fresh copy. The circulated one, by all means."

"It isn't a very presentable copy."

"Please don't apologize for it."

With something that might have been a wink, if the librarian had been anyone else, she took down the battered book.

"This is only half price," she observed. "It's been in circulation so much that we can't sell it as a new book."

"I'll give you double price if you want it!"

"That wouldn't be right."

She looked at the shelves thoughtfully.

"But as long as you feel a little prodigal this morning, might I suggest another book? It's a novel—not a mystery story—and I happen to know the author. He's such a charming young man that it's rather thrilling to help him along."

"Wrap it up," snapped Jimmy.

Her grateful smile—why so grateful?—made him realize his curtness.

"You must pardon my snappiness," he said. "I'm a little excited this morning."

"I'm sure I don't mind it," she replied meltingly, "and snappiness is much preferable to lethargy. Don't you think so?"

She looked a trifle guilty.

"I can have this book autographed for you, if you like," she volunteered. "The author writes captivating inscriptions."

"Certainly. I'll bring it in."

Jimmy paused. There was something refreshing about this girl. She was always cool and pleasant, and her voice had a comforting note in it.

"I'm going to ask you something," he said, "and if you think I'm too presuming, please say so. I don't even know your name—"

"Myrna Quaid," she said. "That's harder to spell than to say, but it really is my name."

"Myrna Quaid" sang its way musically into Jimmy's ear. He liked pretty sounds and he thought that the librarian's name presented a euphonic treat.

"Very well, Miss Quaid. Before I go on, I ought to tell you something of myself. I'm a bachelor, temporarily on leave from my office, which happens to be with a big sugar refining house, and I'm doing a little work on the outside. Someday, perhaps, I may be able to tell you what it is. Just now it's in the nature of a confidential mission.

"Not to make a novel of a very short story, I've been working rather hard on this job, and I feel the need of a little innocent recreation. Would you consider me fearfully bold, designing and impudent if I asked you whether you would care to dine with me tonight at some reasonably respectable place where there is dancing?"

Miss Quaid fingered a book reflectively.

"Of course, as you say, Mr. Wrome, you didn't even know my name, and we're strangers, and we haven't been properly introduced, and for all I know you may be the Sheik of Araby, etcetera and so forth. But, as you don't look very dangerous, and as your business habits, such as are involved in the returning of books, are above reproach, I dare say that I might risk the adventure."

"And the author of the book which you so delicately sold to me— will he object?"

"Not if I can explain it so persuasively as you can."

"When may I call for you—and where would you like to go?"

"You may call at six, this being a day on which I'm relieved at that hour. Our destination is in your hands, Mr. Wrome."

Jimmy was delighted. Miss Quaid was different from any girl that he had known. She was something new. In her company he might be able to forget for a while the convolutions of his detective work.

"How about Banquo's? The smart crowd hasn't discovered it yet, and the music's quiet."

Miss Quaid laughed.

"Banquo's would be excellent. I'd feel as safe in Banquo's as I would in this store."

"That's a peculiar remark."

"I know it. But it's true."

A customer entered.

"Well—then I'll be here at six," concluded Jimmy.

"That'll be charming."

He had a feeling that Miss Quaid had bowed him out ever so gracefully, but his little conversation with her had buoyed him up.

Then he remembered the book.

He hurried home and ran quickly through the pages of *The Porterhouse Murder*. He marked a few passages, noted the pages on a slip of paper, and carefully relegated the book to the strong box which contained the threatening letter and the false mustache.

"That's a pretty mènage," he murmured, as he locked the little safe.

With nothing more important at hand, Jimmy dipped into the opus composed by Miss Quaid's friend. It was a book about a young girl who was brought up to imagine herself a great singer and who came to believe it. Some of it puzzled him, but he came to the conclusion that Miss Quaid was a person of literary taste. A remarkable girl, Miss Quaid.

After a close battle with the razor, Jimmy reported at Curtin's for his evening at Banquo's.

Miss Quaid somehow had gouged enough time out of her working day to be ready in an attractive gray gown. She didn't blossom forth, as young librarians are commonly supposed to sprout. She didn't have to.

There was a surprise for Jimmy at Banquo's. In the small and colorful dining hall, with its modest dancing space, he heard an orchestra of unusual silkiness. And leading this persuasively harmonious ensemble was Eddie Endle.

Eddie wagged a greeting with his saxophone.

"So you have friends here, too," observed Miss Quaid.

"Why not? Haven't you?"

"Why yes. My friend is even a more important official."

"Not the author of that novel, is it?"

"Dear me, no! The proprietor and I are on very good terms."

"The proprietor? Do you mean Mr. Banquo?"

"There isn't any Mr. Banquo. Did you ever hear of Mr. Standard of the Standard Oil Company?"

Jimmy requested an explanation.

"The owner of this place is Mr. Curtin. He runs his book stores for profit and devotes some of his earnings to art. Hence Banquo's."

"Such being the case, let's dance."

Such being the case they danced, and Jimmy discovered in the demure Miss Quaid as artistic an exponent of what passes for the fox-trot as ever he had encountered. She was a delightful companion, a charming partner—but adjectives were unnecessary. Miss Quaid simply was There.

After several blissful sessions on the floor with Miss Quaid, Jimmy found that he wasn't to be the sole partner of the librarian on this evening. A smiling, red-haired young man, stepped to the table and inquired whether he might have the privilege of dancing with Miss Quaid.

"This is Mr. Gumbage," explained Miss Quaid. "He's a poet, and I've managed to force some of his books on innocent customers. But if you don't mind, Mr. Wrome, I'll dance with Mr. Gumbage in spite of that."

Jimmy felt a little lost in this cosey resort, with his partner away. Apparently Eddie noticed his solitude, for he dropped his saxophone, turned over the orchestra to the solemn violinist and sat at Jimmy's table.

"Nice little girl," commented the saxophonist. "First time I've seen you with one, but you sure picked a good one."

The notion of girls somehow brought up the thought of Claire and Jimmy looked pensive.

"Lookin' a little blue," Eddie went on. "That guy take her off you?"

"No. I don't know her very well. Just a friend."

"A-ha!"

Eddie nodded wisely.

"That's how those things start," he continued. "I know. I've been there."

He leaned across the table, obviously anxious to relieve his soul, speaking in a kind of rhythm. He gave a recital with orchestral accompaniment.

"She reminds me of the first girl I ever went with," he said, reflectively. "Only they didn't have no bob hair in those days. She was a sweet trick and it sure looked like a hook-up. That's where the bets was off. They're always off. I and she was just friends, you know. Nothin' more. I didn't know so much then. I used to go up to her house in Bayonne and play the clarinet—that's what I played then— and she'd worry along somehow on the piano. That's all there was to it. Me, clarinet. She, piano. Gee! It makes me laugh to think how simple it all was.

"Well, you can't keep no good thing to yourself. This clarinet-piano stuff was all right until some bird turned up who didn't ask her to do no work when he called. He was a fresh guy, and his old man had a lot o' money which he didn't keep to himself. Some of it went into a car, and the car went to this bird. Well, you can guess how long I lasted. You can't stack a clarinet against a roadster. I couldn't, anyway. And one night she says to me, 'Eddie, I got a big surprise for you.' I should of known what that meant, but I was only a kid and I thought maybe she'd bought some new music or somethin'. Boy, you ain't got no idea how dumb I was then! Then she took hold of my hand—that was the first time she'd ever done that and I sure was surprised—and said, 'You been such a good friend, I want you to be the first to know.' Just like that. 'I want you to be the first to know.' Well, I had a hunch right then somebody was goin' to drop an ax nice and gentle, and she did. 'Eddie,' she says, 'I'm engaged.'

"Well, what was I to say to that? Remember, I was awful innocent then. I just sat around and made faces and when I couldn't make no more faces, I got out and went home and cried like hell."

Something akin to ferocity came over Eddie's expression.

"I didn't care what happened. I was goin' out to kill that bird, I didn't care what. I was bigger'n he was and I would of clouted the lights out o' him. I'd of sent him back to her and said 'Here's your beau. How do you like him now?' But I never saw him again, nor her either until a few nights ago, when she turns up here. She's got bob hair now, just like your girl, and she's filled out a little, but she don't look no older than she did back in Bayonne when she used to pick out tunes on the piano. She wasn't such a hell of a good piano player, at that, but I didn't notice it then.

"Just to be mean, I had the boys put on one o' the tunes she and I used to play. She looked a little surprised when she heard it, and when I dug out the clarinet and played like I used to in her parlor she certainly was knocked for a loop. After that dance I went to her table and said hello and how was she gettin' on. There was a guy with her and I said 'I guess that's your husband,' and she got fussed as hell.

"Little later the bird danced with another jane, and she sent for me and said that wasn't her husband, she'd gotten divorced three years ago, and she was awful unhappy.

"Well, that would of been the cue for me to come in with a big solo if I'd still felt the way I did that night in Bayonne, but I seen too much since. I don't go in much for the rough stuff, but women are my meat, and I could have made this kid without tryin'. But it's funny, boy. I didn't care about her no more. She'd got what was comin' to her. I guess that husband of hers sure raised hell with her."

Eddie motioned to his band, which had stopped, to continue.

"But as I was thinkin' it all over, what she got was what she deserved. She sure pulled a dirty one on me when I was a kid and I'd of been inside my rights to get even.

"It ain't so much that she chucked me for that other bird. We all got a right to change our mind, even women. But it ain't right and it ain't decent to keep company with a guy and next day to say you're goin' to marry somebody else who's got a roadster."

Eddie juggled a glass of water.

"If you talk to some folks about me, you'll hear I don't always act like a perfect gentleman should, and I guess I done a few things that I ain't so proud of, but who ain't? Some things I used to do I don't go in for no more now. But I certainly went wild after she skipped off on me. I'm not sayin' it's her fault, but if she would of played on the level, I wouldn't of pulled some o' the stuff I did.

"But that's women, and what are you goin' to do about it?"

Jimmy admitted that he didn't know.

"Well, I'll tell you!" Eddie announced. "Let 'em know who's who first, and there won't be no second. If a jane was to play around with me a lot today, like she really cared for me, and I was to work the same way, and then she said 'Eddie, I got a big surprise for you,' I wouldn't wait around for no ax to drop. I'd say 'Stand up!' and if she didn't stand up I'd slam her against the wall. And then I'd say, 'Lady, this ain't no surprise to me, but I sure got a surprise for you, and what have you got to say for yourself before it lands on your young jaw?' And then I'd just haul off—"

Eddie stopped with his orchestra.

"You get me, I guess," he concluded. "When a man's up against a woman, he's got to be a man, that's all."

Gumbage returned Miss Quaid to Jimmy with a much too pretty bow and retired, uttering thanks.

"Meet Mr. Endle, Miss Quaid," remarked Jimmy. "Miss Quaid, have you got a big surprise for me?"

"Not that I know of."

"That's good. Mr. Endle just advised me what to do in case you had."

Eddie backed away in confusion.

"I got a new tune for you," he said. "It ain't really a new one, but I just fixed it up for the boys and it's goin' fine. I'll have 'em put it on for you."

"That'll be more than good of you, Mr. Endle," beamed the librarian.

"Oh, it's good, all right."

The orchestra struck up the air immediately, and after some preliminary modulations, the melody became recognizable. Jimmy became agitated as he heard it. His grip on his partner relaxed.

"Anything troubling you, Mr. Wrome?" inquired Miss Quaid solicitously.

"Only memories," sighed Jimmy. "It's very good of him to play something for our especial benefit, but I wish that it had been anything else."

> *"Just a little love, a little kiss;*
> *I would give you all my life for this;*
> *As I hold you fast and bend above you,*
> *Murmuring the little word—'I love you.'"*

The melody seared Jimmy.

"Don't worry about me, Miss Quaid," he apologized. "Some tunes are ghost tunes. They bring back—well, never mind."

"I know," assented Miss Quaid. "That's one of my hobbies—the psychological effect of music, you know. I used to know a phlegmatic, peaceful man who suddenly would jump up and fly at the first person in sight when he heard 'O Promise Me.' He'd promised, I think, but she hadn't, and somehow the tune was associated with the misunderstanding. Then there was a girl who burst into tears whenever she heard the Spring Song. It was the same sort of case."

"What sort of case?"

"There's usually a heartbreak at the bottom of these aversions to certain tunes."

Jimmy scanned the librarian's serene countenance. Could she have guessed what lay behind his complaint about Eddie's new foxtrot? But if she had guessed, she concealed it masterfully.

"Music's such a melting thing," she continued. "I'm sure that Mr. Endle's band would be of great assistance to any young man who came to Banquo's to woo. 'Say it with music' is right. 'Say it *to* music' is even better. If someone wanted to make love to me, and he picked a pretty place, with a good orchestra—"

She broke off with a little laugh.

"Goodness knows what would happen!"

She looked up charmingly but not at all flirtatiously.

"That wasn't an invitation," she explained, "and I won't be offended if you don't take a hint that wasn't a hint."

"Were you ever in love with a violinist?" demanded Jimmy.

She halted in her dancing, and then resumed quickly. "What made you ask that?" she inquired.

"If you'll answer the question," he grinned, "I'll give you a diagram."

"Sure!"

She laughed again.

"I was in love with a violinist when I was sixteen. I'm still in love with him."

"Is he in love with you?"

"Produce your diagram, and I'll answer your question."

The music stopped, and they returned to the table.

"Now then," Jimmy said, "when you were talking about the aphrodisiac effect of music, you had your hand on my shoulder. As you talked you tapped my shoulder with your fingers. You didn't move them up and down, as though you were thinking of piano playing, but you stretched them as a violinist might. I used to take fiddle lessons when I was a kid, and though I can't play a note today, I know that your method isn't the right one. That's why I figured you were thinking of a violinist rather than about playing the violin."

He stirred his orangeade.

"And in addition," he went on, "I did some nice, blind guessing."

"Are you a detective?" inquired Miss Quaid. "That's almost as far-fetched as the deductions of Bernard Gartlin. And about as accurate. I must put you on another diet if detective stories help you to unearth the love secrets of young women."

"You were to answer a question," remarked Jimmy, irrelevantly.

"The fiddler I loved? Certainly. It was Fritz Kreisler. But I haven't any idea how Fritz feels about me, and never having met him, I can't imagine."

After that, they talked like dancers, and if Miss Quaid hadn't recalled that her duties started at nine in the morning, they might be there yet.

Redeeming his hat in the cloakroom, Jimmy spied a familiar-looking piece of headgear on a peg.

"Do you mind if I look at that big straw hat over there?" he asked the attendant, slipping him a monstrous tip.

"Help yourself," bowed the boy.

There was no doubt about this shabby straw. It belonged to the shadow. But where had the shadow been this evening. Banquo's was small enough so that one could see all of the diners as one danced around the floor. The shadow hadn't been visible, There were no discreet nooks—Banquo's wasn't that sort of institution—where he might hide. The shadow couldn't have been there disguised as a waiter, nor was he one of Endle's ensemble.

Jimmy looked puzzled as he rejoined Miss Quaid in the lobby.

"Something wrong?" she inquired gently.

"No—nothing very wrong—I'm a little bothered by something. It doesn't amount to much, though."

"Can I be of any help?"

He was on the point of telling her of Payne, of Claire, of Brinze, of the shadow, of everything. It would help him to retail the story to one so calm and poised. Yet—Gartlin wouldn't have done it. And even if Gartlin might have, Jimmy wouldn't. The murder part of it could have been told. But Claire was too painful a subject to discuss.

"It'll pass away," he said.

"It isn't digestive, is it?" she bantered. "That would be a reflection on Banquo's, and, in a way, I'm connected with Banquo's."

"Merely indigestible facts," Jimmy remarked. "I can't swallow them, and yet they seem to be in my system."

She waved her hands gaily.

"How very Russian!" she cried. "You mustn't be a Slav in your thoughts!"

But the shadow's hat hung over Jimmy's head on the way to Miss Quaid's apartment.

"Really, you must cheer up," she remarked at parting. "Come in tomorrow and I'll give you a fearfully gloomy book. Nothing could be as terrible as that book and you'll feel fine afterwards."

Books! They had done enough!

Jimmy constructed a smile.

"It was so good of you to come with me tonight," he said.

"Don't thank me. I had a better time than you did!"

A lyric good night ended the evening with Miss Quaid.

Jimmy returned home in a taxicab. He looked for the shadow on the street. The shadow apparently had gone to bed.

Jimmy undressed slowly. Miss Quaid occupied his thoughts. What a delightful girl she was! If he had been fancy free and heart whole this evening might have been the beginning of something wonderful. But—

"Claire!" he sighed.

Then he snatched off his collar viciously.

"Don't get so damn sentimental!" he commanded himself.

Clack! Clack!

There was a light patter of footsteps below his window. He looked out. The shadow was back.

Jimmy wondered whether a pail of water poured over this patrolman mightn't be beneficial. No. It was a little too grotesque.

He looked down undecidedly. The shadow wouldn't be likely to come up and disturb him. If he did, there would be a fine battle! He pulled a gift cane from the closet and laid it near the bed, within reach. He locked the doors carefully and pulled down the dark shades.

"Well, I hope it rains on you or something," he muttered, as he switched out the lights.

After all, dancing is exercise, and Jimmy was a little tired. He went to sleep uneventfully.

XIII
UNLUCKY

Morning brought a relaxation in the shadow's vigil and a sudden focusing of attention on the Payne case in the newspapers. Jimmy was fascinated by a front page which was concentrated on the activities or lack of them by the Bellechester authorities. There was a menacing summary of events, neatly boxed in heavy, bold face type, stretching across three columns:

"LEED PAYNE 'DIED' THREE WEEKS AGO.
"SINCE THEN—
"A charge of murder was made by one of the guests in the house on the day of the 'death.'
"An unofficial hearing was held by a member of a prominent family in the county.
"The district attorney has done ? ? ?
"The police have done ? ? ?
"A member of the state legislature has been held on suspicion and dismissed.
"Well—? ? ?"

Jimmy chuckled as he visualized Brinze facing this broadside. Then he opened his little strong-box thoughtfully and looked over the contents as though to make certain that all were intact.

"I may need you sooner than I thought," he murmured.

It was a warm, sultry morning, and Jimmy's apartment was comparatively cool. He sat by the window with a newspaper in his hand, but he couldn't read. He felt restless. The heat had driven people from the streets and even the traffic on Broadway, dimly visible from the window, was sporadic and listless. Jimmy wanted to go out, but the steaming pavement was a deterrent. He ran through his papers again, studying the accounts of the case. The newspapers knew even less than Brinze.

Something ought to be in these stories. He felt that some element had been lacking in the long columns of print, and he had an uneasy, intuitive idea that he would encounter it before long.

"Gossip in Bellechester says that a woman is involved."

There it was!

Jimmy read quickly, hoping that no names would appear. If Claire's name were mentioned, even remotely, it would stand out before him like a burning headline.

"One of the female guests at the house party—"

He tumbled through the rest of it.

No. They hadn't identified the guest.

"Said to be young and exceptionally pretty."

No doubt whom that meant!

"It is said that the guests included—"

But while the list was confined to labels, such as "a member of the state legislature," "a musician," "Mr. Payne's personal physician," and "friends," Claire was relatively safe.

"Friends!"

Claire, Hesbe, and Jimmy. It would be only a day or two before inquiring reporters would inquire into the names of these friends, and then the young and exceptionally pretty woman could be dragged into the case by name.

Jimmy stared at the paper blankly.

"It looks bad for you, Claire," he muttered. "Bad. They can make out a pretty good case against you, and I wonder what you'll have to say. If I had a little more dope—only a little more—I could—"

He indulged himself in a mental motion picture. Claire on the stand, breaking down under the questioning of the police. Witnesses contributing unfavorable evidence. Brinze gloating. Reporters plunging to telephones to unburden Claire's history to re-write men in New York. Jimmy standing up coolly. "Well, what do you want?" "Just a moment, Mr. Brinze." Sensation in the room. "Get it over with quick." "All right, I'll get it over with quick!" A patter of applause, squelched by the officials. Claire looking up in amazement. Question. Answer. Question. Answer. Brinze confused. Jimmy clear, logical. Claire exonerated. Cheers. Claire weeping. Kisses in court. "Jimmy, I never knew—" "It was nothing, Claire. I only wish I could have spared you—this."

"*You damn fool!*"

Jimmy snatched himself from the fantasy. He compared his romantic vision with the facts and shoved aside the papers in disgust. He rose and stretched. A little walk, even in the heat, would help him to think more clearly. He selected a lively neck piece, adjusted it painstakingly and went below.

He stood on the curb wondering in which direction to turn. Glances up and down the street showed that the sun had melted or otherwise disposed of the shadow. He strolled to the corner, bought a few additional newspapers, and returned to his apartment to study the latest bulletins of the case.

"You was to call a Mr. Brinze," said the doorman. "He phoned twice while you was out."

Ah, yes. Brinze probably didn't feel so elated and confident on this charming morning. The district attorney naturally would have vented his irritation on the local detective, who would now be smarting under the lash. The local detective who opposed Gartlin always smarted under the lash, although Jimmy didn't know just what this smarting consisted of. He twirled his hat merrily as he telephoned to Brinze.

"Where've you been all morning?" demanded the detective. "When I don't want you, you ring me up at midnight. When I do want you, you're off at the end of the world."

"Merely up the street."

"Well, go up a few more streets, take the train and come out here as fast as you can."

Jimmy chuckled and Brinze demanded what the noise was.

"Some atmospheric disturbance, I suppose," drawled Jimmy. "Do you really want to see me today?"

"Quit talking and come."

"I thought you knew all you wanted to know."

"I know I don't want any more funny talk from you. Hurry up. That's all."

"That's all." How reminiscent of the dear departed! How Brinze was growing into a regulation police official! Perhaps he, too, had been reading detective stories. But his model had been not the Man of a Million Masks but the veteran police captain who said things curtly, sharply and severely.

Jimmy studied more newspaper reports on the way to Bellechester. He was surprised to see his old friend Heidelman risen to the dignity of a writer for a New York evening paper—not only that, but a writer who was permitted to sign his articles on the Payne case.

A box of black type told the readers that Heidelman had been first on the ground and in touch with the mystery as no other New York reporter had been. Heidelman, who had learned his journalism from a correspondence course.

Whistling a too-prevalent ditty, Jimmy drifted into the Bellechester police station and walked down the dark corridor to Brinze's office. He knocked ironically, and a policeman opened the door.

"Well, here's Sherlock!"

Brinze's voice blazed like his incandescent cravat.

Jimmy bowed meekly, and hung his hat on a peg.

"You know, I never knew it to work, either," he said irrelevantly.

"What to work?" roared Brinze.

Yes, he certainly was the veteran captain today.

"Wax."

"What are you talking about?"

"That mustache you're trying to grow. Mustaches look terrible in the early stages, and smearing wax on them only makes them look worse instead of covering up their youth."

Brinze fingered the untidy growth on his upper lip.

"Shut up!"

The policeman made so poor a job of killing off a guffaw that Brinze turned on him angrily.

"Shut up or get out!" he ordered.

The policeman saluted and turned his back.

"I didn't invite you here for an exhibition of your deductive powers. Wrome," snapped Brinze. "Not now, at any rate. In a little while, you may need all you've got—and then some!"

He smiled with impressive grimness.

"Tell Mr. Kenworthy I'm ready for him. And bring in that reporter."

The policeman saluted again and left.

"Is this to be what they call a conference?" asked Jimmy.

He didn't like Brinze's manner today, and the despatch of the Bellechester watchdog for the district attorney and the reporter boded things which he had not anticipated.

"You'll know what to call it when it's over," retorted Brinze. "Just sit down there next to this table and make yourself at home. It'll be your home for some time!"

"Thanks."

"Don't try to get fresh."

Brinze settled back and lit a cigarette. Jimmy also extracted one.

"Anybody invite you to smoke?" Brinze shot out. "This is an office of the law."

"*Es ist verboten*," sighed Jimmy, restoring the cigarette to its container.

"And don't try any funny talk."

"I don't know what you mean by funny talk. You've talked about funny talk a good deal today but what you're getting at is over my head."

"Well, keep your head up."

This repartee pleased Brinze immensely, for he smiled long and lovingly after it.

The door swung open and Kenworthy entered, followed by Heidelman. Kenworthy, a tall, tawny-haired individual, with a long, cleft chin and soft but penetrating gray eyes, looked over his shell-rimmed glasses.

"So that's the man, eh, Brinze?"

His voice was dry and brisk.

"Come in, Heidelman. Sit down. And if you print a word of this before I say so, you'll be through with a lot of things."

Kenworthy ushered the reporter to a chair on the side of the table opposite Jimmy. He pulled up a chair facing Brinze. Heidelman's face radiated interest and importance. He clasped his hands about his knees and looked on intently.

"You're Wrome, I take it," said Kenworthy. "I'm the district attorney."

"So I gathered," remarked Jimmy.

"He's a detecatif," interpolated Brinze, looking from Kenworthy to Heidelman for an appreciative laugh.

"So it seems, so it seems."

Kenworthy lit a long cigar, rested his elbows on the arms of the chair, and then decided to take off his coat. He snapped his blue suspenders as he spoke.

"Now, Mr. Wrome," he began slowly, "I don't want to go beating about the bush. I want to get at facts and get at them quickly. So I'm going to ask you some questions and I want answers."

Jimmy began to feel uncomfortable. It was evident that an inquisition lay ahead. He had never been the inquisitioned party in such an event, and he could feel perspiration that wasn't attributable to the heat on his forehead. Nerves. Damn his nerves, anyhow.

"You know this man, Heidelman," Kenworthy proceeded. "Now, what did you tell him on the morning following the death of Payne?"

"He told me he knew how it was done and who did it," interrupted Heidelman eagerly.

"I don't want your version of it. I want Mr. Wrome's."

"Mr. Heidelman is correct," said Jimmy.

"In other words, you claimed knowledge of the crime, as we must call it if your statements are accurate, and of its perpetrator."

Jimmy didn't relish Kenworthy's gaze. Yet men who didn't outstare their questioners always were considered dishonest, and he glared violently at the district attorney as he answered.

"Not for publication."

"Not for publication!" echoed Kenworthy scornfully.

"No. I gave him a hint. That was all."

"A hint!" Kenworthy repeated Jimmy's words with a rising inflection that annoyed Jimmy. He resented being called a liar by a tone of voice. "That certainly was the broadest hint I ever heard of. You knowingly made an accusation of murder and you call it a hint. Very good, Mr. Wrome. Call it a hint, if you will. It's immaterial to me what you call it. What I want to know—"

Kenworthy rose from his chair and snapped his suspenders loudly.

"What I want to know is who, in your opinion, killed Leed Payne?"

Jimmy felt all kinds of murmurings inside him. He looked blankly at the district attorney, who had shoved his long jaw down almost into his face.

"Answer me!" shouted Kenworthy. "Who killed Leed Payne?"

He swung his lean arms violently against the arm of Jimmy's chair. Jimmy folded his hands tightly. He wouldn't answer Kenworthy. He wasn't compelled to. When he had any charges to make he would make them in a regular way. He wasn't going to be bullied into admissions of opinion. And anything that he might say now would involve Claire. He knew that a premature disclosure of his notions would lead to the Barton household.

"Is this an official hearing?" Jimmy heard himself saying.

"That doesn't matter!" screamed Kenworthy. "Answer my question! Who killed Leed Payne?"

The district attorney's reiterated query sounded so much like the first line of a jacket description for a Bernard Gartlin story!

"You have no right to ask me that question—assuming that I know the answer," Jimmy said mildly.

District attorneys always bulldozed people. He thought of Vankel, the attorney in *The Porterhouse Murder*. That official might have been modeled after Kenworthy.

"I have every right to demand an answer," howled Kenworthy, who was wrought up tremendously and whose perspiration threatened to flood the room.

"You have not!"

Jimmy snapped out his assertion boldly.

"If I were on the stand in a regular proceeding," he went on, "you might ask some such question. It would be a little melodramatic, but I don't doubt you'd ask it. This session hasn't any legal ground."

"So you're a lawyer as well as a detective," sneered Kenworthy.

"And if he isn't any better as a lawyer than he is as a detective," remarked Brinze, "he's no lawyer."

Heidelman didn't laugh at this, and Brinze seemed chagrined.

"I don't care if he's a lawyer or a detective or what he is," Kenworthy went on aggressively. "Now, Wrome, you told this reporter that you knew who killed Payne and how it was done. I want you to tell me right here and now what was back of that."

"The statement wasn't made for publication—"

"You didn't say I couldn't print it," interrupted Heidelman, his journalistic honor touched.

"No," Jimmy admitted. "But I didn't intend it to be printed. As I remember, I asked you not to use my name in connection with the case."

"I didn't!" protested the reporter.

"You certainly told Mr. Brinze," retorted Jimmy.

"That wasn't printing it," demurred the reporter.

"It was worse," said Jimmy.

"Shut up, both of you!" bellowed Kenworthy. "I don't care who told anybody else anything. The point is you made the statement and I want you to explain it without any more tomfoolery."

"I decline to explain it."

Jimmy's mouth was drawn in a sharp line and his brown eyes were militant. Earlier, he might have given Kenworthy a few suggestions. Now, he wouldn't offer anything.

"Then don't!" Kenworthy shouted.

He turned to Brinze.

"Commit this man to jail on suspicion," he ordered. He swung on Jimmy with a leer.

"If you want to keep quiet, we'll give you a nice place to keep quiet in," he mocked.

"You can't commit me to jail without cause," said Jimmy. "If you do, there'll be a fine political upheaval inside a week."

"Without cause?"

Kenworthy raised his eyebrows momentously.

"If you want cause, you'll get it! Brinze, hold this man on suspicion of murdering Leed Payne."

"Don't be silly," Jimmy remarked. "You haven't the slightest ground for holding me. To begin with, I wasn't within several miles of the place when it happened."

"Is that so?"

Kenworthy spaced out his ancient sarcasm carefully.

"To be frank with you, Wrome, we'd expected you to tell us theories about this case. Now, I suppose it's up to me to tell you some.

Have you any proof that Payne was killed at the time that Stelke says he was?'

"Stelke didn't say anything about that."

"He said he heard the shot, summoned the doctor, and when the door was broken in, Payne was found dead. That should be sufficient. But—"

Kenworthy was enjoying himself.

"It's conceivable that the first shot may have had nothing to do with it."

"For all you know," Jimmy said, "there were twenty shots. The point is that Payne was dead when the door was broken in."

"Very good. I merely threw that out as a suggestion. Here's something more important. Why did you come tearing over to Olean almost immediately after Stelke telephoned?"

The real reason would sound foolish. Jimmy couldn't confess that he had scented a mystery and that he wanted to be in on it. Besides, Kenworthy wouldn't believe it. And if Kenworthy really had any suspicions, this would help to confirm them. Jimmy fidgeted.

"You wouldn't believe me if I told you," he said weakly.

"So that's the way you feel about it!"

"Anyhow," Jimmy went on, pulling himself together, "Payne was dead when I got there."

"How do you know?" Kenworthy shot at him. "Did you see the body?"

"No, but—"

"When did you hear for the first time that Payne was dead?

"The next morning—"

Jimmy stopped. It annoyed him to think how he had slept, with the mystery he sought almost in the next room and how he had had to hear of it from a country coroner.

"And you knew all about it!"

Kenworthy released his clincher triumphantly.

"I guess there's enough smoke," he went on. "I don't accuse you of murdering Payne, but you know too damn much about it to be allowed at large. Brinze, pick out a nice cell and put it at Wrome's disposal."

Brinze pushed a buzzer and two policeman entered.

"Lock him up," commanded Brinze, glowing in his authority. "And see that nobody talks to him. As for you, Heidelman, one word of this in your paper and we'll settle you so quick you won't know what hit you!"

Jimmy knew that it would be futile to resist. He followed the policemen upstairs to a large corridor. There were many little wooden doors and a compartment with steel gratings at either end of the hall.

"Here are the cells," explained Brinze, who had come up. "Which will you have?"

He giggled, as a policeman clumsily opened one of the steel doors and marched Jimmy in.

Brinze slammed the door.

"That'll hold you for a while," he remarked.

Jimmy sat on a broken chair. This was all a trick to keep him quiet. The district attorney hadn't relished the attacks of the newspapers. They had lured him here to lock him up. He'd get out. He'd sue them for false arrest. He'd wipe Kenworthy out of office and he'd show up Brinze for the conceited incompetent that he was.

"Good night!"

Brinze's giggle died out as the detective descended the stairs. The two policemen looked curiously at Jimmy and left.

Jimmy tried the bars. There could be no escape from them. There was no window or other opening at the back or sides of the cubicle. He wondered about the other doors. Were these cells? The dust in his own prison proved that it had long been in disuse. The policemen returned and entered one of the doors. Jimmy had a glimpse of a desk inside the room. Then these were offices. And only two cells for the criminals of Bellechester!

The policemen stepped out again. Jimmy called them. They came to him.

"Orders are nobody's to talk to you," said one.

"Well, where are the rest of the prisoners?" demanded Jimmy.

The smaller policeman laughed.

"First time we've used this cell since old Mac knocked hell out of his wife. That was before I was on the force."

The other also laughed.

"You can't talk to him, Dick," he said, remembering the instructions. "Let's go."

A curious jail, thought Jimmy. He was the first prisoner in—how many years?

He'd get out. He'd even matters with Brinze and Kenworthy. Again he tried the bars. He struggled for a while, and then sat down, exhausted. How long would this farce continue.

The chair was uncomfortable. He took off his coat and stretched it on the stone flooring as a mattress. He lay down.

He woke up, feeling sore. He looked at the luminous dial of his watch. He'd been asleep for hours. The building was quiet. There were no lights in the corridor and no illumination creeping from under the doors of the little rooms. He called out. There was no answer. He pulled viciously at the bars.

He heard a voice. It was a weak voice, somewhere outside the building. He listened. Someone was singing. Singing badly. He called again. The voice only continued singing. The singing became louder, as though the singer were straining. Then he recognized the tune:

> *"Just a little love, a little kiss;*
> *I would give you all my life for this;*
> *As I hold you fast and bend above you*
> *And I hear you murmuring 'I love you!'"*

XIV
THE SHADOW THAT NEVER GREW LESS

A little drowsy, more than a little angry, and completely bewildered, Jimmy tried to find his bearings, physically and mentally. That Brinze had conspired to clap him in prison was obvious; but the singing of the tune which had more than once unnerved him presented a new problem. Was all of this a huge plot to break down his morale, to undermine his processes of thought, perhaps to destroy his mind?

The melancholy voice subsided, and Jimmy waited anxiously to hear what would emanate next from the singer's throat. How, he wondered, could the machinations of Brinze be connected with this assault on his emotions? How could Brinze know that this melody carried with it unbearable associations and shattering memories?

But did Brinze know? Could this not be coincidence? It had been a highly popular air, and might be sung even by people who loitered about rural police stations.

> *"Just a little love, a little kiss;*
> *I would give you—"*

Again the reedy voice intoned its passion. Why should anyone be so fervidly fond of this melody as to stand beside a court house on a warm summer night and sing it without end? For whom was this serenade intended?

Jimmy decided that he was the object of these devotions. If only he could get a glimpse of the singer! Perhaps it was the shadow. The shadow probably would have a weak, tuneless voice.

"And I hear you whispering—"

If this kept up, the pursuers would achieve their purpose. His nerves, quiet for several weeks, were beginning to manifest themselves. He tried to walk them off. He couldn't walk off his depressions in the tiny area of the cell. Again he jerked at the bars and cursed himself for wasting time over such fruitless exertion.

The song died away. Jimmy sat on his chair, trying to think out his next move. Shouting and screaming would bring no one to his rescue. He felt in his pocket for anything that might be a weapon. A few cigarettes and a paper of matches were his only finds. He lit a cigarette and gazed at the burning match. He might set fire to the building—Gartlin had done something of the sort when he had been incarcerated in a deserted barn. But this was no barn, and a fire would not assist him to freedom. Fire or no fire, he couldn't break through the bars. And if the fire department were as efficient as the police department, he probably would burn up with the building. This was no time to be burned.

He speculated on the possibilities of cutting through the floor. It was a stone floor, but seemed to cover only the expanse of the cell. Perhaps he could gouge away the cement at the sides, and drop below with the flooring. But a pocket knife was not designed to dislodge cement. And anyhow, the notion was too imaginative.

Sleep seemed to be the only comforting thing at hand. He arranged his coat and lay down on this impromptu mattress. Soothing as slumber might be, it was hard to obtain. All manner of unpleasant thoughts assailed him. In a half-doze he saw Claire dragged into court, with Kenworthy hurling dangerous questions at her. Kenworthy's jaw constantly approached closer to Claire's beautiful but frightened face. Brinze was interpolating cutting inquiries and giggling over them.

KENWORTHY. Where were you on the night of the murder?

CLAIRE'S ATTORNEY (*who might he be?*). I object to the form of that question.

KENWORTHY (*sneering*). All right. Where were you on the night that Mr. Payne "died?"

CLAIRE (*almost inaudibly*). I was at Shuffle Inn.

KENWORTHY (*cruelly*). You shuffled in while Payne shuffled off!

BRINZE (*roaring*). That's a good one!

THE JUDGE. Order, please.

KENWORTHY (*growing meaner and meaner*). Please answer my questions more directly, Miss Barton. Did you ever own a revolver?

CLAIRE (*always softly and weakly*). No.

KENWORTHY. Are you sure of that? Remember— you are under oath.

CLAIRE. I never owned a revolver.

KENWORTHY. You never owned one—but did you ever buy one?

CLAIRE'S ATTORNEY. I object. This question is irrelevant.

THE JUDGE. Objection overruled.

KENWORTHY (*like a villain*). Now, Miss Barton, will you answer my question? Did you ever buy a revolver?

CLAIRE (*almost fainting*). Yes.

KENWORTHY and BRINZE (*in unison*). A-ha!

Jimmy twisted around on his improvised cot. This melodrama with which he was torturing himself oppressed him. He shook his head as though to clear it. What sort of fiction was this that he was inventing? Claire hadn't gone to trial. Claire hadn't even been arrested. But he knew that Brinze's investigations were following a trail which could lead only to Claire.

Jimmy closed his eyes and began to count sheep. Twenty-seven woolly animals leaped awkwardly over an indefinite stile.

KENWORTHY. And what did you do after you bought this revolver?

(*Claire does not answer*).

KENWORTHY. I asked you a plain question. What did you do—

Twenty-eight, twenty-nine, thirty. The sheep were in the courtroom now, hopping across the railing in front of the bench. Where did they disappear to after they jumped?

KENWORTHY. Did you buy the gun for your own use?

CLAIRE'S ATTORNEY. I object.

THE JUDGE. Objection sustained.

KENWORTHY. All right. To whom did you give the gun after you bought it?

Thirty-one, thirty-two, thirty-three, thirty-four, thirty—

Kenworthy's jaw and Claire's bright hair and the ambulant sheep folded up in a heap and dropped out of sight. A heavy rattling awoke Jimmy from an unrestful sleep. The taller policeman was slamming his club against the bars.

"Get up!" he cried. "Do you know what time it is? It's past nine!"

"I thought they woke the prisoners at daybreak," murmured Jimmy sleepily.

"They'd have to wake the guards first," answered the policeman, "and I'd like to see any man get me out of bed at that hour!"

"Oh! You're the guard."

"Yes, I suppose I'm the guard. I'm the bailiff and the assistant sheriff and the traffic cop—what's the use of me telling you all the things I am. Get up and I'll take you out so you can wash up if you want to."

The irregularity of the proceedings dazed Jimmy. This Poo-Bah didn't conform to his idea of a jailer.

"Hurry up!" shouted the policeman impatiently. "Do you want to keep me waiting all morning? I've got work to do."

"What kind of work?" asked Jimmy, as he entered on a blind struggle with his cravat.

"Tend the shop for the wife."

"Shop?"

"Candy store. The Dainty Sweet Shop down at Main and Bausinger Street."

"You run a shop?"

In his bewilderment at this comic-opera constable, Jimmy repeated his question blankly.

"Hell, yes. I told you I run a shop."

He jammed a key into the lock and managed to wrench the door open.

"Hurry up and get washed. The boss is waiting for you."

"What boss?"

"Brinze."

Jimmy nodded sagely and followed the policeman into a small, dirty washroom.

"Don't use that clean towel," commanded the officer. "'That's the boss'. Use the other one."

Jimmy went through a few motions with soap and water.

"Got a comb?" he asked.

"No," answered the policeman, as though that were the most natural possible question for a prisoner to ask. "But you'll find the boss' in the cabinet. Rinse it out when you're through and he won't know the difference."

Jimmy applied a beautiful part to his brown hair and surveyed himself in the dusty mirror.

"I really need a shave," he suggested.

"Barber comes in later," snapped the policeman. "If he don't come in time you can go down to the barber shop. Ask for Rooks. He's my brother and he'll give you a swell shave."

Mr. Rooks of the Dainty Sweet Shop and the Bellechester police force stirred restlessly.

"Come on down," he insisted.

Jimmy stalked down the stairs into Brinze's office. Kenworthy, in white flannels, a sport coat, and a brilliant neckpiece of red and gold, was smoking a cigar and tapping the floor with heavily rubber-soled white shoes.

"Good morning, Mr. Kenworthy," said Jimmy cheerfully. "The greens certainly ought to be in good shape today."

"What are you talking about?" demanded Kenworthy.

"You're in a hurry to get off to play golf, aren't you?" queried Jimmy sweetly.

"That's some of his detective stuff," laughed Brinze. "Rooks probably told him."

"I did not!"

Wounded virtue blazed from the confectionery policeman.

"He didn't," confirmed Jimmy. "But, my dear Mr. Kenworthy, your costume tends suspiciously in that direction, and why do you grip the slat of your chair as though it were a golf club? Especially, as though it were a putter?"

"Rubbish!" scoffed Brinze.

Kenworthy looked up.

"Any damn fool could have guessed that I was going out golfing," he observed, "but where did you get this stuff about the putter?"

"That was the easiest part of it," said Jimmy. "You had your eyes concentrated on a spot on the floor about six inches away and you were swinging your wrists gently, as though you were about to sink the ball."

Kenworthy's expression confirmed Jimmy's hypothesis.

"And what am *I* going to do this morning?" demanded Brinze scathingly.

"You?"

Jimmy pondered.

"You're going to try to make fearfully caustic cracks."

A slight chuckle from Kenworthy enraged Brinze.

"That's enough from you!" bellowed Brinze. "You seem to forget you're under arrest."

"What for?"

"You know well enough what for."

Kenworthy held up his hand.

"Look here, Wrome," he said, coldly. "You know more about Payne's death than you've told us. Now, I've got a simple proposition for you. If you come clean, you can go. If you don't, you can stay. Do you get the idea?"

"I get it," answered Jimmy, "but I've said all that has any bearing on the matter."

"You said you knew how Payne was killed and who did it," insisted Kenworthy. "As soon as you explain that, you can go—unless it's necessary to hold you."

Jimmy didn't want to spend more time in the Bellechester prison, even under the gentle supervision of Rooks. But what could he tell without incriminating Claire? Probably Brinze and Kenworthy had a pretty good case against her now. His half-dream of the night before passed through his mind. It would be heroic to languish in this curious jail to help Claire. But how could he help her from here?

"All right," he said meekly. "I'll tell you what I meant."

Both men sat up eagerly.

"I'll be frank with you," Jimmy continued. "I don't know who killed him."

"You said you did!"

The voices snarled in unison.

"I was terribly excited over—everything, and I said it, but I didn't really know."

"You suspected somebody," snapped Kenworthy, "or you wouldn't have said so. No matter what you think now, whom did you have in mind then?"

"Was it a man or a woman?" asked Brinze.

"You'll think it absurd," said Jimmy, "when I tell you, and in telling you I'm doing an injustice, to an innocent person. I thought for a moment it was Stelke."

Brinze winked at Kenworthy.

"What made you give up that idea?" asked Kenworthy.

"Stelke hung around so much afterwards. A guilty man wouldn't stay calmly at the scene of the crime."

Both inquisitors laughed.

"This man isn't such a genius," observed Kenworthy. "I thought of that myself, Brinze."

"And I suppose you thought Stelke bought the gun, shot Payne, locked the door, and made it out a suicide," Brinze added lightly.

Jimmy bowed his head.

"Well, that was simple-minded enough for anybody," jeered Kenworthy.

Jimmy bowed his head a little deeper and looked up suddenly. The bowing had brought the blood to his face, and he looked as though he were blushing. Somebody in *The Rosenbaum Case* had used this ruse brilliantly, and he wondered whether it would be effective now.

"Such a maidenly blush!" giggled Brinze.

"I'd blush too," added Kenworthy. "Now listen, Wrome. You know what it feels like to be locked up. Let that be a warning to you. After this, keep your mouth shut, and if you must do detective work, stick to doping out things about putters. Now, we're going to release you—but you've got to promise that you won't say a word about this to anyone, and that you'll keep your hands off this business. Another peep out of you, and—!"

He paused eloquently.

"It's a go," mumbled Jimmy.

"Then get out!" screamed Brinze, suddenly, and Jimmy rushed from the room.

He heard uproarious guffaws as he got into the hall. Quickly he walked to the street and turned the corner.

And then Jimmy laughed as loudly as Brinze and Kenworthy and any three other men.

"Not so bad," he murmured. "They'll be chasing poor Stelke all over town now. Acting ought to be your line, Jimmy. That Rosenbaum blush—"

He laughed again as he sought the barber shop of Rooks.

It was not difficult to recognize the tonsorial Rooks, who seemed to be flattered when Jimmy greeted him by name.

"Quite a mystery you've been having here," remarked Jimmy, as Rooks spread buckets of lather over his cheeks.

"Quite a mystery," agreed Rooks, with the air of one who might say more, were he so minded. "They'll get that woman yet."

"What woman?"

Jimmy upset Rook's systematic plastering as he straightened up in the chair.

"That's what I've been asking," said Rooks, tilting back Jimmy's chin for the razor. "All I know is she's a blonde and one of these nifty blondes. Wish they'd give me the job of taking care of her."

"What sort of eyes has she?" inquired Jimmy as casually as he could.

All roads led to Claire!

"How should I know? I never saw her. Don't twist your head. How do you expect me to shave you?"

Rooks slapped a segment of lather against a towel.

"Shave yourself, don't you?" he asked unpleasantly.

"Yes—don't you?"

The retort startled the barber and ended the colloquy. Jimmy tried to resume the conversation, but grunts were his only answer. He had committed a deadly sin. He had blunted a barber's sarcasm, and his penalty was a moody treatment at the hands of Rooks. Jimmy tried to salve the injury with a spectacular tip, but the damage had been done. Rooks pocketed the change without a word, and stroked his mottled hair as who should say "You can't redeem your insult with money, my good man."

On the way back, Jimmy puzzled over the weak-voiced interpreter of "A Little Love, A Little Kiss." If there had been a deliberate effort to break down his nerves, no better device could have been called into service. How could Brinze have known—but who was to say that Brinze knew?

Brinze obviously was aware of more important things. The barber's allusion to the nifty blonde proved that the constabulary Rooks was none too discreet and that Brinze imparted certain official secrets to his underlings. How did Brinze happen to be on the trail? They had traced the gun. Claire had had it initialed. That was indisputable. Had she bought it as well? The conclusion seemed to be a certainty.

Assuming that Claire was in every way responsible for the gun, how much further evidence was there against her? She had an alibi. On the other hand, an accessory in the murder would be equally guilty with the person who had fired the shot. But why did he take it for granted that Claire had purchased the revolver for an illegal purpose?

This consideration somehow seemed weak. Claire wasn't the sort of girl who would give a man an engraved revolver as a gift. Anything was possible, of course, but this contingency was not only implausible but any attempt to bring forth such a theory in court would be damaging. He could see Kenworthy's long mouth turn into a sneering grin as the district attorney said, "And she gave it to him as a present, gentlemen. Think of it—a present!"

If only Claire would tell him everything!' Didn't she know that he would understand, that he would sympathize, that he would, if necessary, forgive? Probably he was conjuring up a situation far more unfavorable than that which actually existed. He hoped so.

Jimmy left the train thoughtfully and trooped up Fifth Avenue, gay in the sunlight which decorated its white buildings. He reviewed the case from the time of Stelke's hurried message to his own imprisonment and release. He brushed heedlessly into itinerants as he worked out the details on the premise that Claire was the motivating force behind the shooting.

"Why didn't I let it go as a suicide?" he exclaimed so loudly that a stout old lady swerved out of his path and hurried on agitatedly.

"I suppose that's my reward for trying to be clever!"

He cursed Hugh, who had introduced him to Bernard Gartlin. He cursed Bernard Gartlin and all of his stratagems. He prayed for the wrath of heaven on Bernard's creator and condemned the inventor of detective stories to an unprintable doom.

"Nerves, nerves, nerves," he reflected, as he passed into Central Park. "I could be strolling here, enjoying the scenery and contemplating the beauties hidden in a great city if it weren't for nerves. Nerves drove me into this."

He placed a particularly drastic curse upon his neurotic tendencies.

"But if Claire did it, why—?"

He could make out a case against Claire. So could Brinze. Yet Claire wasn't a wanton murderess. She wouldn't have had Payne assassinated for entertainment. What relationship had existed between her and the dead financier? Payne was gone. He couldn't answer. And so far as Jimmy was concerned, Claire, too, was gone.

He trudged to his apartment and lay down wearily. His slumber was short and uneasy and when he awoke he thought he was still in the Bellechester prison. He looked out into the dusk. Another night ahead of him, and nothing to do, nothing to occupy his mind except thoughts of Claire. He wanted to go to her. He wanted to appeal to her, to take her away.

"Out of it all!"

The sentimental tag moved him and amused him.

"I'm getting to be Sidney Carton," he reflected. "Next thing, I'll be confessing to the murder and going to the chair saying 'And I did it all for you, little girl!'"

Through the twilight came an easily recognizable voice, singing quaveringly an all too recognizable melody.

Jimmy jumped from his chair and rushed to the street without waiting for the elevator. He stopped and tiptoed to the little area leading into the basement of the apartment.

"So that's who it was!"

The shadow, hiding in a dark corner, was singing.

Jimmy crept up beside the man and grasped him by the shoulders. The song stopped suddenly. The shadow tore himself from Jimmy's hold and made for the stairs. As Jimmy rushed after him, the shadow wheeled and shoved the pursuer down the steps. Jimmy landed sharply on the stones, but leaped to his feet and bounded up the stairs and down the street. The shadow again had vanished.

Jimmy shook his head. He was stronger than this frail, unwelcome adherent. Why couldn't he have had sense enough to knock him down first, to beat him into unconsciousness, if necessary, and to hold him a prisoner until he learned from him who was the principal who employed this tenacious but evanescent agent?

"Who's after me, anyhow?" he wondered.

He went to his little strong box and laid the exhibits on his desk. There was a threatening letter, and a false mustache along with a marked copy of *The Porterhouse Murder*.

"That's a silly collection," remarked Jimmy. "My nerves ought to be in that box, too."

He lit a cigarette.

"My nerves ought to be—"

As he repeated this to himself, he glanced again at Exhibit C—the Bernard Gartlin adventure tale. He narrowed his eyes, as Gartlin himself was wont to do when in deep research. Then he locked his trophies carefully in the box.

"So *that* is it!" he murmured sagely.

XV
TARGETS

Thunder squalls early in the morning—ten o'clock was early for Jimmy in these days—led Jimmy to believe that he could venture where he wished without the unseen observation of the shadow. Nevertheless his rain coat and his gray tweed cap almost amounted to a disguise. As he inspected himself in the mirror in the lobby he fancied a resemblance to Bernard Gartlin. Gartlin, in most of his manifestations, had worn a linen duster, but at least one of his million masks involved a raincoat. And the tweed cap was so much a favorite headgear with the great detective as occasionally to invalidate his ingenious transformations.

"Even beginning to dress like a detective," thought Jimmy.

It had not been so long since he had last visited the financial district, but Wall Street seemed like a strange thoroughfare today. He was glad that it was raining. The usual loungers in the streets had been driven indoors. The younger brokers, of whom he knew many, didn't care to risk their expensive clothing in the downpour. Jimmy could make his way about without fear of an inconvenient meeting with an acquaintance who would say that he hadn't seen him for a long time and what had he been doing? There would be no encounter with some official of the Universal Sugar Refining Company who would animadvert that he thought Jimmy was ill.

Jimmy entered Ye Arabian Coffee House. It was a collection of rafters, old sporting prints—just what you might have expected to find in Arabia—and bare, pine tables.

The bill of fare presented a study. "Arabian and American" lunches were promised, and there was genuine Arabian coffee, which might be taken home "for home use." The mimeographed bill flaunted undecipherable names, followed by parenthetical "meat balls with sauce" and "roast beef." Jimmy pointed to the Arabian for roast beef and asked the waiter to bring him "some of this."

As he disposed of the dish in a leisurely manner— the motto of Ye Arabian Coffee House was "festino lente"—he watched the door. Men in raincoats swished in out of the streets and sat inconspicuously at the wooden tables. Novices were struggling with the Arabic nomenclature of the menu. The food, Jimmy thought, was nothing that could not be obtained at a lower price in any marble-topped caravansary, but there was atmosphere. The young men who escorted pretty girls descanted on the charming Arabian aura in respectful adjectives. Jimmy thought that he would help his firm to raise the price of sugar by renaming the corporation, "Ye Universalle Sugar Refining Company." They could add another cent per pound by making it "Ye Olde."

His survey of the economic implications of quaint titles came to an abrupt end as Claire entered, followed by Hesbe. Jimmy was glad that he had eaten. The sight of Claire still paralyzed his emotions and dissolved his interest in food. So Hesbe was still a favored suitor. Well, why shouldn't he be? Wasn't he her fiancé?

Jimmy picked up the punched check which the waiter had dropped and made his way to the cashier's desk. He halted at Claire's table. At least she would give some sign of recognition. He paused hesitantly, and looked directly at Claire. Her golden hair glittered ravishingly in the mild glow of the yellow lamp. Hesbe, as usual, seemed pale and menacing in a spineless way. He was a human eel, and not so very human.

Was Claire oblivious of his presence? Jimmy summoned a light cough. Claire had noticed it. She had noticed him when she entered ye coffee house. But she bent all too intently over the bill of fare, as though to hide in it until Jimmy had passed.

"Good morning."

The salutation direct brought no response. Jimmy grunted as though he had been struck by a foul blow and shuffled listlessly on. A hortatory clearing of the throat from the cashier prompted him to toss the check and a bill on his desk. He shuffled further.

Rain, rain, rain. Rain was in his mood now. Claire had given him the cut direct. He no longer meant anything in her life. His greetings were not even worthy of acknowledgment. He wasn't even a passing acquaintance who might say "Hello" and receive a formal smile in return.

Disheartened, ill in several senses, and utterly depressed, Jimmy wandered home. Sleep sometimes had relieved him in this condition. He tried to lose consciousness. The bleak, damp day was ideal for slumber. But again, slumber was not to be captured. He tossed wretchedly. The old quivers began to come over him. What a hell of a thing it was to be in love! It was worse than ever now. Once it had been only a simple case of unrequited affection. Now it was complicated by murder, the entanglement of his beloved, double-edged clews and shadows. Why couldn't he have left life alone? He would never tamper with his nervous system again by falling in love. Live and let live would be enough. Love and let love would be debarred.

He felt feverish. Perhaps he had caught cold in the rain. He hoped that his discomfort could be attributed to the weather. He really ought to see a doctor in any case.

It was too wet for a man with a fever to go out. His forehead didn't seem abnormally warm, but there was moisture on it. He felt stinging pains in his knees.

He called Dr. Farrigan on the telephone.

"Can't you come over?" demanded Hugh, who had been put out of sorts by the weather.

"I feel too rotten, I'm afraid to."

"Not enough exercise and too much brooding," diagnosed Hugh. "Keep quiet, don't think of anything, and I'll be over."

The little clock on the desk seemed to lose interest in life, as Jimmy paced about, waiting for Hugh. Why didn't he come? He wasn't a busy physician. Didn't he realize that this was an urgent call? He wanted to telephone again, and the clock told him reproachfully that he had been waiting only four minutes.

Hugh stepped into the apartment rather suddenly, carrying a little black bag.

"Been walking around?" he asked aggressively. The accusing, "steely" look disturbed Jimmy.

"I can't lie down. I feel worse lying down than walking around."

"You'll feel worse if you keep on walking. Sit down, at least, and let me look you over."

Hugh took his pulse and his temperature. He looked at the thermometer curiously.

"How long have you felt this way?" he inquired.

"Just for a couple of hours."

Jimmy had a foolish sensation as he answered.

"Is it much temperature?" he asked.

"It strikes me you're developing into a hypochondriac," remarked Hugh. "You've got a good pulse, and dead normal temperature. You don't need a doctor. What you need is a little sense."

He sat down and lit his pipe.

"First you worried yourself into a fine nervous state about a girl," he said. "Then you took these detective stories too seriously and worried yourself with the idea that all suicides were murders and that you were the detective who would unravel them. Whether there's something new now, I don't know. But what you need most is a change of scene. I'll bet that everything in this room reminds you of something that upsets you."

"Something in that," confessed Jimmy.

"Something? Everything!" snorted Hugh. "Another thing is that you haven't followed my instructions."

"Didn't I read a whole library?" moaned Jimmy.

"That isn't what I'm talking about. If you'd only read the books and let it go at that, everything might have been all right. Instead of that, you worked yourself up over this thing of being the Man of a Million Masks or Sherlock Holmes or somebody. Why don't you take up golf seriously or go on a little pleasure trip?"

"I don't want to take a trip, little or big," remonstrated Jimmy. "Heaven only knows what might happen while I was away."

"Enough can happen if you stay here," retorted Hugh. "But don't take my word for it. I'm only an orthopedist, anyhow. See some good neurologist like Villmers down at the hospital."

"I don't want to see anybody," demurred Jimmy. "I'm going to stay right here."

Hugh shrugged his shoulders.

"That's up to you, I suppose," he commented. "But at least you might do something to get out of this atmosphere. You've got a pretty little apartment, but its associations are bad for you."

Jimmy agreed that the plan might be feasible.

"I'll tell you what," suggested the physician. "There's an extra bed in my place. Suppose you sleep there tonight. Sleeping in a strange bed may help to break up the trouble you have right now, and when you feel a little more composed, we can make the cure permanent."

"All right."

Jimmy sighed. Perhaps Hugh was right. There could be no harm in this short hegira, and perhaps the innovation might relieve the tension.

As he sat with Hugh at the open window that evening, enjoying the fresh breeze that blew through the streets after the day of rain, and looking wistfully at the sunset sky—sunset had all manner of sentimental connotations for Jimmy, although he had never observed it in Claire's company—the familiar refrain came wafting up.

"Do you mind if I close the window?" asked Jimmy.

"Too drafty?"

"No, not that, but—"

Hugh closed the window, and the shutting off of the voice seemed to relieve Jimmy.

"Feeling better?" inquired Hugh.

"Somewhat."

Jimmy felt disinclined to discuss the song, its significance and its recurrences with Hugh. So far as the physician was concerned, the nervousness induced by the melody was only another symptom in the case as a whole. And to tell it would be foolish. Jimmy didn't mind thinking of himself as a melodramatic hero, but he didn't want to speak like one.

Finally he picked up an old issue of *Pharmaceutical Phun* and went to bed. The little room was inviting. There were no memories dangling from the walls and no reminders on the chair and table. He went to sleep without much assistance from *Pharmaceutical Phun*.

Jimmy wasn't certain how long he had been asleep when it happened, it being a series of shots somewhere in the street. He jumped from the bed and opened the window wide, staring across the way.

There seemed to be lights in all the houses, and people in night-gowns were gaping from hundreds of windows. He found Hugh's door open, but the physician evidently either hadn't heard the shooting or wasn't interested. He lay in bed and looked around drowsily.

"Didn't you hear the shooting?" called Jimmy.

"Shooting? I heard a tire explode. What do you want?"

"There's been shooting on the street. Everybody's up. I wonder what it was."

"A new mystery for you to solve," droned Hugh. "More work for the undertaker."

"Oh, wake up!"

Jimmy was thoroughly aroused. He was figuring on how long it would take him to get dressed and be in the thick of this affair. He wouldn't wait to be informed by a coroner this time!

"Somebody's been shot!"

Hugh propped himself up on his elbow.

"How do you know?"

Jimmy didn't know.

"Somebody must have been shot!"

"If so, nobody invited you to chase the murderer."

Hugh sat up.

"You got into enough trouble the first time you insisted on monkeying with a shooting," he remarked. "I'd think you'd be satisfied. You'll only make yourself more ridiculous if you go racing around like Sherlock Holmes."

The commotion already was quieting down. Lights were disappearing and windows were slamming. A few men who had been loitering about the street were going slowly into doorways.

"Maybe you're right," said Jimmy. "It looks all over, anyhow."

He saw a policeman taking a few names from men who seemed to be anxious to be mentioned in connection with so public an event.

"Good night!"

Jimmy went back to his room and closed the door. He sat on the bed for a moment. Then he switched out the light and went to sleep.

Thanking his host for a pleasant and almost eventful night, Jimmy returned to his apartment in the morning. The doorman, who generally greeted him with only a perfunctory salute, stared at him thoughtfully. The elevator man left his car and inspected Jimmy from a point of vantage.

"Why all this?" asked Jimmy. "Didn't you expect to see me alive again?"

"It's this way," explained the doorman. "They shot up your apartment last night, Mr. Wrome."

Shooting in his own apartment—and he had missed it! Jimmy was more disappointed than surprised.

"Who's 'they'?" he asked. "Who shot up my apartment?"

"Nobody knows. I tried to break in, but the door was locked, and when I got in, somebody covered me with a gun, and when the night man came up, the man had gotten away down the fire-escape and we couldn't find him."

The shadow, of course.

"That's too bad," said Jimmy.

"Take me up," he told the elevator man.

"You come along, too," he added to the doorman.

The door was closed, but the lock had been broken.

"We left everything as it was," explained the doorman, "in case you wanted to call the police."

"I don't," said Jimmy. "That wouldn't be much use—not now, anyhow. Let's see what he took."

The chairs and tables had been upset, and the intruder obviously had rummaged through the closets and the bureau drawers, but nothing seemed to be missing.

"I guess he didn't find what he was after," observed Jimmy.

"Maybe we scared him off," said the doorman.

"Maybe you did."

Jimmy was looking at the bed. The maid, who came in once a day to tidy up, had fixed it, but of course no one had slept in it. The covers were wrinkled, and the pillow was in disarray. There was a hole in the pillow slip.

"You say he shot in here?"

"I certainly heard the shot," said the doorman proudly.

"What was he shooting at?"

The doorman bowed to indicate that he had had the honor of being the target.

"You weren't lying on the bed, were you?"

The doorman resented the question and reiterated volubly that he had broken in when he heard the shot.

"Then how could he have been shooting at you?"

"Well, he pointed the gun at me, anyhow," said the doorman defiantly. "And if I'd been there when he shot, he would have shot me."

Jimmy handed him a dollar.

"That'll help you cover the damage," he observed.

Another dollar went into the waiting hand of the elevator man.

"Don't say anything about this," Jimmy cautioned them. "As far as I can see it was just some madman running around and shooting. There's been nothing taken. All I'm out is a little rest and two dollars."

The attendants backed out gracefully and gratefully.

Jimmy lifted the pillow carefully. The hole in it was made by a bullet. There were powder marks on the slip. The shadow, for some fantastic reason, had punctured the linen. Examination revealed that the bullet had lodged in the mattress. Jimmy dug it out, and laid it on the desk.

He lifted the mattress to turn it around. It wouldn't do to have the maid ask too many questions. There was a torn scrap of paper under the mattress. He held up the paper and saw several lines of scribbling on it.

"Don't make a fool of yourself, you are no detective. You are only making trouble for yourself. Let this be a warning to you, we knew you were out but next time the bullet will go to the same spot when you are asleep.

"BEWARE!"

Jimmy held the note under the light. He opened his strong box and dropped in it the bullet and the note.

"I wonder how Gartlin would figure out this assortment," he mused.

XVI
POMP AND CIRCUMSTANCE

If Jimmy hadn't stopped to test the door of his apartment after locking it, he might not have noticed the chalk marks on it. He had planned a day of relaxation at Coney Island, and he was starting out early for a session in the chutes. But the daubs of white dust on the door attracted his attention.

In the darkness of the hallway they seemed to indicate nothing, yet a white trail smeared across a door was not the usual thing in these apartments. Evidently the chalk formed a design, a design indistinguishable in the gloom. He returned to the apartment and examined the chalk marks by the light of a pocket lamp.

Someone had been trying to decorate the panel with a skull and crossbones.

"All part of the game," mused Jimmy.

There was a message traced under the design.

"*The End is Near,*" was the legend.

Jimmy went to the strong box and extracted the threatening message. He compared the writing with that on the door. They were, as Bernard Gartlin liked to say, as like as two peas in a pod, except that the resemblance was far more striking.

"Rather stupid of him," he murmured. "That wasn't subtle."

He was a little aggrieved at his unknown persecutor. The pillow shooting of the night before had had its dramatic values, but this exhibit was crude.

"So the end is near," he reflected, looking at himself in a mirror.

He wondered how the brown-haired young man before him would look if the neat gray suit were removed in favor of a shroud.

Once he had harbored the fugitive notion that death would be preferable to life without Claire. On that occasion, too, he had paused before the same mirror.

"No Coney Island today," he remarked to his image. "You've got work to do, Jimmy."

He removed the chalk marks with a damp cloth and descended for an interview with the doorman. The doorman hadn't seen anybody come in during the night. If anybody had come in it must have been early last night, when he was off duty. Positively! He knew what he was talking about!

Jimmy stopped at the door, looking for any symptoms of his shadow. Finding none, he walked down the street, up Broadway and into Curtin's.

Miss Quaid, cool and demure as ever, greeted him with her delicious smile.

"Are you buying or borrowing this morning?" she asked.

"Neither. I want to ask another favor. I must be asking a lot of favors nowadays, but I'd appreciate this one more than anything you've done for me."

"The store is yours," she said graciously.

"How did you know that I wanted just that?" he demanded.

"Oh, do you?"

"Exactly. I want to be the librarian for about an hour."

"I'm afraid that we couldn't pay you enough to make it worth your while."

"I'll pay you to let me have the job for an hour. How much do you want?"

"Are you serious?"

The cryptic brown eyes manifested amusement.

"Really. Won't you take an hour off, and let me take your place? I know the routine well enough."

"Well," she said judicially, "I could trust you here, of course, but I don't know what Mr. Curtin would think if he happened to come here."

"Leave him to me!"

There was belligerence in Jimmy's voice.

"But why?"

"If you'll trust me with the books, perhaps you'll trust me with a secret. You'll know some day."

"That sounds rather thrilling, although I don't see any excitement in being a librarian."

"I do! It's about nine-thirty now. I'll see you again at ten-thirty."

"How very masterful!"

She awarded to Jimmy a lightly ironic smile.

"I can't disobey so commanding a personality," she went on, "and I did want to do some shopping. So I'll see you again at ten-thirty. The understanding is that if I lose the job, you're to get me a better one!"

"Not only that—I'll get you a good one!" laughed Jimmy, "Don't be gone more than an hour."

He watched her admiringly as she adjusted a gray feather turban and walked gracefully out. Here was a girl, who—

Never mind about that. There was more urgent business at hand.

He investigated the card indices on the desk. He grinned as he learned what some of his friends had been reading. Finally he found two cards that had unusual interest. He put them aside and looked for blank cards. A fussy old gentleman, who declined to pay a fine on a book a week overdue on the ground that the regular librarian wasn't in, interrupted his search, but he unearthed the blanks. He copied the two cards, substituted the copies for the originals, and tucked away the Curtin records in his pocket.

"That'll take some explaining," he mused, "but so will the cards!"

He found nothing difficult about the technique of renting out books although he was hard put to it when a mild lady asked for a book that she could conscientiously recommend as something that would influence her daughter's life for the better. She almost growled when Jimmy suggested *The Shower Bath Enigma.*

"It was a great influence in my life," he said.

"For the better?" she insisted.

"For better or for worse—I hope," he replied, and she hurried out in consternation.

Miss Quaid was a little surprised to find that Jimmy showed no disposition to speak of his adventures as a librarian.

"If you find anything unusual," he said, "don't worry."

"I'll be worried if I don't," she said.

It was back to Wall Street for Jimmy. He would have to interview at least one man—possibly two. The noisy ride was restful and he almost passed his station.

Blinking as he came up to the street, he was aware of a familiar figure at the corner. So Brinze had come to town! Was this developing into a race with Brinze? It would be worth knowing the object of Brinze's visit. He slouched carelessly toward the Bellechester functionary, jostling him mildly as he passed. Brinze whirled about.

"Oh, it's you!" he called out.

"Mr. Brinze!" exclaimed Jimmy, as though he were pleased to renew an acquaintance. "Welcome to our city."

"I guess you won't forget your last welcome to *our* city," laughed Brinze.

"You have a very charming and unique jail," said Jimmy. "I've never seen one like it."

Brinze scowled at his levity.

"It's ready for you again at any time," he said. "I suppose you've decided not to continue in the detective business."

"I'm not in the detective business."

"I don't know what else to call your meddling around with police affairs that don't concern you, but we won't need your valuable services, Mr. Wrome. We've proved our case."

Jimmy put his hands in his pockets. Hands often betrayed excitement.

"Against whom?"

"You'd like to know that, wouldn't you?" sneered Brinze. "Well, you'll find out when we're good and ready."

"No hurry."

Jimmy waved impertinently at the detective and crossed the street. What did Brinze have up his capacious sleeve now? Which case had he proved? Jimmy adopted the tactics of the shadow and trailed Brinze. The pursuit led to John Street and the building which housed, among others, Hesbe.

This was easy. Blake's little office had an anteroom, and it would be simple to wait for Brinze there. Jimmy's appearance could pass as a coincidence.

The attendant seemed startled as Jimmy entered, but Jimmy acted naturally.

"What do you want to see him about?" asked the wan factotum.

"Personal."

"You can't see him now. He's busy."

"I'll wait."

The attendant looked at him shiftily.

"He'll be a long time."

"With Mr. Brinze?"

The attendant was confused.

"I dunno," he mumbled.

"Well, it was Mr. Brinze I wanted to see, anyhow."

"You can't go in now."

"All right. I'll send him a note."

"Can't be disturbed."

Jimmy stood up militantly.

"You take a note in right now!" he shouted.

He snatched a sheet of paper from the desk and scribbled a few lines.

"Take this in at once," he snapped, "or I'll knock you down and take it in myself."

The bravado was effective, and the attendant took up the sheet listlessly.

"Wait," said Jimmy. "I want a receipt for that note."

An inquiring grunt was the only response.

"Sit down and write this," Jimmy commanded. "'Received, one document for delivery,' and sign your name."

"What for?"

"Write it!"

The sparkling brown eyes and the clenched fists, so impressed the man that he scrawled the required receipt.

"Thanks. Now take it in."

Brinze stalked out of Hesbe's room almost immediately. He bristled.

"What do you mean by this?" he bellowed, waving the note. "Didn't I tell you to keep out of this?"

"I wouldn't be doing my duty if I didn't tell you what I know," purred Jimmy.

"'I've proved my case, too'," recited Brinze, reading from the note. "Since when have you had a case to prove?"

"The last couple of hours," drawled Jimmy.

"All right. You can prove it in the newspapers—like you proved it last time."

"I'll prove it in court."

"The only way you'll get to talk in court is on the stand, after we clap the old man in jail."

Jimmy stopped short. The old man! Brinze was aware of his slip, despite Jimmy's efforts to appear disinterested.

"Yes, the old man!" reiterated Brinze. "What are you going to do about it?"

"Why should I do anything about the old man?" Jimmy ventured. "I don't know which old man you mean. The country's full of old men."

"You'll know which old man inside of twenty-four hours."

Brinze threw out his chest fatuously.

"I can't waste time talking about things," he concluded. "Good morning."

Jimmy stood silently in the ante-room as Brinze reentered Hesbe's office. The old man, of course, was old man Barton. So they had selected him as the murderer! "Chairchez la femm." They had connected Claire with the revolver and probably the revolver with Barton.

Again Jimmy sought motives. If Barton had killed Payne, he must have been in Bellechester at some time prior to the shooting. That point would have to be investigated. But why did he wish to put Payne out of the way? Had the old man stepped in to save his daughter's honor?

This glitteringly sensational hypothesis appealed strongly to Jimmy. Sad but determined fathers always were shooting wealthy but unscrupulous sensualists. There was the old veteran in *The Statue of Liberty Tangle*, who had knifed the senator at midnight in the Statute of Liberty torch. The veteran's daughter—

But it seemed too simple. Payne might well have had designs on Claire. Any man would have desired her. But even had he made advances—anything more was unthinkable—Claire wouldn't have asked the assistance of her father. There was a singular streak of independence in her. She was too reticent. Had she only confided in Jimmy from the outset, matters would have been better for her. Or better for Jimmy. He didn't know whether she was merely a passing guest in Payne's home or whether she had known him for years. Claire rarely volunteered information and it was hard to extract it from her.

It occurred to Jimmy that all of the serious investigations of the death had started with the shooting. It was curious that no one apparently had thought of looking into the events precedent to the murder. Gartlin wouldn't have overlooked them. Jimmy wouldn't overlook them, either.

He hurried from the office to the railroad station and made a tedious local train to Bellechester. Brinze wouldn't be there today to disturb him by putting him in a cell, and the shadow probably wouldn't be on hand to observe his actions.

Bellechester seemed as sleepily suburban as ever when Jimmy stepped off the train. This, he hoped, would be his last trip to this rustic haven. He fingered his chin as he contemplated the road that led to Olean and was pleased to discover that he needed a shave.

The tonsorial Rooks greeted him coldly.

"That was a wonderful shave you gave me the other day," said Jimmy heartily.

The barber emitted an indescribable sound.

"I mean it," Jimmy continued with outrageous sincerity. "My face never felt like that before. We men who have to shave ourselves are victims. If you'd start a shop in New York, you'd be benefiting mankind and you'd make a fortune. Think it over."

He placed himself in the chair.

"Shave?" grunted Rooks.

"Shave, haircut, shampoo, massage and any special treatment you think would be good. I leave myself entirely in your hands."

Carte blanche seemed to sooth the still ruffled pride of the barber, for he went about his cutical ministrations with a wealth of tenderness.

"I used to have a friend here," remarked Jimmy. "Maybe you'd know where I can find him. His name's Stelke."

Rooks deliberately re-sharpened his razor before replying.

"Used to work up at Payne's?"

"I think so. He was his secretary or something."

"Secretary—hell!" sniffed the barber. "He was his butler. That's the kind of big talk he's always handing out. Bet you don't know what he's doing now."

"I couldn't imagine."

"He's nothing but a waiter over at Kimmy's hash house."

"Where's Kimmy's?"

"Down the block. If you're looking for Stelke, that's where you'll find him, but don't eat there if you value your stomach."

"That's very good of you."

"I'm not doing anybody a favor by warning him off that place. I wouldn't eat there myself. Don't move your head so much."

Jimmy closed his eyes and dozed as the barber completed his operations. He surveyed himself in the mirror when the ceremony was over.

"Wonderful!" he murmured. "Wonderful!"

Rewarding Rooks with another unreasonable bonus, Jimmy strolled down Bellechester's Main Street until he reached the beaten white shack which was Kimmy's. Flies and chauffeurs droned over the damp tiled tables. Stelke was rushing between the tables and the long, dripping food bar. Jimmy sat at a dirty slab in the far corner of the establishment and scanned the greasy cardboard bill of fare.

Stelke, carrying a towel, with which he mopped the tables and his forehead, stopped before Jimmy. He seemed abashed when he saw who his patron was.

"Hello, Stelke," was Jimmy's greeting. "Glad to see you."

He motioned swiftly for Stelke to bend over the table.

"I want to talk to you," he whispered.

"I'm too busy," Stelke said hoarsely.

Jimmy pressed a bill into his hand.

"See if you can't go outside with me for a few minutes," he suggested. "It's very important."

Stelke glanced about.

"Only a minute, sir," he said. "It's almost time for the rush."

"I'll go out first and wait at the corner," said Jimmy. "You come out about a minute later."

He left the restaurant and walked to the Bellechester Second National Bank building. He wondered whether there ever had been a first national bank in this metropolis. Stelke came up to him warily.

"What's up?" he asked.

"Nothing's up," answered Jimmy. "I want to know a few things about what happened just before Mr. Payne died."

Stelke frowned.

"Why do you want to bring that up?" he complained. "I want to forget it. Since it happened, I ain't been able to get a decent place. When people hear I worked for Payne they sort o' shudder and turn away. I tried to get another place, but when they ask me who I worked for last, what can I tell 'em? I was with Payne five years and all I was before that was a handy man. You'd think I killed him myself the way they act when they hear I was with him."

Jimmy shook his head sympathetically.

"When it's all over, I'll see what I can do for you," he said. "Maybe I can use you myself."

"I'll go anywhere!" exclaimed Stelke.

"We'll see. Now, try to remember. Was there anybody except the guests at the house on the day it happened?"

"No. Mr. Payne didn't have much company that he didn't know about beforehand."

"Wasn't there an old man somewhere about the place?"

"If there was, I'd have seen him. We didn't have anybody but you and the rest of them that week-end."

"You didn't see any strangers about the grounds that day?"

"No."

"Could any of the other people in the house have seen any stranger?"

"No. I'm positive of that, sir, because I got all the help together the morning after it happened and asked 'em if they'd seen anybody around and they said no, they hadn't."

"You were in or about the house all day?"

"Yes, sir. My orders was always to be about when we was expectin' company."

"You remember about when each of the guests arrived?"

"Yes, sir."

Stelke looked at the clock on the building.

"If I don't go back now, sir," he said, "like as not they'll fire me, and you don't know what a hard time I've had even gettin' this job."

"I'll walk back with you," volunteered Jimmy, "and I can finish on the way."

They started slowly down Main Street.

"Did you show all the guests to their rooms?" Jimmy went on.

"Yes, sir."

"Now, do you remember the storm? Were you on the ground floor all of the time after Mr. Payne felt ill and went upstairs?"

"Yes, sir."

"Were you there just before that—I mean before tea was served?"

"Almost all the time. I was on the second floor a little while, lookin' to see if there was enough towels and things in the rooms."

"That was when?"

"Just before tea."

"Good. Where was Mr. Payne at that time?"

"He was out in the garden, lookin' over some new plants."

"Not in his room?"

"No, sir. But you'll have to excuse me."

"I'll finish this in a minute. Was Payne's door open or closed all that time?"

Stelke fidgeted.

"I'm not asking whether you went in and out or not," Jimmy explained.

"Can't you let me be?" pleaded Stelke. "Anything I say just makes it that much harder for me to get a good place."

"No matter what happens, I'll protect you. Just answer this: Did you see anybody go into Payne's room before tea?"

Stelke nodded blankly.

"Somebody carrying something?"

Another blank and unwilling nod.

"A small package?" Jimmy hazarded.

"Yes, sir, but please let me go now!"

"All right," Jimmy hurried on. "The person who entered closed the door behind him and came out a moment later, carrying the wrapping of the package, but not the contents."

"It wasn't a he," said Stelke impatiently.

"Now please be accurate," insisted Jimmy.

"It wasn't a he," repeated Stelke. "It was Miss Barton. I've got to go now, sir. I can't afford to stay away. I've been away too long already."

XVII
PREMISES

Several hours later, Jimmy telephoned to Hugh.

"What did you say was the name of that neurologist?" he asked.

"You sound as though you'd been shot," said Hugh. "I guess it's time for you to see a neurologist. Villmers is his name. He's at the hospital."

"Your hospital?"

"Yes. I'll give you a card to him."

"Never mind."

Jimmy struggled to the hospital and found the office of Dr. Villmers. The neurologist was a tall, slender man, with inquiring brown eyes and a handsome brown beard. He looked alert but there was a world-weary manner about him. He was a man who had listened to many sorrows. The interview was brief, and Jimmy emerged from the office with a sad smile.

"I hope this won't be an extended treatment," he thought, "but it seems to be what I needed."

When he returned home, he found a note on his door.

"More threats?" he murmured.

But it was only a message to ring a number. The number gave Jimmy all sorts of palpitations. His hands bobbed about as he called it, and he swayed on the chair until an answering voice came over the wire.

"Oh, Jimmy!"

Fear and relief were in Claire's voice.

"You must have been surprised when you got my message," she went on hurriedly, "and I hated to call you up—after everything."

"It's all right."

"That's good of you, Jimmy. But, Jimmy—I know how you feel and I—"

"What is it?"

Her hesitation maddened him. Was she going to break gently the news of her engagement to Hesbe? This was true feminine delicacy!

"Jimmy, we're in trouble."

A heavy breath.

"Who's 'we'?"

"Father and I—all of us."

The words rushed now.

"Jimmy, father's been arrested for the death of Mr. Payne and I'm going mad!"

So the old man had been captured!

"Jimmy—I wanted to tell you, I thought—"

"You thought I might help you out?"

He stamped his foot angrily as he realized the brutality of the question.

A sob was Claire's only answer.

"Little girl, you haven't treated me right, but I'll stick by you till—"

Wouldn't it have been fine to deliver some such bombast now? The hero of *The Rosenbaum Case* had won his lady in these words. But Jimmy's head was cold, although he felt the rest of him burning and throbbing.

"Is there a hearing?" he asked.

"There's to be an informal hearing before the district attorney tonight."

"Where?"

"In Bellechester."

"Have you retained a lawyer?"

"Yes—Mr. Durand."

"I see. I don't know why you've called on me, Claire. I asked you to tell me everything and you wouldn't. You wouldn't even nod to me when you met me. It seems a little late now."

"Oh, please, Jimmy," she implored. "I was so wrong about everything."

What "everything" might include was a question which Jimmy was aching to put, but it seemed to be an unfair advantage to take of a distressed girl.

"We'll let all that go for the present," he declared a little grandly. "I can't do much between now and tonight, you know."

"Nothing?"

"Only this. There are reasons why I wouldn't be permitted to attend any hearing conducted by the authorities in Bellechester. I don't think they like me. Now, I want you to tell Mr. Durand this: He must have me there tonight. This preliminary examination by the district attorney isn't of legal consequence, although anything your father says can be held against him. I want to be there as Mr. Durand's secretary. I can't explain this now, and I may do nothing but listen tonight. That's about all I can do for the present."

"That's so good of you, Jimmy. I'll never forget it. You don't think father did it, do you?"

"No matter what I think, you'll have to trust me. I'll see you in Bellechester."

Jimmy hung up the receiver on her tearful thanks. He went to the cabinet and withdrew his strong box. He rang for a taxi.

"You're safer in a safe deposit vault right now," Jimmy remarked to the box.

He felt relieved when he had received a receipt for his treasure. And somehow he managed to sleep quietly for several hours until it was time to go to Bellechester. A great man was Dr. Villmers!

Barton was a sullen, frightened figure, Mrs. Barton was a quivering, frightened figure, Claire was a beautiful, frightened figure, and Durand was a quiet, efficient figure. Brinze and Kenworthy scowled and fumed at Jimmy's presence, but Durand was obdurate. His client had a right to have counsel, and counsel had a right to have assistance.

Kenworthy shrugged his shoulders in disgust and motioned for Brinze to end his protests.

"He doesn't matter, anyhow," he said, pointing to Jimmy with his jaw. "We'll begin this thing now, and I expect direct answers to all of my questions. The manner in which Mr. Barton answers will count as heavily as the matter of his answers. I don't want to indict anyone on so grave a charge, but it's my duty to see that justice is done, painful as it may be."

He sat at Brinze's desk, and arranged a pile of memoranda.

"I'll begin, Mr. Barton, by asking whether you had had at any time personal acquaintance with Leed Payne?"

Mrs. Barton was holding her husband's hand as reassuringly as she could, but Durand tactfully removed her to another part of the room. Barton's eyes were dull, and he looked infinitely old. He was a man who had suffered much, undergoing another ordeal, an unexpected ordeal and one that might well be a breaking experience. He answered listlessly and haltingly, with occasional imploring glances at Durand, as though Durand could mollify Kenworthy's severity and perhaps bring peace to Barton's battered morale.

"I knew him."

Kenworthy's examination was under way.

"When did you see him last?"

"I don't remember."

"That'll do you no good here, Mr. Barton. We're trying to get at the facts. I'm not asking now for the exact minute. Approximately how long ago did you last see Leed Payne?"

"About—about twenty-five years ago."

"Where?"

"In Charleston."

"And you've never seen him since?"

"No."

"Tell us of your relations with Payne in Charleston."

"I just knew him."

"We know that! Were you friendly with him? Did you have business relations with him? Please be more specific."

"I just knew him."

Kenworthy referred to his papers.

"Isn't it a fact that you and Payne were rivals in love?"

Jimmy, who had been slipping into a leisurely attitude, sat up. So Brinze also had found the trail to Charleston! How many other trails had he found?

"Well—you might call it that."

"Thank you. And Payne was in love with the present Mrs. Barton?"

"Is it necessary to go into that?" interrupted Durand.

"It certainly is. Will you answer my question, please, Mr. Barton?"

"He liked her. Many young fellows liked her."

Mrs. Barton smiled sweetly.

"Liked her, did he? Wasn't he a pretty heavy suitor?"

"You might call it that."

"With your permission, I will call it that. And you, as it were, won her from him?"

"No," broke in Mrs. Barton. "From the minute I met my husband, there wasn't any other man."

"Very touching, I'm sure, and I'll accept your answer in place of Mr. Barton's. But I'd like Mr. Barton to answer for himself hereafter. There was some sort of fight between you and Payne right after the marriage, wasn't there!"

"How?"

Kenworthy read from a typewritten sheet an account of the shooting in the saloon. The wording of the statement convinced Jimmy that Ormer had told his story again for the benefit of Brinze or one of his agents.

"Is that substantially correct?" concluded Kenworthy.

"Yes."

"Payne made statements to the effect that he would get you. He also said that he had something on you. What did he mean by that?"

"I decline to let my client answer that question," said Durand.

"That's a pity. His own statement would have been valuable. We'll drop the matter for a moment. Mr. Barton—when you were married, you were employed in a bank, were you not?"

"Yes."

"And setting up housekeeping was an expensive proposition—compared, I mean, to bachelorhood."

"You might call it that."

"I think I would call it that. And you needed funds—that is, within the month before your marriage?"

"Yes."

Jimmy noted the deadening of Barton's voice and the tension of Mrs. Barton and Claire. He feared Kenworthy's next question.

"By the way, you eloped, didn't you?"

"Is that material?" asked Durand.

"You might call it that," mimicked Kenworthy, "but we'll let it go, if you don't like it. At any rate, Mr. Barton needed money. That much is admitted. And how did Mr. Barton get the money? I'll ask Mr. Barton whether he didn't do a little speculating?"

A nod answered.

"And when the speculation went astray, didn't Payne come to the rescue?"

"Yes."

"Payne, as we learn, came to the rescue. He came to the rescue, in answer to an imploring letter. I have it here. It was in Payne's effects. Perhaps Mr. Barton can tell us the contents."

Barton bowed his head over his hands.

"This letter is one of a series of three, which Payne, for reasons of his own, kept in his safe. I shall now read them, and ask Mr. Barton to offer any comment he chooses."

Kenworthy took three envelops from the desk. "Number one. The post-mark is 1897, and it was written in Charleston.

"'Dear Friend Payne: For God's sake, help me out with three hundred dollars. If you do not, I shall be unable to make good this sum to the bank, and I cannot face the consequences of my folly. Anything I have or ever shall have is yours.'

"Number two. 'Dear Friend Payne: In God's name I beg you not to exact further payments from me. I have paid you over and over again for your accommodation in those early days, and I need every cent to keep my little business alive. Can you not have mercy on me?'

"That was written in 1907. Number three was written ten years later. There is no salutation, but the address and the handwriting are sufficient to identify it.

"'I am giving up my business, for I can no longer pay tribute to you. I have nothing left in the world, and it is only the goodness of God that makes it possible for me to support my wife and little daughter. For their sake, I ask you to let me live in peace. I do not know what wrong I may have done you, but if my ruin and poverty will serve as your compensation, you have gained it.'"

Kenworthy replaced the letters.

"I read them, Mr. Durand," he remarked, with a mocking bow to Barton's attorney, "to prove that Mr. Barton had good reason for being none too kindly disposed towards Payne."

"They seem to prove," retorted Durand, "that Payne was a blackmailer of the lowest order."

"We're not trying Payne," snapped Kenworthy, "Somebody else seems to have taken that duty on himself, and that's why we're here this pleasant evening."

He stroked back his hair and ordered the pile of papers on his desk.

"Now I'll ask Mr. Brinze a few questions."

Brinze buttoned his sport coat jauntily, and straightened out importantly. His answers were crisp and delivered with due regard for dramatic effect.

"You know a man named Hesbe—Blake Hesbe, do you not?"

"Yes, sir."

"This Hesbe is in the brokerage business, is he not?"

"In a small way. He handles no large accounts. He has no seat on the exchange and he deals through larger houses for small customers."

"Very good. You have investigated him?"

"Thoroughly."

"He was, in a sense, a business agent for Payne?"

"Yes. Payne handled only big transactions, and referred small business to Hesbe."

"In the course of business, Hesbe became fairly familiar with Payne? They were friendly?"

"Yes."

"Who told you this?"

"Hesbe."

"Hesbe was also friendly with Miss Claire Barton?"

"Don't you think that you ought to ask Miss Barton that?" suggested Durand.

"Possibly at the trial. You can put her on the stand then, if you care to. Now, Mr. Brinze, describe what you have discovered about the relations between Hesbe, Miss Barton and Payne."

"It was about like this. Hesbe, as I said, got Payne's chicken feed, and sometimes attended to little business matters for him. Payne accepted no commission on this business, although Hesbe says he offered to pay it. Payne took it out in personal errands and things of that sort.

"Payne took a fancy to Miss Barton."

Claire's face turned red, and her mother tried to comfort her.

"Payne knew who she was, and wanted to meet her. Hesbe, having an office in the same building in which Miss Barton worked, was told to arrange a meeting. He managed to scrape up an acquaintance and so Payne got to know Miss Barton.

"I couldn't get from Hesbe whether Payne intended to marry Miss Barton. Hesbe says he doesn't know. Anyhow, Miss Barton soon learned that Payne had some sort of hold on her father. She wouldn't go out with Payne, even when he threatened her."

Jimmy wanted to applaud this bit of testimony. He uttered "good girl!" so audibly that Kenworthy and Brinze frowned savagely.

"Never mind the emotional reactions of intruders, Mr. Brinze," said Kenworthy. "Go on with your story."

"Payne told Hesbe that he was going to invite Miss Barton for a week-end. Hesbe told Miss Barton and induced her to invite him to go along—for her protection, as he said. He also told her that he knew about Payne's ideas, and that he would save her from him."

"Double-crossed Payne, in short," interpolated Durand.

"We're not passing on Hesbe's motives," announced Kenworthy.

"I suggest that Miss Barton tell her version of this matter," said Durand.

"Mr. Brinze's account seems adequate."

"I insist that Miss Barton check it up."

Kenworthy hesitated.

"All right," he assented. "Of course, I'm not bound by anything she says here. Miss Barton, do you care to add your version of this affair to Mr. Brinze's?"

Claire stood up. Jimmy saw that she was summoning all her forces to speak coherently and to avert a collapse.

"Mr. Brinze's story is substantially correct—that part of it which concerns me," she said in a voice that was beautiful for all its

restrained agitation. "Mr. Hesbe made my acquaintance, introduced me to Mr. Payne, and then made use of his knowledge of my
father's misfortunes to thrust his company on me. I might add that
in a minor way, he forced silence on me. He forbade me to discuss in
any way his relations with him on pain of giving up his efforts with
Payne in behalf of my father. What these efforts may have been, I
don't know.

"He even went so far as to intimate to his friends that I would
marry him. When I protested, he said that we could discuss the matter later, but that I must give the impression of being his fiancée in
order that he might complete his schemes to release my father I see
now that that was all false."

Jimmy almost cheered. His pleasure was so evident, that Durand
cautioned him not to show too much feeling.

"Payne called me to his office one day, and invited me for a week-
end at Bellechester. I declined, but he said that no harm would come
to me and threatened something very unpleasant to my father if I
wouldn't come. I knew then that my father was no longer answer-
able for—for anything that had happened twenty-five years ago, but
I knew that any publicity would break his heart and perhaps kill
him. What else could I do?"

"You told your father?" asked Kenworthy.

"I didn't intend to, but he insisted on knowing where I was going
for the week-end, and I told him the truth."

"That's more than satisfactory," remarked Kenworthy. "That's
all for the present, Miss Barton." He turned suddenly to Barton.

"Where were you on the night that Payne died, Mr. Barton?" he
shouted.

Barton hardly raised his head.

"Nowhere in particular."

"You were somewhere and somewhere in particular. You know
where you were, and there's no use evading the question."

"He doesn't have to answer," objected Durand.

"I say he does! Were you at home that night, Mr. Barton?"

No answer.

Kenworthy shifted to Mrs. Barton.

"Was your husband home on the night to which I refer?"

Mrs. Barton, completely taken aback mumbled a soft negative.

"Where were you then, Mr. Barton? Answer me!"

No answer.

"All right."

Kenworthy pushed a buzzer on the desk, and constable Rooks entered.

"Bring in Hatch," snapped Kenworthy.

Rooks returned in a moment, with a homely, heavyset man of middle age.

"Mr. Hatch," said Kenworthy, "you were the clerk on duty at the Coliseum Hotel here on the night on which Leed Payne died?"

'Yes, sir."

"There were not many visitors?"

"No, sir—not for that time of year."

"You could identify any of the guests who registered while you were on duty?"

"Certainly."

"Very good. Look at this man here and tell me whether he stopped at the hotel that night."

Hatch squinted at Barton.

"Yes, sir."

"Do you recall under what name he registered?"

"Yes, sir. Mr. Brown of New York."

"That's all, Mr. Hatch. You may go."

As Hatch retired, Kenworthy turned triumphantly to Barton.

"Naturally, we looked up all the strangers in town after the shooting, Mr. Barton. We identified all except a mysterious Mr. Brown of New York. The camera-eyed Mr. Hatch described the unknown Mr. Brown so accurately that we knew where to find him if we needed him. Do you deny that you were registered at the Coliseum Hotel on that night under the name of Brown?"

"No," moaned Barton. "My God, I only came out here so I could be on the ground if anything happened to Claire. I didn't know what Payne was up to. I wanted to be here to protect my daughter—that was all."

"That was enough. Mr. Durand, is there anything you want to say before I hold Mr. Barton for the grand jury?"

Jimmy pulled Durand's sleeve.

"You keep out of this!" screamed Brinze. "You know what we'll do to you if you butt in again!"

"I have a right to consult with my—secretary," said Durand blandly. "So far you've shown nothing to indicate that my client was in any way connected with the death of Payne."

"We don't have to tell you everything," retorted Kenworthy, "and we have enough evidence to hold him."

"It's late now," demurred Durand, "and there are a few bits of evidence I want to lay before you. May we continue this in the morning? You can see for yourself that my client is in no condition to answer further questions now."

"As a courtesy to you, I'll defer making out the papers until ten o'clock tomorrow morning. But I may as well tell you that we've only touched the evidence in our possession."

"There's the gun—" Brinze started grandly.

"Shut up, you fool!" barked Kenworthy.

Again he pressed the buzzer for Rooks.

"We'll hold this man overnight," the district attorney ordered.

Jimmy looked for a tearful scene, but Barton meekly followed the constable, without looking at his family. Claire and Mrs. Barton were huddled together, paying little attention to the soothing words of Durand. Kenworthy locked his papers in the desk, took his hat from the rack and started for the door with Brinze.

"Pardon me," said Jimmy. "May I look at your New York telephone book?"

With a grunt, Brinze flung it at him.

"Good night," jeered the detective. "Maybe you'll find the murderer's name in it."

Jimmy opened the book at the H's, and ran his finger down a row of names. Then he wrote a few lines on a slip of paper.

"I don't care how you do it," he told Durand, "but get this man here at ten tomorrow. That's the address."

"Nonsense!" exclaimed the lawyer.

"Do it!" insisted Jimmy, striding quickly from the room. "I've got to telephone to New York."

XVIII
CONCLUSIONS

There was one addition to the melancholy gathering chaperoned by Durand in Brinze's office the next morning. He was Dr. Villmers, and his brooding calm seemed to soothe the worn nerves of the Bartons. Jimmy was at high tension, but only the brightness of his eyes indicated his mental state. Dr. Villmers had brought with him a sort of restfulness.

"Good morning, everybody!" was the greeting of Kenworthy.

The district attorney evidently expected to clean up the case rapidly, for he was in his golf costume, and a bag of clubs rested against the wall. Brinze, also handsomely arrayed, showed plainly that he expected to have the indictment proceedings over with before many minutes had passed.

"Here," said Kenworthy, "Are the indictment papers—the complaint, in short,—properly drawn up, awaiting my signature. As a courtesy to Mr. Durand, I have postponed the actual signing until this morning. I want you to understand that there is nothing personal about this matter. I am only an instrument of the law, and I must do my duty. It is with deep regret that I am compelled to hold Mr. Barton for the grand jury."

Durand arose.

"This is no time to enter an official plea," he said, "but in the interests of law and justice, I wish to present a few considerations to Mr. Kenworthy. I therefore turn over the statement of these facts to Mr. Wrome here."

"We know Mr. Wrome," said Brinze. "We've heard some of his notions. Is there any good reason, Mr. Durand, why we should hear more of them?"

213

"I prefer to let Mr. Wrome speak," answered Durand stiffly. "Go ahead, Mr. Wrome."

Kenworthy and Brinze exchanged more or less skillful winks, as Jimmy unlocked his little strong box and arranged the contents on a small table.

"What's that mustache for?" inquired Brinze. "Going to a masquerade?"

"Masquerade?" repeated Jimmy. "Something like that."

He sat down, folded his hands, and spoke quietly. The great Gartlin always was supremely calm at this stage of proceedings.

"To begin with," he said. "I'm rather a nervous young man. Dr. Villmers here, whom you may have heard of as a neurologist, will be glad to testify to that. I might add that I didn't make so great an inroad on his valuable time merely to prove that my nerves sometimes go awry.

"Some time ago, my affections were involved deeply for the first time."

"Is this a love story?" interrupted Brinze. "I thought you were going to tell us who killed Payne?"

"'Chairchez la femm' to quote your classical French," Jimmy went on smoothly, "but we must wait for our femm."

"As a result of this entanglement, my nerves were upset and I consulted a physician. He advised me to read detective stories to divert my mind and interests. Dr. Villmers will tell you that the adoption of this curious habit in the frame of mind in which I was then resulted in an obsession. That means that I saw life in terms of detective stories."

"You still do," observed Brinze.

"Fortunately, yes. When Dr. Farrigan invited me to go to Olean with him, I naturally saw the whole scene as the background for a mystery. It was all like the books I had read. Even Payne looked like a character. You know—the strong, irritable, lucky banker, with plenty of enemies. He always turns up in those yarns.

"When I went to Shuffle Inn that night, my mind was full of the possibilities of the situation. The banker ill at home, while his guests were making merry only a little way off. And when I heard Dr.

Farrigan paged, I couldn't resist the impulse to insert myself in the situation.

"You know what I found when I hurried back to Olean. If the darkened room, the mysterious manner of Stelke, the butler, and the grave tones of the doctor weren't typical properties of a, mystery story, I didn't know my mystery stories. Of course, I had to be the last to learn of the event. Throughout this case, I seem to have come upon the scene after everyone else had been over it.

"And here you are again," chirped Brinze.

"This time I'm not so certain that I'm late. My first thought naturally was 'Did Payne really shoot himself?' Why should he commit suicide? Wasn't it more likely that some enemy had squared an old grudge? I managed to look over the ground, and I found that there was no doubt that Payne had fired the shot that ended his life."

"Then what the hell is all this for?" shouted Kenworthy.

"But—it was not suicide. Payne was murdered. He was murdered by someone who was several miles away at the time of the shooting, and the actual murder took place about five or six hours before the shot was fired."

Kenworthy stirred in his chair.

"This is all most diverting," he remarked coldly, "but we're trying to get at facts."

"You're getting at them. The manner in which the murder was committed flashed into my mind instantly. I also thought that I knew who did it. My suspicion was incorrect, but in my enthusiasm I blurted out a few generalities to a reporter. I can prove how the murder was done, and the facts do not vary in the slightest from my original hypothesis. The identity of the murderer, however, may be a little surprising.

"You will recall the initialed revolver and the note which Payne left. I thought it curious that the revolver should be there so opportunely. In fact, I was sure that it had been left there by someone who wanted Payne to use it just as he did and who had had it initialed to make it seem natural. I traced the revolver—by a somewhat different method than that which Mr. Brinze used, but with the same results. You are right, Mr. Brinze. It was purchased by Monica Wells, but I am a little surprised that the name doesn't mean more to you."

"Miss Barton bought it under that name," snapped Brinze. "That's old stuff."

"Granted. But the fact that she used that name was very helpful to me, at least.

"The note was also interesting. You may have heard that there was a story-telling bee at Olean during the storm. Someone told the story of a suicide, and this story tallied almost exactly with Payne's end. In this story, a man retired, woke up at midnight, wrote a note saying that he would end it all, and shot himself. That's what Payne did. But the wording of the note he left was that of the suicide in the story. The paper also was significant. It was unlike any stationery in the house. The top had been torn off to conceal its origin. In short, this scrap of paper had been planted on the desk, so that Payne would not have to search for paper, and so that he could attend to his shooting with as little delay as possible. All very thoughtful, you will agree."

Kenworthy was looking at Jimmy seriously.

"Go on," he said crisply, as Jimmy paused.

"On the basis of this, and my hypothesis, I tried to run down the murderer. And now I'll tell you what that hypothesis was.

"Payne was killed by auto-suggestion. Everybody knows what that is. An idea takes possession of what we call the sub-conscious mind. We are hardly aware that it is present. But at some moment, when the psychological safeguard known as the 'censor' isn't aware of it, this sub-conscious idea takes possession of the conscious mind, and, under favorable conditions, results in action. Payne had been given the suggestion to kill himself in just the manner that he did, and arising sleepily, weakly, and also feeling ill, he acted on it. Even the waking was part of the suggestion."

"Hold on," interrupted the district attorney. "Who told that story about the suicide?"

"I thought you'd ask that," remarked Jimmy. "It was Mr. Hesbe."

"So you accuse—"

"I don't accuse anyone yet. You've jumped to a conclusion."

Jimmy held up the false mustache.

"Not long after it became known to some people that I was working on this case, I found that I was under strict surveillance.

Someone had been kind enough to engage a lank, seedy shifter to follow me. I say that this unique shadow was acting for a principal because it's unthinkable that he would operate on his own initiative. Furthermore, a principal wouldn't be likely to take the risks involved in that sort of enterprise. This fake mustache here belonged to the shadow. He and I had a little catch-as-catch-can encounter one day, and I won by a hair, so to speak.

"Now, this shadow was rather an annoyance. He seemed to have no office hours, and I couldn't count on him. He also was addicted to singing, and his favorite song seemed to be a melody which had particularly poignant associations for me. By the way, Mr. Brinze, on the night that you provided me with the questionable hospitality of your jail, the shadow serenaded me from the yard. He certainly knew what was going on. He also is the worst singer I ever heard."

"Is this musical criticism?" asked Brinze.

"No—but remember the song. It's important."

Jimmy looked at his watch.

"I've timed this very nicely, I think. The train ought to be in now, and if the detective Mr. Durand recommended still has the shadow with him, I'll introduce you to the gentleman in a few minutes.

"While we wait, let me say that the shadow—I don't know his name—really proved a very handy thing for me."

"This is all very good I suppose," said Kenworthy, "but what bearing has it on the revolver?"

Jimmy fetched out his copy of *The Porterhouse Murder*.

"Here is a most engaging tale," he said. "The heroine's name is Monica Wells. That was why I was a little startled by Miss Barton's alias. I'll tell you more about the book later.

"About this shadow, now. He seems to have left threatening letters in my room. Here are two. One is a crudely typed warning. Another appeared under the mattress, following a shooting in my room while I was away. It informs me that the next time, my head, not the pillow, will be punctured. This note is in writing. And here is a third exhibit. It's a receipt. I got it in Mr. Hesbe's office the day that I followed you there, Mr. Brinze."

Here Rooks ushered in Durand's detective, who brought with him Hesbe and his assistant.

"Here's Mr. Hesbe," said Jimmy, "and his office helper, who has taken the trouble to follow me so closely. The similarity of the writing on the notes I've offered seems to me to be conclusive. The paper also is the same."

The shadow was trembling.

"Sit down," said Jimmy. "We've met before."

"What's all this about?" blustered Hesbe.

"Does this man work for you?" inquired Jimmy.

"He does."

"That's interesting—but don't jump to a conclusion, Mr. Kenworthy."

"I want to question that man," said Kenworthy.

"Please let me go on. I want to take up a point about Payne. He was a man who worked on hunches. He was extremely susceptible to suggestion. In his weakened condition, the suicide suggestion worked beautifully. Now I must connect this suggestion with motives."

"We showed Barton's motive yesterday," said Kenworthy. "If he's your murderer, I'll waive the rest of your story."

"He's no more the murderer than you are!"

"Mr. Barton had plenty of motive, I'll admit," Jimmy continued, "and if he had done it, nobody could have blamed him, and not a jury in the world would have convicted him. But that's neither here nor there.

"Following up every clew I could find, I found several possibilities. One trail led to Miss Barton, despite her alibi. I apologize to her for ever having even considered her in the matter. And I don't mind saying that if I had found undeniable evidence against her, I would have kept it to myself.

"Another led to Mr. Gulvin. That was a fairly obvious thing, as I believe I proved to Mr. Brinze on one occasion.

"A third took me to Mr. Hesbe. Frankly, I should have enjoyed that, for reasons which no longer obtain—again I apologize to Miss Barton, but only she will understand this—but Mr. Hesbe isn't implicated. Of course, he told the story which served as the suggestion, but he didn't know what he was doing, and his only motive was to tell an entertaining, cheerful narrative in a storm. Any old sport in a storm, you know.

"Then I recalled that the person back of the murder and back of shadowing which I underwent must be someone who had in his hands not only a complete knowledge of Payne, but of me. And there was only one person who had that.

"That person, I regret to say, was Dr. Hugh Farrigan."

"Where is he?" shouted Kenworthy, jumping to his feet.

"I yield the floor to Dr. Villmers," said Jimmy.

The neurologist leaned back wearily in his chair. "This is very painful for me," he said, "and yet I must tell what I know.

"Dr. Farrigan came to our hospital, of which I am one of the directors, as a young physician of great promise. We thought that he would develop into a really great orthopedist. But he made little progress. He had in him a curious experimental streak. He was reprimanded several times for unjustifiable experiments on clinical patients. I made a study of him and discovered that it was a curious kink in his mind that led him to these excesses. He looked like a sturdy, dependable young practitioner. Very often, he performed brilliant operations. But every now and then something morbid in his make-up would lead him into dangerous ways. When we learned that he had made unsound experiments in auto-suggestion, we considered seriously the question of dismissing him from our staff.

"I am more than a little worn this morning, for I have been with Dr. Farrigan all night. I have here his own statement. He has become interested in the idea of inducing suicide by auto-suggestion by a book—"

"Here it is," interrupted Jimmy, tossing *The Porterhouse Murder* to Kenworthy. "It's all in that story. And here are library cards to prove that he borrowed it from a circulating library. This is the copy he borrowed, and he marked some most illuminating passages with a pencil. You can read them for yourself. He even told Miss Barton to use the name of 'Monica Wells' when she bought the pistol. You see, it's all detective story stuff. Only, it happens that I had read the right detective story."

"Just a moment, Mr. Wrome," said Dr. Villmers. "That explains your procedure. Dr. Farrigan's confession is very complete. It tells how he conceived the idea, how he coerced Miss Barton to place the pistol and the paper in Payne's room—"

"Did you know that, Wrome?" broke in Kenworthy.

"Sure," said Jimmy. "And it certainly was rough on my nerves. Only, I didn't know that Farrigan knew about Mr. Barton's relations with Payne. And Miss Barton, at one time, didn't care to favor me with information. Perhaps it was because three men were holding things over her, and she didn't want a fourth."

"Dr. Farrigan's original intention was not to kill Mr. Payne," continued the neurologist. "He didn't believe that suggestion would go that far. But he had a fiendish notion about trying the experiment and learning Payne's reactions on finding the pistol and paper. Mr. Hesbe played into his hands with that story. As Dr. Farrigan led Payne upstairs he all but hypnotized him—he has amazingly compelling eyes—into following the suggestion. If Hesbe hadn't told the story, he would merely have given Payne a mild suggestion before retiring and awaited results. But all that is in the confession.

"When Dr. Farrigan learned of Mr. Wrome's activities, he became frightened, and tried to drive him from his purpose by playing on his nerves. It was clever of him to engage Mr. Hesbe's office assistant for the purpose. You see, Mr. Wrome, you told Dr. Farrigan that you would like to 'hang it on Hesbe,' and he proposed to lead you in that direction if he couldn't frighten you off altogether. May I ask, as a matter of interest, whether you had him under suspicion the night you stayed at his rooms?"

"I had him spotted ever since I heard so much of that melody," said Jimmy. "He was the only person I'd told about it until I told you last night. He played into my hands by referring me to you. But he thought I was consulting you about myself. That's where he slipped."

"And of course you see," concluded the neurologist, "why he insisted throughout that it was suicide."

Kenworthy took Farrigan's confession from Dr. Villmers.

"Where's Farrigan now?" he asked.

"After I called on him and told him what Mr. Wrome had told me, he collapsed. He's a complete wreck. I doubt whether he'll ever recover completely. I have had him committed to our neurological ward. It is not for me to interfere, but is it necessary to prosecute this unfortunate young man, who is, in a way, a mental cripple? From what I have learned of this case, it seems to me that the state would be performing no divine act of justice by persecuting the slayer of a man like Payne."

Kenworthy tore up some papers.

"Barton is released," he snapped. "I want Farrigan."

"Listen, Mr. Kenworthy," said Jimmy. "You couldn't convict him. First of all, it would be too easy to prove that he was mentally incompetent. Second—this form of murder isn't so easy to use as a basis for a good conviction. Think it over."

"There's his confession," insisted Kenworthy.

"What of it?"

"You know what the papers have been doing to us ever since you broke into print. How can we back down now?"

Jimmy walked over to Claire and took her hand.

"Let me do the backing down," he said. "I'm out of the detective business now, and, after all, it *was* a suicide. I'll give Heidelman a perfectly stunning retraction. It won't bother me much, because I expect to be out of town on a honeymoon or something like that."

XIX
INCIDENTALLY

There was a light mist along upper Broadway, as Myrna Quaid decided that it was time for Curtin's to close for the night. She looked from the door to the corner and was confirmed in her decision by the sight of a familiar figure standing under an awning at the orangeade stand on the corner. A pleasant young man, wearing a light brown suit and smoking a cigarette was looking at his watch. He rubbed the mist from his shell-rimmed glasses, and shook his head with a smile.

It was a pity to keep him waiting. In a way, it served him right, for he really should have called for her at the shop and waited until she was ready to go. But he was shy. And she liked him for it.

As she was putting on a charming new summer hat, and taking her little umbrella from the stand, two persons entered. She looked about a little aggrieved, for she had already delayed her meeting too long. But she smiled amiably as she saw Jimmy and the lovely young woman who accompanied him, arm in arm.

"Well, Miss Quaid," said Jimmy, "here is Miss Barton. Miss Barton is to become a regular patron of your establishment within the next few weeks."

"I'm happy to meet Miss Barton," answered the librarian.

"Here, by the way, are some records I abstracted from your files," said Jimmy, handing her two cards. "It was absent-minded of me to take them when I substituted for you."

"And absent-minded to leave copies?"

Jimmy was embarrassed.

"You're a curious man, Mr. Wrome," continued Miss Quaid. "I half suspect you of many things. Your card is full of detective stories—far more than the doctor ordered. Are you learning a new profession?"

"No," said Claire, "Mr. Wrome is going back to his old job. But you're right. He's a very curious man."

"Is any additional deposit required when two members of the same family draw books?" asked Jimmy.

"Not for your family," returned Miss Quaid.

"Well, Mrs. Wrome will draw some when we return. And I know that you'll give her the same charming service that you gave to her husband."

"Certainly."

Miss Quaid shook hands with them heartily as they passed out of the door into the mists. She looked up Broadway until Jimmy's bright hat-band and Claire's twinkling ankles had disappeared in the night.

She patted the rows of books into symmetry and carefully locked the desk. With a faint smile she opened it again and dropped Jimmy's cards into their proper places. She pulled down the shade and, looking around once more at her neat little institution, set the lock on the door, and switched off the lights. Curtin's was closed until nine o'clock the next morning.

As she stepped out of the door, she looked again to the corner. The young man was still there, still looking amiable, still waiting. She felt a little guilty about keeping him standing there so long. But he would understand. He was charming, she thought, and above all sympathetic. Yes, she reflected, he was a delightful person.

She closed the door and started down the street to keep her somewhat deferred appointment with the author of this book.

COACHWHIP PUBLICATIONS
COACHWHIPBOOKS.COM

SAMUEL ROGERS

YOU'LL BE
SORRY!

YOU LEAVE
ME COLD!

COACHWHIP PUBLICATIONS
CoachwhipBooks.com

COACHWHIP PUBLICATIONS
CoachwhipBooks.com

COACHWHIP PUBLICATIONS
CoachwhipBooks.com

THE EDINGTONS

THE HOUSE OF THE
VANISHING
GOBLETS

COACHWHIP PUBLICATIONS
CoachwhipBooks.com

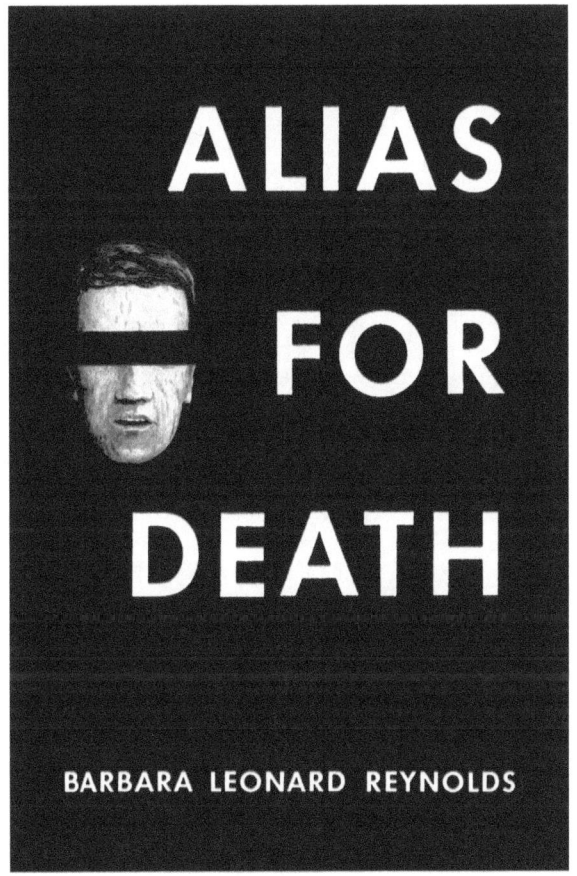

ALIAS

FOR

DEATH

BARBARA LEONARD REYNOLDS

COACHWHIP PUBLICATIONS
CoachwhipBooks.com

THE
SARA ELIZABETH
MASON
MYSTERIES

MURDER RENTS A ROOM

THE CRIMSON FEATHER

COACHWHIP PUBLICATIONS
CoachwhipBooks.com

THE
SARA ELIZABETH
MASON
MYSTERIES

THE HOUSE THAT HATE BUILT

THE WHIP

www.ingramcontent.com/pod-product-compliance
Lightning Source LLC
Chambersburg PA
CBHW020641260626
47157CB00008B/2848